AN
AFRICAN
MILLIONAIRE

AN AFRICAN MILLIONAIRE

Episodes in the Life of the Illustrious Colonel Clay

GRANT ALLEN

With an Introduction by Norman Donaldson
Author of "In Search of Dr. Thorndyke"

Dover Publications, Inc.

New York

Published in Canada by General Publishing Company, Ltd.,
30 Lesmill Road, Don Mills, Toronto, Ontario.
Published in the United Kingdom by Constable and Company, Ltd., 10 Orange Street, London WC2H 7EG.

This Dover edition, first published in 1980, is an unabridged
and unaltered republication of the work as originally published by Grant Richards, London, in 1897. An introduction
has been written especially for the Dover edition by Norman
Donaldson.

International Standard Book Number: 0-486-23992-6
Library of Congress Catalog Card Number: 80-65318

Manufactured in the United States of America
Dover Publications, Inc.
180 Varick Street
New York, N.Y. 10014

INTRODUCTION

In this remarkable book you will meet Colonel Clay, "the first great thief of short mystery fiction," as Fred Dannay has correctly described him. Not only was he first on the scene, beating E. W. Hornung's amateur cracksman A. J. Raffles into hard covers by two years, but the stories in which he appears have better stood the test of time. Though Hornung was witty enough in conversation (did he not perpetrate the best of all Sherlockian puns: "Though he might be more humble, there's no police like Holmes"?) the Raffles stories lack the ironic touch found in *An African Millionaire*. Dannay, the bibliographical half of the Ellery Queen partnership, in introducing one of the present stories in their 1945 collection *Rogues Gallery,* wrote, "it is all the more amazing to find 'The Diamond Links' still fresh and ingenious, with none of the dated and slightly decadent quality that envelops, with a Victorian aura, even the best of the Raffles tales."

Charles Grant Blairfindie Allen was an unlikely writer to become, late in life, a pioneer of crook fiction.

A clergyman's son, he rebelled to become a noted anti-cleric and freethinker, a follower of Herbert Spencer.

He was born to an Irish father and French-Canadian mother near Kingston, Ontario, on 24 February 1848. A thoughtful, gentle child of delicate health and sensibilities (R. L. Stevenson's *Travels with a Donkey* was spoiled for him by the description of how the beast was beaten), he was a born naturalist whose happiest hours were spent alone in the countryside.

Allen was educated in Connecticut by a tutor from Yale, and later at Dieppe and King Edward's School, Birmingham. He married early to an invalid who was soon to die. Hampered by his own poor health, his fight, ultimately successful, to gain a baccalaureate degree at Merton College, Oxford, was heroic and prolonged. From 1873 to 1876 he taught at a newly founded college for black students in Jamaica, and when that institution failed he returned to a life of grinding poverty in Oxford.

A hundred articles on scientific subjects were, one after the other, turned down by magazine editors, and a book, *Physiological Aesthetics,* published with his meager savings, failed to find a public. (As the title indicates, it was the kind of volume that, once put down, was difficult to pick up again.) The first money earned by his pen was the twelve guineas sent to him by the *Cornhill* magazine for his article "Carving a Cocoa-nut," but this small success was followed by further disappointments and a brief unhappy stint as a London journalist.

It was an accident that nudged Grant Allen onto the "downward path"—as he himself regarded it—to fiction writing ("the upward path," wrote Andrew Lang later, "judging by his many excellent stories"). Here is Allen's own account:

> . . . about the year 1880 . . . , wishing to contribute an article to "Belgravia" on the improbability of a man's being able to recognize a ghost as such, even if he saw one, and the impossibility of his being able to apply any test of credibility to an apparition's statements, I ventured for the better development of my subject to throw the argument into the form of a narrative. I did not regard this narrative as a story: I looked upon it merely as a convenient method of displaying a scientific truth. However, the gods and Mr. Chatto thought otherwise. For, a month or two later, Mr. Chatto wrote to ask me if I could supply "Belgravia" with "another story." Not a little surprised at this request, I sat down, like an obedient workman, and tried to write one at my employer's bidding. I distrusted my own ability to do so, it is true; but Mr. Chatto, I thought, being a dealer in the article, must know better than I; and I was far too poor a craftsman at that time to refuse any reasonable offer of employment. So I did my best, "crassa Minerva." To my great astonishment, my second story was accepted and printed like my first . . .

These stories and subsequent ones were submitted to *Belgravia* and the *Cornhill* under a pseudonym, J. Arbuthnot Wilson. It was only when the author received two notes simultaneously from James Payn, editor of the *Cornhill,* one of them rejecting Allen's

latest scientific piece and the other begging "Mr.
Wilson" to supply more fiction, that the impoverished
writer gave his full attention to imagined tales and
shortly produced two of his best efforts, "The Reverend
John Creedy" and "The Curate of Churnside." These
powerful, rather unpleasant character studies can be
found in Grant Allen's 1884 collection, *Strange Stories*.

But the fastidious Allen felt keenly his abandon-
ment of what he saw as his noble mission to bring
enlightenment to the scientifically benighted masses. The
more popular his novels and stories became, the deeper
was his conviction that he had betrayed his principles,
and the more ardently he begged friends not to read his
potboilers. In 1893 he acquired a house at Hindhead
in Surrey, the highest spot in the southeast of England,
and there wrote several novels, each of which carried a
social message. He called them his "hilltop novels," and
there was more than a hint of misplaced arrogance in
the term. Among those who thought so was the popular
novelist Margaret Oliphant who, wearied by years of
supporting her children and invalid husband by her
pen, contemptuously drew a farmyard analogy between
Allen's "hilltop" and its smaller and smellier counter-
part.

Andrew Lang, a friend of Allen's and his colleague
during his short career as a journalist, also pooh-
poohed these pretensions. In particular, "one could never
quite believe in his want of interest as to his own
novels. No doubt he would liefer have been writing
about the loves of the pismires, but he must have been

a little concerned about those of his own characters."

Grant Allen's second marriage was lifelong and serene. He was a frail man who, in contrast to his public character, exhibited to his friends a gentle, if animated, demeanor. They would often consult his encyclopedic knowledge on subjects that puzzled them. "Let us look it up in Grant," they would joke among themselves. He was remarkably industrious, using the then uncommon appliance, a typewriter, while his houseguests crowded around. When Richard Le Gallienne, laid low by a personal bereavement, was staying with him, he dashed off in ten minutes or so a 500-word book review that he knew Le Gallienne had undertaken to write, and did it moreover with five admiring visitors leaning over the machine.

His output was remarkably varied. In 1897, the year *An African Millionaire* was published (by his nephew Grant Richards in London, by Edward Arnold in New York), there also appeared three historical guides (to Paris, Florence, and the cities of Belgium), a book for children *(Tom Unlimited* by "Martin Leach Warborough"), a religious work *(The Evolution of the Idea of God)* and a lightweight novel *(The Type-Writer Girl* by "Olive Pratt Rayner").

The best-known of the "hilltop novels" was *The Woman Who Did* (1895), a sensational, over-earnest thesis defending a woman's right to desert a dipsomaniac husband and find happiness with a second choice without benefit of wedlock. But, though this humorless tract brought him instant fame (or notoriety), it is neither for this nor for his many scientific and philosophical books that Grant Allen is remembered today. His modern reputation, shocked though he would be to know it, rests on his experiments in the literature of lighthearted detection and villainy.

In *The Detective Short Story: A Bibliography* (1942) Ellery Queen lists, in addition to *An African Millionaire,* two stories collected in *Ivan's Greet's Masterpiece etc* (1893), namely, "The Great Ruby Robbery" and "The Conscientious Burglar," and also two of Grant Allen's final books, *Miss Cayley's Adventures* (1899) and the posthumous *Hilda Wade: A Woman with Tenacity of Purpose* (1900).

It may have been the influence of Arthur Conan Doyle, who had recently become a neighbor, that turned Grant Allen's thoughts increasingly toward detective fiction. He benefited so much himself from the bracing air of Hindhead that he recommended the district to Doyle as an excellent place to bring his tuberculous first wife Touie, and the creator of Sherlock Holmes followed his advice. As he lay dying of liver disease, Allen begged Doyle to complete *Hilda Wade,* then running as a serial in the *Strand* magazine. He was worried by the knowledge that two numbers still needed to be written. Doyle made bedside notes of the dying man's ideas and from them wrote the final stories. In his *Memories and Adventures* he recalled the experience: "It was a pleasure for me to do them for him, and so relieve his mind, but it was difficult collar work, and I expect they were pretty bad." It is from the same source that we obtain a final glimpse of our author:

> I well remember that death-bed of Grant Allen's. He was an agnostic of a type which came very near to atheism, though in his private life an amiable and benevolent man. Believing what he did, the approach of death must have offered rather a bleak prospect, and as he had paroxysms of extreme pain the poor fellow seemed very miserable. I had often argued the case with him, I from a Theistic and he from a negative point of view, but I did not intrude my opinions or disturb his mind at that solemn moment. Death-bed changes, though some clergy may rejoice in them, are really vain things. His brain, however, was as clear as ever, and his mind was occupied with all manner of strange knowledge, which he imparted, in the intervals of his pain, in the curious high nasal voice which was character-istic. I can see him now, his knees drawn up to ease internal pain, and his long thin nose and red-dish-grey goatee protruding over the sheet, while he croaked out: "Byzantine art, my dear Doyle, was of three periods, the middle one roughly coinciding with the actual fall of the Roman Empire. The characteristics of the first period——" and so on, until he would give a cry, clasp his hands across his stomach, and wait till the pain passed before resuming his lecture. . . .

Grant Allen died at Hindhead on 25 October 1899, aged only fifty-one. The "bleak prospect" of death mentioned by Conan Doyle was perhaps an exaggera-tion of Allen's beliefs, which were better expressed in one of his poems. At the cremation ceremony, Le

Gallienne attached to his wreath a couple of lines:

Perchance a little light will come with morning,
Perchance I shall but sleep.

Although *Miss Cayley's Adventures* and *Hilda Wade* have their place in the adventure fiction of the 1890s, it is *An African Millionaire* that makes the most serious claim on a modern reader's interest. It was the first entry in a field that attracted several authors in various countries during the next fifteen years. After Hornung's *Raffles* in 1899 came Romney Pringle, the fictional thief created by Clifford Ashdown (R. Austin Freeman and J. J. Pitcairn) and then several rogues depicted by William Le Queux. In the U.S., Jeff Peters, O. Henry's "Gentle Grafter," provided a welcome spot of high humor in a field that, despite the intrinsic allure of its subject matter, sometimes tends to dullness of style. But it was France that seized the laurels with Maurice Leblanc's immortal Arsène Lupin.

An African Millionaire first appeared in twelve successive issues of London's *Strand* magazine, beginning in June 1896. The episodes are by no means unrelated, a fact that arises from the peculiar nature of the overall plot and that has no doubt restricted the appearance of the separate tales in anthologies. The series is unique in the genre in relating a series of robberies by the same thief *from the same victim!* Time and time again a financier, Sir Charles Vandrift, is ruthlessly mulcted of his millions by the relentless Colonel Clay who, Dannay has written, "playfully pilfered, purloined and pluck-pigeoned his way to pecuniary profits." Such is the

predator's cunning that no amount of caution—or pre-
caution—on Vandrift's part can save him from this
confidence man par excellence.

As we of a later age observe Clay, a master of disguise, gradually separating the millionaire from his
wealth by playing on his shifty business morality, we
may be left incredulous at these achievements in impersonation. We know that, however expertly an Alec
Guinness or Peter Sellers may transform his features,
the voice, if nothing else, can usually be depended upon
to give the game away. So some suspension of dis-
belief may be needed as we read these chapters.

At the same time, the psychology of swindler and
dupe are well enough founded in our own experience
for us to find ourselves dividing our sympathies. One
contemporary reviewer characterized the book as almost
an inverted series of Sherlock Holmes adventures, and
added :

> What we should like to read now would be a story
> in which Colonel Clay should be pitted against
> Sherlock Holmes in a desperate struggle of wits, and
> we confess that we do not know which of the two
> would come out ahead, which is perhaps the best
> tribute we can pay to the entertaining qualities of
> Mr. Allen's book.

The narrator of the tales is Vandrift's brother-in-law
and private secretary, who regards his employer's pre-
dicament with ironic detachment and who is not above
feathering his nest at the millionaire's expense.

But in the end villainy earns its just reward at the
Old Bailey. To this extent Grant Allen reconciles his

story to the requirements of orthodox morality, but even in the courtroom scene the financier is made to look as great a rogue as the swindler.

By the end of the book the reader learns Clay's true identity and the secret of his modus operandi, and the series is revealed to be not so much a set of isolated episodes as a fully developed picaresque novel.

NORMAN DONALDSON

Columbus, Ohio
January 1980

CONTENTS

		PAGE
1.	THE EPISODE OF THE MEXICAN SEER	1
2.	THE EPISODE OF THE DIAMOND LINKS	26
3.	THE EPISODE OF THE OLD MASTER	56
4.	THE EPISODE OF THE TYROLEAN CASTLE	80
5.	THE EPISODE OF THE DRAWN GAME	107
6.	THE EPISODE OF THE GERMAN PROFESSOR	137
7.	THE EPISODE OF THE ARREST OF THE COLONEL	161
8.	THE EPISODE OF THE SELDON GOLD-MINE	191
9.	THE EPISODE OF THE JAPANNED DISPATCH-BOX	217
10.	THE EPISODE OF THE GAME OF POKER	243
11.	THE EPISODE OF THE BERTILLON METHOD	267
12.	THE EPISODE OF THE OLD BAILEY	291

LIST OF ILLUSTRATIONS

PAGE

Yes, I go 6
In blood-red letters, my brother-in-law read the name . . 14
I guess you've been victimised 18
Madame Picardet withdrew her balance . . . 24
The man with the big eyebrows sidled up . . . 30
Charles, I shall never be happy again till I get them . . 40
The concierge stepped forward with a little note for Amelia . 43
She took out the links from her husband's cuffs . . 48
Have you bought them, Seymour? 50
Would you allow me to offer you one?. . . . 58
There sat our friend, Dr. Polperro 66
In his judgment, it was not a Rembrandt at all . . 69
It's all right, my man, he said 73
A cheerful little note 78
Merci, Monsieur! 82
Césarine returned with a full, true, and particular list . . 86
As to price, the lawyers were obdurate . . . 92
Commission? he inquired 97
We were met at the door by the surly steward . . . 100
Two letters 105
Césarine took it as directed 111
She was endowed with a slight squint . . . 115
Ten is more usual 117
A groom was dispatched with a telegram . . . 120
Ta-ta! 125
Charles was half beside himself 128
I climbed to the top of the cliff 132
His spirits revived 135
This nonsense must be stopped, he said . . . 141
The scientific men craned their necks in their eagerness . 144
Three uncomfortable, unhappy-faced men . . . 149

	PAGE
Charles was beside himself with anger	157
I am bamboozled and led a dance	163
Medhurst	165
Césarine took a violent dislike to him	168
Medhurst suddenly emerged from the bookcase . .	173
The discovery was most important	178
Breathless expectation	180
He accuses me of forgery, fraud, and theft . . .	185
Peering at the rocks in a suspicious manner . . .	196
I hope Sir Charles won't come and catch us . . .	198
Ten per cent, he murmured, is more usual . . .	208
Oh, my stars, what a lovely one !	212
He brandished it thrice in Charles's eyes . . .	215
Finglemore's brother	220
Charles insisted	225
He seized the doctor's hair	228
The pretty little woman burst in	231
A fiery Virginian	235
Still a rogue	241
The lion of the hour	247
I shall imitate Mary	249
Moody	253
We burst down the stairs in a body	259
I rolled backward	261
Show me the signature	269
Dr. Beddersley	274
How blind you men are !	277
A convenient policeman	287
Where's that hansom gone ?	289
I want you to help me in a most painful difficulty . .	295
A pretty little woman stood, pale and anxious . . .	300
The prisoner	302
Unwillingly, shamefacedly, Charles was compelled to confess .	307
Modelled by Dr. Beddersley	310
The jury filed slowly back	314

AN
AFRICAN
MILLIONAIRE

I

THE EPISODE OF THE MEXICAN SEER

MY name is Seymour Wilbraham Wentworth. I am brother-in-law and secretary to Sir Charles Vandrift, the South African millionaire and famous financier. Many years ago, when Charlie Vandrift was a small lawyer in Cape Town, I had the (qualified) good fortune to marry his sister. Much later, when the Vandrift estate and farm near Kimberley developed by degrees into the Cloetedorp Golcondas, Limited, my brother-in-law offered me the not unremunerative post of secretary; in which capacity I have ever since been his constant and attached companion.

He is not a man whom any common sharper can take in, is Charles Vandrift. Middle height, square build, firm mouth, keen eyes—the very picture of a sharp and successful business genius. I have only known one rogue impose upon Sir Charles, and that one rogue, as the Commissary of Police at Nice remarked, would doubtless have imposed upon a syndicate of Vidocq, Robert Houdin, and Cagliostro.

We had run across to the Riviera for a few weeks in the season. Our object being strictly rest and recreation from the arduous duties of financial combination, we did not think it necessary to take our wives out with us. Indeed, Lady Vandrift is absolutely wedded to the joys of London, and does not appreciate the rural delights of the Mediterranean littoral. But Sir Charles and I, though immersed in affairs when at home, both thoroughly enjoy the complete change from the City to the charming vegetation and pellucid air on the terrace at Monte Carlo. We *are* so fond of scenery. That delicious view over the rocks of Monaco, with the Maritime Alps in the rear, and the blue sea in front, not to mention the imposing Casino in the foreground, appeals to me as one of the most beautiful prospects in all Europe. Sir Charles has a sentimental attachment for the place. He finds it restores and freshens him, after the turmoil of London, to win a few hundreds at roulette in the course of an afternoon among the palms and cactuses and pure breezes of Monte Carlo. The country, say I, for a jaded intellect! However, we never on any account actually stop in the Principality itself. Sir Charles thinks Monte Carlo is not a sound address for a financier's letters. He prefers a comfortable hotel on the Promenade des Anglais at Nice, where he recovers health and renovates his nervous system by taking daily excursions along the coast to the Casino. This particular season we were snugly ensconced

at the Hôtel des Anglais. We had capital quarters
on the first floor—salon, study, and bedrooms—and
found on the spot a most agreeable cosmopolitan
society. All Nice, just then, was ringing with talk
about a curious impostor, known to his followers as
the Great Mexican Seer, and supposed to be gifted
with second sight, as well as with endless other
supernatural powers. Now, it is a peculiarity of my
able brother-in-law's that, when he meets with a
quack, he burns to expose him; he is so keen a
man of business himself that it gives him, so to
speak, a disinterested pleasure to unmask and detect
imposture in others. Many ladies at the hotel,
some of whom had met and conversed with the
Mexican Seer, were constantly telling us strange
stories of his doings. He had disclosed to one the
present whereabouts of a runaway husband; he had
pointed out to another the numbers that would win
at roulette next evening; he had shown a third the
image on a screen of the man she had for years
adored without his knowledge. Of course, Sir
Charles didn't believe a word of it; but his curiosity
was roused; he wished to see and judge for himself
of the wonderful thought-reader.

'What would be his terms, do you think, for a
private *séance*?' he asked of Madame Picardet, the
lady to whom the Seer had successfully predicted
the winning numbers.

'He does not work for money,' Madame Picardet
answered, 'but for the good of humanity. I'm sure

he would gladly come and exhibit for nothing his miraculous faculties.'

'Nonsense!' Sir Charles answered. 'The man must live. I'd pay him five guineas, though, to see him alone. What hotel is he stopping at?'

'The Cosmopolitan, I think,' the lady answered. 'Oh no; I remember now, the Westminster.'

Sir Charles turned to me quietly. 'Look here, Seymour,' he whispered. 'Go round to this fellow's place immediately after dinner, and offer him five pounds to give a private *séance* at once in my rooms, without mentioning who I am to him; keep the name quite quiet. Bring him back with you, too, and come straight upstairs with him, so that there may be no collusion. We'll see just how much the fellow can tell us.'

I went as directed. I found the Seer a very remarkable and interesting person. He stood about Sir Charles's own height, but was slimmer and straighter, with an aquiline nose, strangely piercing eyes, very large black pupils, and a finely-chiselled close-shaven face, like the bust of Antinous in our hall in Mayfair. What gave him his most characteristic touch, however, was his odd head of hair, curly and wavy like Paderewski's, standing out in a halo round his high white forehead and his delicate profile. I could see at a glance why he succeeded so well in impressing women; he had the look of a poet, a singer, a prophet.

'I have come round,' I said, 'to ask whether you

will consent to give a *séance* at once in a friend's rooms ; and my principal wishes me to add that he is prepared to pay five pounds as the price of the entertainment.'

Señor Antonio Herrera—that was what he called himself — bowed to me with impressive Spanish politeness. His dusky olive cheeks were wrinkled with a smile of gentle contempt as he answered gravely—

'I do not sell my gifts ; I bestow them freely. If your friend—your anonymous friend—desires to behold the cosmic wonders that are wrought through my hands, I am glad to show them to him. Fortunately, as often happens when it is necessary to convince and confound a sceptic (for that your friend is a sceptic I feel instinctively), I chance to have no engagements at all this evening.' He ran his hand through his fine, long hair reflectively. 'Yes, I go,' he continued, as if addressing some unknown presence that hovered about the ceiling ; 'I go ; come with me !' Then he put on his broad sombrero, with its crimson ribbon, wrapped a cloak round his shoulders, lighted a cigarette, and strode forth by my side towards the Hôtel des Anglais.

He talked little by the way, and that little in curt sentences. He seemed buried in deep thought ; indeed, when we reached the door and I turned in, he walked a step or two farther on, as if not noticing to what place I had brought him. Then he drew himself up short, and gazed around him for a

moment. 'Ha, the Anglais,' he said—and I may
mention in passing that his English, in spite of a
slight southern accent, was idiomatic and excellent.

YES, I GO.

'It is here, then; it is here!' He was addressing
once more the unseen presence.

I smiled to think that these childish devices
were intended to deceive Sir Charles Vandrift. Not

quite the sort of man (as the City of London knows) to be taken in by hocus-pocus. And all this, I saw, was the cheapest and most commonplace conjurer's patter.

We went upstairs to our rooms. Charles had gathered together a few friends to watch the performance. The Seer entered, wrapt in thought. He was in evening dress, but a red sash round his waist gave a touch of picturesqueness and a dash of colour. He paused for a moment in the middle of the salon, without letting his eyes rest on anybody or anything. Then he walked straight up to Charles, and held out his dark hand.

'Good-evening,' he said. 'You are the host. My soul's sight tells me so.'

'Good shot,' Sir Charles answered. 'These fellows have to be quick-witted, you know, Mrs. Mackenzie, or they'd never get on at it.'

The Seer gazed about him, and smiled blankly at a person or two whose faces he seemed to recognise from a previous existence. Then Charles began to ask him a few simple questions, not about himself, but about me, just to test him. He answered most of them with surprising correctness. 'His name? His name begins with an S I think: —You call him Seymour.' He paused long between each clause, as if the facts were revealed to him slowly. 'Seymour—Wilbraham—Earl of Strafford. No, not Earl of Strafford! Seymour Wilbraham Wentworth. There seems to be some connection in somebody's mind now present between Wentworth and Strafford.   I am not English.   I do not know what it means.   But they are somehow the same name, Wentworth and Strafford.'

He gazed around, apparently for confirmation. A lady came to his rescue.

'Wentworth was the surname of the great Earl of Strafford,' she murmured gently; 'and I was wondering, as you spoke, whether Mr. Wentworth might possibly be descended from him.'

'He is,' the Seer replied instantly, with a flash of those dark eyes.   And I thought this curious; for though my father always maintained the reality of the relationship, there was one link wanting to complete the pedigree.   He could not make sure that the Hon. Thomas Wilbraham Wentworth was the father of Jonathan Wentworth, the Bristol horse-dealer, from whom we are descended.

'Where was I born?' Sir Charles interrupted, coming suddenly to his own case.

The Seer clapped his two hands to his forehead and held it between them, as if to prevent it from bursting.   'Africa,' he said slowly, as the facts narrowed down, so to speak.   'South Africa; Cape of Good Hope; Jansenville; De Witt Street.   1840.'

'By Jove, he's correct,' Sir Charles muttered. 'He seems really to do it.   Still, he may have found me out.   He may have known where he was coming.'

'I never gave a hint,' I answered;   till he reached

the door, he didn't even know to what hotel I was piloting him.'

The Seer stroked his chin softly. His eye appeared to me to have a furtive gleam in it. 'Would you like me to tell you the number of a bank-note inclosed in an envelope?' he asked casually.

'Go out of the room,' Sir Charles said, 'while I pass it round the company.'

Señor Herrera disappeared. Sir Charles passed it round cautiously, holding it all the time in his own hand, but letting his guests see the number. Then he placed it in an envelope and gummed it down firmly.

The Seer returned. His keen eyes swept the company with a comprehensive glance. He shook his shaggy mane. Then he took the envelope in his hands and gazed at it fixedly. 'AF, 73549,' he answered, in a slow tone. 'A Bank of England note for fifty pounds—exchanged at the Casino for gold won yesterday at Monte Carlo.'

'I see how he did that,' Sir Charles said triumphantly. 'He must have changed it there himself; and then I changed it back again. In point of fact, I remember seeing a fellow with long hair loafing about. Still, it's capital conjuring.'

'He can see through matter,' one of the ladies interposed. It was Madame Picardet. 'He can see through a box.' She drew a little gold vinaigrette, such as our grandmothers used, from her dress-

pocket. 'What is in this?' she inquired, holding it
up to him.

Señor Herrera gazed through it. 'Three gold
coins,' he replied, knitting his brows with the effort
of seeing into the box: 'one, an American five
dollars; one, a French ten-franc piece; one, twenty
marks, German, of the old Emperor William.'

She opened the box and passed it round. Sir
Charles smiled a quiet smile.

'Confederacy!' he muttered, half to himself.
'Confederacy!'

The Seer turned to him with a sullen air. 'You
want a better sign?' he said, in a very impressive
voice. 'A sign that will convince you! Very well:
you have a letter in your left waistcoat pocket—a
crumpled-up letter. Do you wish me to read it
out? I will, if you desire it.'

It may seem to those who know Sir Charles
incredible, but, I am bound to admit, my brother-in-
law coloured. What that letter contained I cannot
say; he only answered, very testily and evasively,
'No, thank you; I won't trouble you. The exhibi-
tion you have already given us of your skill in this
kind more than amply suffices.' And his fingers
strayed nervously to his waistcoat pocket, as if he
was half afraid, even then, Señor Herrera would
read it.

I fancied, too, he glanced somewhat anxiously
towards Madame Picardet.

The Seer bowed courteously. 'Your will, señor,

is law,' he said.   'I make it a principle, though I
can see through all things, invariably to respect the
secrecies and sanctities.   If it were not so, I might
dissolve society.   For which of us is there who could
bear the whole truth being told about him?'   He
gazed around the room.   An unpleasant thrill super-
vened.   Most of us felt this uncanny Spanish
American knew really too much.   And some of us
were engaged in financial operations.

'For example,' the Seer continued blandly, 'I
happened a few weeks ago to travel down here from
Paris by train with a very intelligent man, a company
promoter.   He had in his bag some documents—
some confidential documents:' he glanced at Sir
Charles.   'You know the kind of thing, my dear sir:
reports from experts—from mining engineers.   You
may have seen some such; marked *strictly private.*'

'They form an element in high finance,' Sir
Charles admitted coldly.

'Pre-cisely,' the Seer murmured, his accent for
a moment less Spanish than before.   'And, as they
were marked *strictly private*, I respect, of course, the
seal of confidence.   That's all I wish to say.   I
hold it a duty, being intrusted with such powers,
not to use them in a manner which may annoy or
incommode my fellow-creatures.'

'Your feeling does you honour,' Sir Charles
answered, with some acerbity.   Then he whispered
in my ear: 'Confounded clever scoundrel, Sey;
rather wish we hadn't brought him here.'

Señor Herrera seemed intuitively to divine this wish, for he interposed, in a lighter and gayer tone—

'I will now show you a different and more interesting embodiment of occult power, for which we shall need a somewhat subdued arrangement of surrounding lights. Would you mind, señor host—for I have purposely abstained from reading your name on the brain of any one present—would you mind my turning down this lamp just a little? . . . So! That will do. Now, this one; and this one. Exactly! that's right.' He poured a few grains of powder out of a packet into a saucer. 'Next, a match, if you please. Thank you!' It burnt with a strange green light. He drew from his pocket a card, and produced a little ink-bottle. 'Have you a pen?' he asked.

I instantly brought one. He handed it to Sir Charles. 'Oblige me,' he said, 'by writing your name there.' And he indicated a place in the centre of the card, which had an embossed edge, with a small middle square of a different colour.

Sir Charles has a natural disinclination to signing his name without knowing why. 'What do you want with it?' he asked. (A millionaire's signature has so many uses.)

'I want you to put the card in an envelope,' the Seer replied, 'and then to burn it. After that, I shall show you your own name written in letters of blood on my arm, in your own handwriting.'

Sir Charles took the pen. If the signature was

to be burned as soon as finished, he didn't mind giving it. He wrote his name in his usual firm clear style—the writing of a man who knows his worth and is not afraid of drawing a cheque for five thousand.

'Look at it long,' the Seer said, from the other side of the room. He had not watched him write it.

Sir Charles stared at it fixedly. The Seer was really beginning to produce an impression.

'Now, put it in that envelope,' the Seer exclaimed.

Sir Charles, like a lamb, placed it as directed.

The Seer strode forward. 'Give me the envelope,' he said. He took it in his hand, walked over towards the fireplace, and solemnly burnt it. 'See—it crumbles into ashes,' he cried. Then he came back to the middle of the room, close to the green light, rolled up his sleeve, and held his arm before Sir Charles. There, in blood-red letters, my brother-in-law read the name, 'Charles Vandrift,' in his own handwriting !

'I see how that's done,' Sir Charles murmured, drawing back. 'It's a clever delusion ; but still, I see through it. It's like that ghost-book. Your ink was deep green ; your light was green ; you made me look at it long ; and then I saw the same thing written on the skin of your arm in complementary colours.'

'You think so ?' the Seer replied, with a curious curl of the lip.

'I'm sure of it,' Sir Charles answered.

Quick as lightning the Seer again rolled up his sleeve. 'That's your name,' he cried, in a very clear voice, 'but not your whole name. What do you say, then, to my right? Is this one also a complementary colour?' He held his other arm out. There, in sea-green letters, I read the name, 'Charles

IN BLOOD-RED LETTERS, MY BROTHER-IN-LAW READ THE NAME.

O'Sullivan Vandrift.' It is my brother-in-law's full baptismal designation; but he has dropped the O'Sullivan for many years past, and, to say the truth, doesn't like it. He is a little bit ashamed of his mother's family.

Charles glanced at it hurriedly. 'Quite right,' he said, 'quite right!' But his voice was hollow. I could guess he didn't care to continue the *séance*. He could see through the man, of course; but it

was clear the fellow knew too much about us to be
entirely pleasant.

'Turn up the lights,' I said, and a servant turned
them. 'Shall I say coffee and benedictine?' I
whispered to Vandrift.

'By all means,' he answered. 'Anything to keep
this fellow from further impertinences! And, I say,
don't you think you'd better suggest at the same
time that the men should smoke? Even these
ladies are not above a cigarette—some of them.'

There was a sigh of relief. The lights burned
brightly. The Seer for the moment retired from
business, so to speak. He accepted a partaga with
a very good grace, sipped his coffee in a corner, and
chatted to the lady who had suggested Strafford
with marked politeness. He was a polished
gentleman.

Next morning, in the hall of the hotel, I saw
Madame Picardet again, in a neat tailor-made
travelling dress, evidently bound for the railway-
station.

'What, off, Madame Picardet?' I cried.

She smiled, and held out her prettily-gloved
hand. 'Yes, I'm off,' she answered archly.
'Florence, or Rome, or somewhere. I've drained
Nice dry—like a sucked orange. Got all the fun I
can out of it. Now I'm away again to my beloved
Italy.'

But it struck me as odd that, if Italy was her
game, she went by the omnibus which takes down

to the *train de luxe* for Paris.   However, a man of
the world accepts what a lady tells him, no matter
how improbable ; and I confess, for ten days or
so, I thought no more about her, or the Seer
either.

At the end of that time our fortnightly pass-book
came in from the bank in London.   It is part of
my duty, as the millionaire's secretary, to make up
this book once a fortnight, and to compare the
cancelled cheques with Sir Charles's counterfoils.
On this particular occasion I happened to observe
what I can only describe as a very grave discrepancy,
—in fact, a discrepancy of £5000.   On the wrong
side, too.   Sir Charles was debited with £5000
more than the total amount that was shown on the
counterfoils.

I examined the book with care.   The source of
the error was obvious.   It lay in a cheque to Self
or Bearer, for £5000, signed by Sir Charles, and
evidently paid across the counter in London, as it
bore on its face no stamp or indication of any other
office.

I called in my brother-in-law from the salon to
the study.   ' Look here, Charles,' I said, ' there's a
cheque in the book which you haven't entered.'
And I handed it to him without comment, for I
thought it might have been drawn to settle some
little loss on the turf or at cards, or to make up some
other affair he didn't desire to mention to me.
These things will happen.

He looked at it and stared hard. Then he pursed up his mouth and gave a long low 'Whew!' At last he turned it over and remarked, ' I say, Sey, my boy, we've just been done jolly well brown, haven't we ? '

I glanced at the cheque. ' How do you mean ? ' I inquired.

' Why, the Seer,' he replied, still staring at it ruefully. ' I don't mind the five thou., but to think the fellow should have gammoned the pair of us like that—ignominious, I call it ! '

' How do you know it's the Seer ? ' I asked.

' Look at the green ink,' he answered. ' Besides, I recollect the very shape of the last flourish. I flourished a bit like that in the excitement of the moment, which I don't always do with my regular signature.'

' He's done us,' I answered, recognising it. ' But how the dickens did he manage to transfer it to the cheque ? This looks like your own handwriting, Charles, not a clever forgery.'

' It is,' he said. ' I admit it—I can't deny it. Only fancy his bamboozling me when I was most on my guard ! I wasn't to be taken in by any of his silly occult tricks and catch-words ; but it never occurred to me he was going to victimise me financially in this way. I expected attempts at a loan or an extortion ; but to collar my signature to a blank cheque—atrocious ! '

' How did he manage it ? ' I asked.

'I haven't the faintest conception. I only know those are the words I wrote. I could swear to them anywhere.'

'Then you can't protest the cheque?'

'Unfortunately, no; it's my own true signature.'

I GUESS YOU'VE BEEN VICTIMISED.

We went that afternoon without delay to see the Chief Commissary of Police at the office. He was a gentlemanly Frenchman, much less formal and red-tapey than usual, and he spoke excellent English with an American accent, having acted, in fact, as a detective in New York for about ten years in his early manhood.

'I guess,' he said slowly, after hearing our story,

'you've been victimised right here by Colonel Clay, gentlemen.'

'Who is Colonel Clay?' Sir Charles asked.

'That's just what I want to know,' the Commissary answered, in his curious American - French - English. 'He is a Colonel, because he occasionally gives himself a commission; he is called Colonel Clay, because he appears to possess an india-rubber face, and he can mould it like clay in the hands of the potter. Real name, unknown. Nationality, equally French and English. Address, usually Europe. Profession, former maker of wax figures to the Musée Grévin. Age, what he chooses. Employs his knowledge to mould his own nose and cheeks, with wax additions, to the character he desires to personate. Aquiline this time, you say. *Hein!* Anything like these photographs?'

He rummaged in his desk and handed us two.

'Not in the least,' Sir Charles answered. 'Except, perhaps, as to the neck, everything here is quite unlike him.'

'Then that's the Colonel!' the Commissary answered, with decision, rubbing his hands in glee. 'Look here,' and he took out a pencil and rapidly sketched the outline of one of the two faces—that of a bland-looking young man, with no expression worth mentioning. 'There's the Colonel in his simple disguise. Very good. Now watch me: figure to yourself that he adds here a tiny patch of wax to his nose—an aquiline bridge—just so; well,

you have him right there ; and the chin, ah, one
touch : now, for hair, a wig : for complexion, nothing
easier : that's the profile of your rascal, isn't it ? '

'Exactly,' we both murmured. By two curves of
the pencil, and a shock of false hair, the face was
transmuted.

'He had very large eyes, with very big pupils,
though,' I objected, looking close ; 'and the man in
the photograph here has them small and boiled-
fishy.'

'That's so,' the Commissary answered. 'A drop
of belladonna expands—and produces the Seer ;
five grains of opium contract—and give a dead-alive,
stupidly-innocent appearance. Well, you leave this
affair to me, gentlemen. I'll see the fun out. I
don't say I'll catch him for you ; nobody ever yet
has caught Colonel Clay ; but I'll explain how he
did the trick ; and that ought to be consolation
enough to a man of your means for a trifle of five
thousand ! '

'You are not the conventional French office-
holder, M. le Commissaire,' I ventured to interpose.

'You bet ! ' the Commissary replied, and drew
himself up like a captain of infantry. 'Messieurs,'
he continued, in French, with the utmost dignity, ' I
shall devote the resources of this office to tracing
out the crime, and, if possible, to effectuating the
arrest of the culpable.'

We telegraphed to London, of course, and we
wrote to the bank, with a full description of the

suspected person. But I need hardly add that
nothing came of it.

Three days later the Commissary called at our
hotel. 'Well, gentlemen,' he said, 'I am glad to say
I have discovered everything!'

'What? Arrested the Seer?' Sir Charles cried.

The Commissary drew back, almost horrified at
the suggestion.

'Arrested Colonel Clay?' he exclaimed. '*Mais*,
monsieur, we are only human! Arrested him? No,
not quite. But tracked out how he did it. That is
already much—to unravel Colonel Clay, gentlemen!'

'Well, what do you make of it?' Sir Charles
asked, crestfallen.

The Commissary sat down and gloated over his
discovery. It was clear a well-planned crime amused
him vastly. 'In the first place, monsieur,' he said,
'disabuse your mind of the idea that when monsieur
your secretary went out to fetch Señor Herrera that
night, Señor Herrera didn't know to whose rooms
he was coming. Quite otherwise, in point of fact.
I do not doubt myself that Señor Herrera, or Colonel
Clay (call him which you like), came to Nice this
winter for no other purpose than just to rob you.'

'But I sent for him,' my brother-in-law interposed.

'Yes; he *meant* you to send for him. He forced
a card, so to speak. If he couldn't do that I guess
he would be a pretty poor conjurer. He had a lady
of his own—his wife, let us say, or his sister—

stopping here at this hotel; a certain Madame Picardet. Through her he induced several ladies of your circle to attend his *séances*. She and they spoke to you about him, and aroused your curiosity. You may bet your bottom dollar that when he came to this room he came ready primed and prepared with endless facts about both of you.'

'What fools we have been, Sey,' my brother-in-law exclaimed. 'I see it all now. That designing woman sent round before dinner to say I wanted to meet him; and by the time you got there he was ready for bamboozling me.'

'That's so,' the Commissary answered. 'He had your name ready painted on both his arms; and he had made other preparations of still greater importance.'

'You mean the cheque. Well, how did he get it?'

The Commissary opened the door. 'Come in,' he said. And a young man entered whom we recognised at once as the chief clerk in the Foreign Department of the Crédit Marseillais, the principal bank all along the Riviera.

'State what you know of this cheque,' the Commissary said, showing it to him, for we had handed it over to the police as a piece of evidence.

'About four weeks since——' the clerk began.

'Say ten days before your *séance*,' the Commissary interposed.

'A gentleman with very long hair and an aquiline

nose, dark, strange, and handsome, called in at my
department and asked if I could tell him the name
of Sir Charles Vandrift's London banker. He said
he had a sum to pay in to your credit, and asked if
we would forward it for him. I told him it was
irregular for us to receive the money, as you had no
account with us, but that your London bankers were
Darby, Drummond, and Rothenberg, Limited.'

'Quite right,' Sir Charles murmured.

'Two days later a lady, Madame Picardet, who
was a customer of ours, brought in a good cheque
for three hundred pounds, signed by a first-rate
name, and asked us to pay it in on her behalf to
Darby, Drummond, and Rothenberg's, and to open
a London account with them for her. We did so,
and received in reply a cheque-book.'

'From which this cheque was taken, as I learn
from the number, by telegram from London,' the
Commissary put in. 'Also, that on the same day
on which your cheque was cashed, Madame Picardet,
in London, withdrew her balance.'

'But how did the fellow get me to sign the
cheque?' Sir Charles cried. 'How did he manage
the card trick?'

The Commissary produced a similar card from
his pocket. 'Was that the sort of thing?' he
asked.

'Precisely! A facsimile.'

'I thought so. Well, our Colonel, I find, bought
a packet of such cards, intended for admission to a

religious function, at a shop in the Quai Masséna. He cut out the centre, and, see here——' The Commissary turned it over, and showed a piece of paper pasted neatly over the back ; this he tore off,

MADAME PICARDET WITHDREW HER BALANCE.

and there, concealed behind it, lay a folded cheque, with only the place where the signature should be written showing through on the face which the Seer had presented to us. ' I call that a neat trick,' the Commissary remarked, with professional enjoyment of a really good deception.

'But he burnt the envelope before my eyes,' Sir Charles exclaimed.

'Pooh!' the Commissary answered. 'What would he be worth as a conjurer, anyway, if he couldn't substitute one envelope for another between the table and the fireplace without your noticing it? And Colonel Clay, you must remember, is a prince among conjurers.'

'Well, it's a comfort to know we've identified our man, and the woman who was with him,' Sir Charles said, with a slight sigh of relief. 'The next thing will be, of course, you'll follow them up on these clues in England and arrest them?'

The Commissary shrugged his shoulders. 'Arrest them!' he exclaimed, much amused. 'Ah, monsieur, but you are sanguine! No officer of justice has ever succeeded in arresting le Colonel Caoutchouc, as we call him in French. He is as slippery as an eel, that man. He wriggles through our fingers. Suppose even we caught him, what could we prove? I ask you. Nobody who has seen him once can ever swear to him again in his next impersonation. He is *impayable*, this good Colonel. On the day when I arrest him, I assure you, monsieur, I shall consider myself the smartest police-officer in Europe.'

'Well, I shall catch him yet,' Sir Charles answered, and relapsed into silence.

II

THE EPISODE OF THE DIAMOND LINKS

'LET us take a trip to Switzerland,' said Lady Vandrift. And any one who knows Amelia will not be surprised to learn that we *did* take a trip to Switzerland accordingly. Nobody can drive Sir Charles, except his wife. And nobody at all can drive Amelia.

There were difficulties at the outset, because we had not ordered rooms at the hotels beforehand, and it was well on in the season; but they were overcome at last by the usual application of a golden key; and we found ourselves in due time pleasantly quartered in Lucerne, at that most comfortable of European hostelries, the Schweitzerhof.

We were a square party of four—Sir Charles and Amelia, myself and Isabel. We had nice big rooms, on the first floor, overlooking the lake; and as none of us was possessed with the faintest symptom of that incipient mania which shows itself in the form of an insane desire to climb mountain heights of disagreeable steepness and unnecessary snowiness, I will venture to assert we all enjoyed ourselves. We

spent most of our time sensibly in lounging about the
lake on the jolly little steamers ; and when we did
a mountain climb, it was on the Rigi or Pilatus
—where an engine undertook all the muscular work
for us.

As usual, at the hotel, a great many miscellaneous
people showed a burning desire to be specially nice
to us.   If you wish to see how friendly and charming
humanity is, just try being a well-known millionaire
for a week, and you'll learn a thing or two.   Wher-
ever Sir Charles goes he is surrounded by charming
and disinterested people, all eager to make his
distinguished acquaintance, and all familiar with
several excellent investments, or several deserving
objects of Christian charity.   It is my business in
life, as his brother-in-law and secretary, to decline
with thanks the excellent investments, and to throw
judicious cold water on the objects of charity.   Even
I myself, as the great man's almoner, am very much
sought after.   People casually allude before me to
artless stories of 'poor curates in Cumberland, you
know, Mr. Wentworth,' or widows in Cornwall,
penniless poets with epics in their desks, and young
painters who need but the breath of a patron to open
to them the doors of an admiring Academy.   I smile
and look wise, while I administer cold water in
minute doses ; but I never report one of these cases
to Sir Charles, except in the rare or almost unheard-
of event where I think there is really something in
them.

Ever since our little adventure with the Seer at Nice, Sir Charles, who is constitutionally cautious, had been even more careful than usual about possible sharpers. And, as chance would have it, there sat just opposite us at *table d'hôte* at the Schweitzerhof —'tis a fad of Amelia's to dine at *table d'hôte ;* she says she can't bear to be boxed up all day in private rooms with 'too much family'—a sinister-looking man with dark hair and eyes, conspicuous by his bushy overhanging eyebrows. My attention was first called to the eyebrows in question by a nice little parson who sat at our side, and who observed that they were made up of certain large and bristly hairs, which (he told us) had been traced by Darwin to our monkey ancestors. Very pleasant little fellow, this fresh-faced young parson, on his honeymoon tour with a nice wee wife, a bonnie Scotch lassie with a charming accent.

I looked at the eyebrows close. Then a sudden thought struck me. 'Do you believe they're his own?' I asked of the curate ; 'or are they only stuck on—a make-up disguise? They really almost look like it.'

'You don't suppose——' Charles began, and checked himself suddenly.

'Yes, I do,' I answered ; 'the Seer!' Then I recollected my blunder, and looked down sheepishly. For, to say the truth, Vandrift had straightly enjoined on me long before to say nothing of our painful little episode at Nice to Amelia ; he was afraid if *she* once heard of it, *he* would hear of it for ever after.

'What Seer?' the little parson inquired, with parsonical curiosity.

I noticed the man with the overhanging eyebrows give a queer sort of start.   Charles's glance was fixed upon me.   I hardly knew what to answer.

'Oh, a man who was at Nice with us last year,' I stammered out, trying hard to look unconcerned. 'A fellow they talked about, that's all.'   And I turned the subject.

But the curate, like a donkey, wouldn't let me turn it.

'Had he eyebrows like that?' he inquired, in an undertone.   I was really angry.   If this *was* Colonel Clay, the curate was obviously giving him the cue, and making it much more difficult for us to catch him, now we might possibly have lighted on the chance of doing so.

'No, he hadn't,' I answered testily; 'it was a passing expression.   But this is not the man.   I was mistaken, no doubt.'   And I nudged him gently.

The little curate was too innocent for anything. 'Oh, I see,' he replied, nodding hard and looking wise.   Then he turned to his wife and made an obvious face, which the man with the eyebrows couldn't fail to notice.

Fortunately, a political discussion going on a few places farther down the table spread up to us and diverted attention for a moment.   The magical name

of Gladstone saved us.   Sir Charles flared up.   I
was truly pleased, for I could see Amelia was boiling
over with curiosity by this time.

THE MAN WITH THE BIG EYEBROWS SIDLED UP.

After dinner, in the billiard-room, however, the
man with the big eyebrows sidled up and began to
talk to me.   If he *was* Colonel Clay, it was evident he
bore us no grudge at all for the five thousand pounds

he had done us out of. On the contrary, he seemed
quite prepared to do us out of five thousand more
when opportunity offered ; for he introduced himself
at once as Dr. Hector Macpherson, the exclusive
grantee of extensive concessions from the Brazilian
Government on the Upper Amazons. He dived
into conversation with me at once as to the splendid
mineral resources of his Brazilian estate—the silver,
the platinum, the actual rubies, the possible diamonds.
I listened and smiled ; I knew what was coming.
All he needed to develop this magnificent concession
was a little more capital. It was sad to see thousands
of pounds' worth of platinum and car-loads of rubies
just crumbling in the soil or carried away by the
river, for want of a few hundreds to work them with
properly. If he knew of anybody, now, with money
to invest, he could recommend him—nay, offer him
—a unique opportunity of earning, say, 40 per cent
on his capital, on unimpeachable security.

'I wouldn't do it for every man,' Dr. Hector
Macpherson remarked, drawing himself up ; 'but if
I took a fancy to a fellow who had command of
ready cash, I might choose to put him in the way
of feathering his nest with unexampled rapidity.'

'Exceedingly disinterested of you,' I answered
drily, fixing my eyes on his eyebrows.

The little curate, meanwhile, was playing billiards
with Sir Charles. His glance followed mine as it
rested for a moment on the monkey-like hairs.

'False, obviously false,' he remarked with his lips ;

and I'm bound to confess I never saw any man speak so well by movement alone ; you could follow every word though not a sound escaped him.

During the rest of that evening Dr. Hector Macpherson stuck to me as close as a mustard-plaster. And he was almost as irritating. I got heartily sick of the Upper Amazons. I have positively waded in my time through ruby mines (in prospectuses, I mean) till the mere sight of a ruby absolutely sickens me. When Charles, in an un-wonted fit of generosity, once gave his sister Isabel (whom I had the honour to marry) a ruby necklet (inferior stones), I made Isabel change it for sapphires and amethysts, on the judicious plea that they suited her complexion better. (I scored one, incidentally, for having considered Isabel's complexion.) By the time I went to bed I was prepared to sink the Upper Amazons in the sea, and to stab, shoot, poison, or otherwise seriously damage the man with the concession and the false eyebrows.

For the next three days, at intervals, he returned to the charge. He bored me to death with his platinum and his rubies. He didn't want a capitalist who would personally exploit the thing ; he would prefer to do it all on his own account, giving the capitalist preference debentures of his bogus company, and a lien on the concession. I listened and smiled ; I listened and yawned ; I listened and was rude ; I ceased to listen at all ; but still he droned on with it. I fell asleep on the steamer one day, and woke

up in ten minutes to hear him droning yet, 'And
the yield of platinum per ton was certified to be——'
I forget how many pounds, or ounces, or pennyweights. These details of assays have ceased to
interest me : like the man who 'didn't believe in
ghosts,' I have seen too many of them.

The fresh-faced little curate and his wife, however,
were quite different people. He was a cricketing
Oxford man ; she was a breezy Scotch lass, with a
wholesome breath of the Highlands about her. I
called her 'White Heather.' Their name was
Brabazon. Millionaires are so accustomed to being
beset by harpies of every description, that when they
come across a young couple who are simple and
natural, they delight in the purely human relation.
We picnicked and went excursions a great deal with
the honeymooners. They were so frank in their
young love, and so proof against chaff, that we all
really liked them. But whenever I called the pretty
girl 'White Heather,' she looked so shocked, and
cried : 'Oh, Mr. Wentworth !' Still, we were the
best of friends. The curate offered to row us in a
boat on the lake one day, while the Scotch lassie
assured us she could take an oar almost as well as
he did. However, we did not accept their offer, as
row-boats exert an unfavourable influence upon
Amelia's digestive organs.

'Nice young fellow, that man Brabazon,' Sir
Charles said to me one day, as we lounged together
along the quay ; 'never talks about advowsons or

next presentations. Doesn't seem to me to care two pins about promotion. Says he's quite content in his country curacy; enough to live upon, and needs no more; and his wife has a little, a very little, money. I asked him about his poor to day, on purpose to test him: these parsons are always trying to screw something out of one for their poor; men in my position know the truth of the saying that we have that class of the population always with us. Would you believe it, he says he hasn't any poor at all in his parish! They're all well-to-do farmers or else able-bodied labourers, and his one terror is that somebody will come and try to pauperise them. "If a philanthropist were to give me fifty pounds to-day for use at Empingham," he said, "I assure you, Sir Charles, I shouldn't know what to do with it. I think I should buy new dresses for Jessie, who wants them about as much as anybody else in the village—that is to say, not at all." There's a parson for you, Sey, my boy. Only wish we had one of his sort at Seldon.'

'He certainly doesn't want to get anything out of you,' I answered.

That evening at dinner a queer little episode happened. The man with the eyebrows began talking to me across the table in his usual fashion, full of his wearisome concession on the Upper Amazons. I was trying to squash him as politely as possible, when I caught Amelia's eye. Her look amused me. She was engaged in making signals to Charles at her side to observe the little curate's curious sleeve-links. I glanced at them, and saw at once they were a singular possession for so unᵣobtrusive a person. They consisted each of a short gold bar for one arm of the link, fastened by a tiny chain of the same material to what seemed to my tolerably experienced eye—a first-rate diamond. Pretty big diamonds, too, and of remarkable shape, brilliancy, and cutting. In a moment I knew what Amelia meant. She owned a diamond *rivière*, said to be of Indian origin, but short by two stones for the circumference of her tolerably ample neck. Now, she had long been wanting two diamonds like these to match her set; but owing to the unusual shape and antiquated cutting of her own gems, she had never been able to complete the necklet, at least without removing an extravagant amount from a much larger stone of the first water.

The Scotch lassie's eyes caught Amelia's at the. same time, and she broke into a pretty smile of good-humoured amusement. 'Taken in another person, Dick, dear!' she exclaimed, in her breezy way, turning to her husband. 'Lady Vandrift is observing your diamond sleeve-links.'

'They're very fine gems,' Amelia observed incautiously. (A most unwise admission if she desired to buy them.)

But the pleasant little curate was too transparently simple a soul to take advantage of her slip of judgᵣment. 'They *are* good stones,' he replied ; 'very good stones—considering. They're not diamonds at all, to tell you the truth. They're best old-fashioned Oriental paste. My great-grandfather bought them, after the siege of Seringapatam, for a few rupees, from a Sepoy who had looted them from Tippoo Sultan's palace. He thought, like you, he had got a good thing. But it turned out, when they came to be examined by experts, they were only paste—very wonderful paste ; it is supposed they had even imposed upon Tippoo himself, so fine is the imitation. But they are worth—well, say, fifty shillings at the utmost.'

While he spoke Charles looked at Amelia, and Amelia looked at Charles. Their eyes spoke volumes. The *rivière* was also supposed to have come from Tippoo's collection. Both drew at once an identical conclusion. These were two of the same stones, very likely torn apart and disengaged from the rest in the *mêlée* at the capture of the Indian palace.

'Can you take them off?' Sir Charles asked blandly. He spoke in the tone that indicates business.

'Certainly,' the little curate answered, smiling. 'I'm accustomed to taking them off. They're always noticed. They've been kept in the family ever since the siege, as a sort of valueless heirloom, for the sake of the picturesqueness of the story, you know ; and nobody ever sees them without asking, as you do, to examine them closely. They deceive even experts at first. But they're paste, all the same ; unmitigated Oriental paste, for all that.'

He took them both off, and handed them to Charles. No man in England is a finer judge of gems than my brother-in-law. I watched him narrowly. He examined them close, first with the naked eye, then with the little pocket-lens which he always carries. 'Admirable imitation,' he muttered, passing them on to Amelia. 'I'm not surprised they should impose upon inexperienced observers.'

But from the tone in which he said it, I could see at once he had satisfied himself they were real gems of unusual value. I know Charles's way of doing business so well. His glance to Amelia meant, 'These are the very stones you have so long been in search of.'

The Scotch lassie laughed a merry laugh. ' He sees through them now, Dick,' she cried. ' I felt sure Sir Charles would be a judge of diamonds.'

Amelia turned them over. I know Amelia, too ; and I knew from the way Amelia looked at them that she meant to have them. And when Amelia means to have anything, people who stand in the way may just as well spare themselves the trouble of opposing her.

They were beautiful diamonds. We found out afterwards the little curate's account was quite correct : these stones *had* come from the same necklet as Amelia's *rivière,* made for a favourite wife of Tippoo's, who had presumably as expansive personal charms

as our beloved sister-in-law's.   More perfect diamonds
have seldom been seen.   They have excited the
universal admiration of thieves and connoisseurs.
Amelia told me afterwards that, according to legend,
a Sepoy stole the necklet at the sack of the palace,
and then fought with another for it.   It was believed
that two stones got spilt in the scuffle, and were
picked up and sold by a third person—a looker-on
—who had no idea of the value of his booty.   Amelia
had been hunting for them for several years to
complete her necklet.

'They are excellent paste,' Sir Charles observed,
handing them back.   'It takes a first-rate judge to
detect them from the reality.   Lady Vandrift has a
necklet much the same in character, but composed
of genuine stones ; and as these are so much like
them, and would complete her set, to all outer
appearance, I wouldn't mind giving you, say, £10
for the pair of them.'

Mrs. Brabazon looked delighted.   'Oh, sell them
to him, Dick,' she cried, 'and buy me a brooch with
the money !   A pair of common links would do for
you just as well.   Ten pounds for two paste stones !
It's quite a lot of money.'

She said it so sweetly, with her pretty Scotch
accent, that I couldn't imagine how Dick had the
heart to refuse her.   But he did, all the same.

'No, Jess, darling,' he answered.   'They're worthless, I know ; but they have for me a certain sentimental value, as I've often told you.   My dear

mother wore them, while she lived, as ear-rings ; and
as soon as she died I had them set as links in order
that I might always keep them about me.   Besides,
they have historical and family interest.   Even a
worthless heirloom, after all, *is* an heirloom.'

Dr. Hector Macpherson looked across and inter-
vened.   'There is a part of my concession,' he said,
'where we have reason to believe a perfect new
Kimberley will soon be discovered.   If at any time
you would care, Sir Charles, to look at my diamonds
—when I get them—it would afford me the greatest
pleasure in life to submit them to your consideration.'

Sir Charles could stand it no longer.   'Sir,' he
said, gazing across at him with his sternest air, 'if
your concession were as full of diamonds as Sindbad
the Sailor's valley, I would not care to turn my head
to look at them.   I am acquainted with the nature
and practice of salting.'   And he glared at the man
with the overhanging eyebrows as if he would devour
him raw.   Poor Dr. Hector Macpherson subsided
instantly.   We learnt a little later that he was a
harmless lunatic, who went about the world with
successive concessions for ruby mines and platinum
reefs, because he had been ruined and driven mad
by speculations in the two, and now recouped himself
by imaginary grants in Burmah and Brazil, or anywhere else that turned up handy.   And his eyebrows,
after all, were of Nature's handicraft.   We were sorry
for the incident ; but a man in Sir Charles's position
is such a mark for rogues that, if he did not take

means to protect himself promptly, he would be for ever overrun by them.

When we went up to our *salon* that evening, Amelia flung herself on the sofa. 'Charles,' she broke out in the voice of a tragedy queen, 'those are

CHARLES, I SHALL NEVER BE HAPPY AGAIN TILL I GET THEM.

real diamonds, and I shall never be happy again till I get them.'

'They are real diamonds,' Charles echoed. 'And you shall have them, Amelia. They're worth not less than three thousand pounds. But I shall bid them up gently.'

So, next day, Charles set to work to higgle with

the curate.   Brabazon, however, didn't care to part
with them.   He was no money-grubber, he said.
He cared more for his mother's gift and a family
tradition than for a hundred pounds, if Sir Charles
were to offer it.   Charles's eye gleamed.   ' But if
I give you *two* hundred ! ' he said insinuatingly.
' What opportunities for good !   You could build a
new wing to your village school-house ! '

' We have ample accommodation,' the curate
answered.   ' No, I don't think I'll sell them.'

Still, his voice faltered somewhat, and he looked
down at them inquiringly.

Charles was too precipitate.

' A hundred pounds more or less matters little to
me,' he said ; ' and my wife has set her heart on
them.   It's every man's duty to please his wife—
isn't it, Mrs. Brabazon ?—I offer you three hundred.'

The little Scotch girl clasped her hands.

' Three hundred pounds !   Oh, Dick, just think
what fun we could have, and what good we could
do with it !   Do let him have them.'

Her accent was irresistible.   But the curate shook
his head.

' Impossible,' he answered.   ' My dear mother's
ear-rings !   Uncle Aubrey would be so angry if he
knew I'd sold them.   I daren't face Uncle Aubrey.'

' Has he expectations from Uncle Aubrey ? ' Sir
Charles asked of White Heather.

Mrs. Brabazon laughed.   ' Uncle Aubrey !   Oh,
dear, no.   Poor dear old Uncle Aubrey !   Why, the

darling old soul hasn't a penny to bless himself with, except his pension. He's a retired post captain.' And she laughed melodiously. She was a charming woman.

'Then I should disregard Uncle Aubrey's feelings,' Sir Charles said decisively.

'No, no,' the curate answered. 'Poor dear old Uncle Aubrey! I wouldn't do anything for the world to annoy him. And he'd be sure to notice it.'

We went back to Amelia. 'Well, have you got them?' she asked.

'No,' Sir Charles answered. 'Not yet. But he's coming round, I think. He's hesitating now. Would rather like to sell them himself, but is afraid what "Uncle Aubrey" would say about the matter. His wife will talk him out of his needless consideration for Uncle Aubrey's feelings; and to-morrow we'll finally clench the bargain.'

Next morning we stayed late in our *salon*, where we always breakfasted, and did not come down to the public rooms till just before *déjeûner*, Sir Charles being busy with me over arrears of correspondence. When we *did* come down the *concierge* stepped forward with a twisted little feminine note for Amelia. She took it and read it. Her countenance fell. 'There, Charles,' she cried, handing it to him, 'you've let the chance slip. I shall *never* be happy now! They've gone off with the diamonds.'

Charles seized the note and read it. Then he passed it on to me. It was short, but final :—

'*Thursday*, 6 *a.m.*

'DEAR LADY VANDRIFT— *Will* you kindly excuse our having gone off hurriedly without bidding you good-bye?   We have just had a horrid telegram to say that Dick's favourite sister is *dangerously* ill of

THE CONCIERGE STEPPED FORWARD WITH A LITTLE NOTE FOR AMELIA.

fever in Paris.   I wanted to shake hands with you before we left—you have all been so sweet to us— but we go by the morning train, absurdly early, and I wouldn't for worlds disturb you.   Perhaps some day we may meet again—though, buried as we are

in a North-country village, it isn't likely ; but in any
case, you have secured the grateful recollection of
Yours very cordially,   JESSIE BRABAZON.

'P.S.—Kindest regards to Sir Charles and those
dear Wentworths, and a kiss for yourself, if I may
venture to send you one.'

'She doesn't even mention where they've gone,'
Amelia exclaimed, in a very bad humour.

'The *concierge* may know,' Isabel suggested,
looking over my shoulder.

We asked at his office.

Yes, the gentleman's address was the Rev. Richard
Peploe Brabazon, Holme Bush Cottage, Empingham,
Northumberland.

Any address where letters might be sent at once,
in Paris ?

For the next ten days, or till further notice,
Hôtel des Deux Mondes, Avenue de l'Opéra.

Amelia's mind was made up at once.

'Strike while the iron's hot,' she cried.   'This
sudden illness, coming at the end of their honeymoon, and involving ten days' more stay at an
expensive hotel, will probably upset the curate's
budget.   He'll be glad to sell now. You'll get them
for three hundred.   It was absurd of Charles to offer
so much at first ; but offered once, of course we must
stick to it.'

'What do you propose to do ? ' Charles asked.
'Write, or telegraph ? '

'Oh, how silly men are!' Amelia cried. 'Is this the sort of business to be arranged by letter, still less by telegram? No. Seymour must start off at once, taking the night train to Paris; and the moment he gets there, he must interview the curate or Mrs. Brabazon. Mrs. Brabazon's the best. She has none of this stupid, sentimental nonsense about Uncle Aubrey.'

It is no part of a secretary's duties to act as a diamond broker. But when Amelia puts her foot down, she puts her foot down—a fact which she is unnecessarily fond of emphasising in that identical proposition. So the self-same evening saw me safe in the train on my way to Paris; and next morning I turned out of my comfortable sleeping-car at the Gare de Strasbourg. My orders were to bring back those diamonds, alive or dead, so to speak, in my pocket to Lucerne; and to offer any needful sum, up to two thousand five hundred pounds, for their immediate purchase.

When I arrived at the Deux Mondes I found the poor little curate and his wife both greatly agitated. They had sat up all night, they said, with their invalid sister; and the sleeplessness and suspense had certainly told upon them after their long railway journey. They were pale and tired, Mrs. Brabazon, in particular, looking ill and worried—too much like White Heather. I was more than half ashamed of bothering them about the diamonds at such a moment, but it occurred to me that Amelia was

probably right—they would now have reached the
end of the sum set apart for their Continental trip,
and a little ready cash might be far from unwelcome.

I broached the subject delicately. It was a fad
of Lady Vandrift's, I said. She had set her heart
upon those useless trinkets. And she wouldn't go
without them. She must and would have them.
But the curate was obdurate. He threw Uncle
Aubrey still in my teeth. Three hundred?—no,
never! A mother's present ; impossible, dear Jessie!
Jessie begged and prayed ; she had grown really
attached to Lady Vandrift, she said ; but the curate
wouldn't hear of it. I went up tentatively to four
hundred. He shook his head gloomily. It wasn't
a question of money, he said. It was a question of
affection. I saw it was no use trying that tack any
longer. I struck out a new line. ' These stones,' I
said, ' I think I ought to inform you, are really
diamonds. Sir Charles is certain of it. Now, is it
right for a man of your profession and position to
be wearing a pair of big gems like those, worth
several hundred pounds, as ordinary sleeve-links ?
A woman ?—yes, I grant you. But for a man, is it
manly ?' And you a cricketer !'

He looked at me and laughed. ' Will nothing
convince you ?' he cried. ' They have been examined
and tested by half a dozen jewellers, and we know
them to be paste. It wouldn't be right of me to sell
them to you under false pretences, however unwilling
on my side. I *couldn't* do it.'

'Well, then,' I said, going up a bit in my bids to meet him, 'I'll put it like this. These gems are paste. But Lady Vandrift has an unconquerable and unaccountable desire to possess them. Money doesn't matter to her. She is a friend of your wife's. As a personal favour, won't you sell them to her for a thousand?'

He shook his head. 'It would be wrong,' he said,—'I might even add, criminal.'

'But we take all risk,' I cried.

He was absolute adamant. 'As a clergyman,' he answered, 'I feel I cannot do it.'

'Will *you* try, Mrs. Brabazon?' I asked.

The pretty little Scotchwoman leant over and whispered. She coaxed and cajoled him. Her ways were winsome. I couldn't hear what she said, but he seemed to give way at last. 'I should love Lady Vandrift to have them,' she murmured, turning to me. 'She *is* such a dear!' And she took out the links from her husband's cuffs and handed them across to me.

'How much?' I asked.

'Two thousand?' she answered, interrogatively. It was a big rise, all at once; but such are the ways of women.

'Done!' I replied. 'Do you consent?'

The curate looked up as if ashamed of himself.

'I consent,' he said slowly, 'since Jessie wishes it. But as a clergyman, and to prevent any future misunderstanding, I should like you to give me a

statement in writing that you buy them on my
distinct and positive declaration that they are made of
paste—old Oriental paste—not genuine stones, and
that I do not claim any other qualities for them.'

I popped the gems into my purse, well pleased.

SHE TOOK OUT THE LINKS FROM HER HUSBAND'S CUFFS.

'Certainly,' I said, pulling out a paper. Charles,
with his unerring business instinct, had anticipated
the request, and given me a signed agreement to
that effect.

'You will take a cheque?' I inquired.

He hesitated.

'Notes of the Bank of France would suit me better,' he answered.

'Very well,' I replied. 'I will go out and get them.'

How very unsuspicious some people are! He allowed me to go off—with the stones in my pocket!

Sir Charles had given me a blank cheque, not exceeding two thousand five hundred pounds. I took it to our agents and cashed it for notes of the Bank of France. The curate clasped them with pleasure. And right glad I was to go back to Lucerne that night, feeling that I had got those diamonds into my hands for about a thousand pounds under their real value!

At Lucerne railway station Amelia met me. She was positively agitated.

'Have you bought them, Seymour?' she asked.

'Yes,' I answered, producing my spoils in triumph.

'Oh, how dreadful!' she cried, drawing back. 'Do you think they're real? Are you sure he hasn't cheated you?'

'Certain of it,' I replied, examining them. 'No one can take me in, in the matter of diamonds. Why on earth should you doubt them?'

'Because I've been talking to Mrs. O'Hagan, at the hotel, and she says there's a well-known trick just like that—she's read of it in a book. A swindler has two sets—one real, one false; and he makes you

buy the false ones by showing you the real, and
pretending he sells them as a special favour.'

'You needn't be alarmed,' I answered.   'I am a
judge of diamonds.'

HAVE YOU BOUGHT THEM, SEYMOUR?

'I shan't be satisfied,' Amelia murmured, 'till
Charles has seen them.'

We went up to the hotel.   For the first time in
her life I saw Amelia really nervous as I handed the

stones to Charles to examine. Her doubt was con-
tagious. I half feared, myself, he might break out
into a deep monosyllabic interjection, losing his
temper in haste, as he often does when things go
wrong. But he looked at them with a smile, while
I told him the price.

'Eight hundred pounds less than their value,' he
answered, well satisfied.

'You have no doubt of their reality?' I asked.

'Not the slightest,' he replied, gazing at them.
'They are genuine stones, precisely the same in quality
and type as Amelia's necklet.'

Amelia drew a sigh of relief. 'I'll go upstairs,'
she said slowly, 'and bring down my own for you both
to compare with them.'

One minute later she rushed down again, breathless. Amelia is far from slim, and I never before
knew her exert herself so actively.

'Charles, Charles!' she cried, 'do you know what
dreadful thing has happened? Two of my own stones
are gone. He's stolen a couple of diamonds from my
necklet, and sold them back to me.'

She held out the *rivière*. It was all too true.
Two gems were missing—and these two just fitted
the empty places!

A light broke in upon me. I clapped my hand
to my head. 'By Jove,' I exclaimed, 'the little
curate is—Colonel Clay!'

Charles clapped his own hand to his brow in
turn. 'And Jessie,' he cried, 'White Heather—that

innocent little Scotchwoman! I often detected a
familiar ring in her voice, in spite of the charming
Highland accent. Jessie is—Madame Picardet!'

We had absolutely no evidence ; but, like the
Commissary at Nice, we felt instinctively sure of it.

Sir Charles was determined to catch the rogue.
This second deception put him on his mettle. ' The
worst of the man is,' he said, ' he has a method. He
doesn't go out of his way to cheat us ; he makes us
go out of ours to be cheated. He lays a trap, and
we tumble headlong into it. To-morrow, Sey, we
must follow him on to Paris.'

Amelia explained to him what Mrs. O'Hagan had
said. Charles took it all in at once, with his usual
sagacity. ' That explains,' he said, ' why the rascal
used this particular trick to draw us on by. If we
had suspected him he could have shown the diamonds
were real, and so escaped detection. It was a blind
to draw us off from the fact of the robbery. He went
to Paris to be out of the way when the discovery was
made, and to get a clear day's start of us. What a
consummate rogue ! And to do me twice running ! '

' How did he get at my jewel - case, though ? '
Amelia exclaimed.

' That's the question,' Charles answered. ' You *do*
leave it about so ! '

' And why didn't he steal the whole *rivière* at once,
and sell the gems ? ' I inquired.

' Too cunning,' Charles replied. ' This was much
better business. It isn't easy to dispose of a big

thing like that. In the first place, the stones are large and valuable ; in the second place, they're well known—every dealer has heard of the Vandrift *rivière*, and seen pictures of the shape of them. They're marked gems, so to speak. No, he played a better game—took a couple of them off, and offered them to the only one person on earth who was likely to buy them without suspicion. He came here, meaning to work this very trick ; he had the links made right to the shape beforehand, and then he stole the stones and slipped them into their places. It's a wonderfully clever trick. Upon my soul, I almost admire the fellow.'

For Charles is a business man himself, and can appreciate business capacity in others.

How Colonel Clay came to know about that necklet, and to appropriate two of the stones, we only discovered much later. I will not here anticipate that disclosure. One thing at a time is a good rule in life. For the moment he succeeded in baffling us altogether.

However, we followed him on to Paris, telegraphing beforehand to the Bank of France to stop the notes. It was all in vain. They had been cashed within half an hour of my paying them. The curate and his wife, we found, quitted the Hôtel des Deux Mondes for parts unknown that same afternoon. And, as usual with Colonel Clay, they vanished into space, leaving no clue behind them. In other words, they changed their disguise, no doubt, and reappeared somewhere else that night in altered characters. At any rate, no such person as the Reverend Richard Peploe Brabazon was ever afterwards heard of—and, for the matter of that, no such village exists as Empingham, Northumberland.

We communicated the matter to the Parisian police. They were *most* unsympathetic. ' It is no doubt Colonel Clay,' said the official whom we saw ; ' but you seem to have little just ground of complaint against him. As far as I can see, messieurs, there is not much to choose between you. You, Monsieur le Chevalier, desired to buy diamonds at the price of paste. You, madame, feared you had bought paste at the price of diamonds. You, monsieur the secretary, tried to get the stones from an unsuspecting person for half their value. He took you all in, that brave Colonel Caoutchouc—it was diamond cut diamond.'

Which was true, no doubt, but by no means consoling.

We returned to the Grand Hotel. Charles was fuming with indignation. ' This is really too much,' he exclaimed. ' What an audacious rascal ! But he will never again take me in, my dear Sey. I only hope he'll try it on. I should love to catch him. I'd know him another time, I'm sure, in spite of his disguises. It's absurd my being tricked twice running like this. But never again while I live ! Never again, I declare to you !'

' *Jamais de la vie !* ' a courier in the hall close by

murmured responsive.   We stood under the verandah
of the Grand Hotel, in the big glass courtyard.   And
I verily believe that courier was really Colonel Clay
himself in one of his disguises.

But perhaps we were beginning to suspect him
everywhere.

III

THE EPISODE OF THE OLD MASTER

LIKE most South Africans, Sir Charles Vandrift is anything but sedentary. He hates sitting down. He must always 'trek.' He cannot live without moving about freely. Six weeks in Mayfair at a time is as much as he can stand. Then he must run away incontinently for rest and change to Scotland, Homburg, Monte Carlo, Biarritz. 'I won't be a limpet on the rock,' he says. Thus it came to pass that in the early autumn we found ourselves stopping at the Métropole at Brighton. We were the accustomed nice little family party—Sir Charles and Amelia, myself and Isabel, with the suite as usual.

On the first Sunday morning after our arrival we strolled out, Charles and I—I regret to say during the hours allotted for Divine service—on to the King's Road, to get a whiff of fresh air, and a glimpse of the waves that were churning the Channel. The two ladies (with their bonnets) had gone to church; but Sir Charles had risen late, fatigued from the week's toil, while I myself was suffering from a

matutinal headache, which I attributed to the close
air in the billiard-room overnight, combined, perhaps,
with the insidious effect of a brand of soda-water to
which I was little accustomed ; I had used it to
dilute my evening whisky.   We were to meet our
wives afterwards at the church parade—an institution
to which I believe both Amelia and Isabel attach
even greater importance than to the sermon which
precedes it.

We sat down on a glass seat.   Charles gazed
inquiringly up and down the King's Road, on the
look-out for a boy with Sunday papers.   At last one
passed.   '*Observer*,' my brother-in-law called out
laconically.

'Ain't got none,' the boy answered, brandishing
his bundle in our faces.   ''Ave a *Referee* or a *Pink
'Un ?*'

Charles, however, is not a Refereader, while as to
the *Pink 'Un*, he considers it unsuitable for public
perusal on Sunday morning.   It may be read indoors,
but in the open air its blush betrays it.   So he shook
his head, and muttered, 'If you pass an *Observer*,
send him on here at once to me.'

A polite stranger who sat close to us turned
round with a pleasant smile.   'Would you allow me
to offer you one?' he said, drawing a copy from his
pocket.   'I fancy I bought the last.   There's a run
on them to-day, you see.   Important news this
morning from the Transvaal.'

Charles raised his eyebrows, and accepted it, as I

thought, just a trifle grumpily. So, to remove the false impression his surliness might produce on so benevolent a mind, I entered into conversation with the polite stranger. He was a man of middle age, and medium height, with a cultivated air, and a pair of gold *pince-nez ;* his eyes were sharp ; his voice was refined ; he dropped into talk before long about

WOULD YOU ALLOW ME TO OFFER YOU ONE?

distinguished people just then in Brighton. It was clear at once that he was hand in glove with many of the very best kind. We compared notes as to Nice, Rome, Florence, Cairo. Our new acquaintance had scores of friends in common with us, it seemed ; indeed, our circles so largely coincided, that I wondered we had never happened till then to knock up against one another.

'And Sir Charles Vandrift, the great African millionaire,' he said at last, 'do you know anything of *him* ?   I'm told he's at present down here at the Métropole.'

I waved my hand towards the person in question.

'*This* is Sir Charles Vandrift,' I answered, with proprietary pride ; 'and *I* am his brother-in-law, Mr. Seymour Wentworth.'

'Oh, indeed !' the stranger answered, with a curious air of drawing in his horns.   I wondered whether he had just been going to pretend he knew Sir Charles, or whether perchance he was on the point of saying something highly uncomplimentary, and was glad to have escaped it.

By this time, however, Charles laid down the paper and chimed into our conversation.   I could see at once from his mollified tone that the news from the Transvaal was favourable to his operations in Cloetedorp Golcondas.   He was therefore in a friendly and affable temper.   His whole manner changed at once.   He grew polite in return to the polite stranger.   Besides, we knew the man moved in the best society ; he had acquaintances whom Amelia was most anxious to secure for her 'At Homes' in Mayfair—young Faith, the novelist, and Sir Richard Montrose, the great Arctic traveller. As for the painters, it was clear that he was sworn friends with the whole lot of them.   He dined with Academicians, and gave weekly breakfasts to the members of the Institute.   Now, Amelia is particularly desirous that her *salon* should not be considered too exclusively financial and political in character : with a solid basis of M.P.'s and millionaires, she loves a delicate under-current of literature, art, and the musical glasses. Our new acquaintance was extremely communicative : ' Knows his place in society, Sey,' Sir Charles said to me afterwards, ' and is therefore not afraid of talking freely, as so many people are who have doubts about their position.' We exchanged cards before we rose. Our new friend's name turned out to be Dr. Edward Polperro.

' In practice here ? ' I inquired, though his garb belied it.

' Oh, not medical,' he answered. ' I am an LL.D. don't you know. I interest myself in art, and buy to some extent for the National Gallery.'

The very man for Amelia's ' At Homes ' ! Sir Charles snapped at him instantly. ' I've brought my four-in-hand down here with me,' he said, in his best friendly manner, ' and we think of tooling over to-morrow to Lewes. If you'd care to take a seat I'm sure Lady Vandrift would be charmed to see you.'

' You're very kind,' the Doctor said, ' on so casual an introduction. I'm sure I shall be delighted.'

' We start from the Métropole at ten-thirty,' Charles went on.

' I shall be there. Good morning ! ' And, with a satisfied smile, he rose and left us, nodding.

We returned to the lawn, to Amelia and Isabel.

Our new friend passed us once or twice. Charles
stopped him and introduced him.   He was walking
with two ladies, most elegantly dressed in rather
peculiar artistic dresses.   Amelia was taken at first
sight by his manner.   'One could see at a glance,'
she said, 'he was a person of culture and of real
distinction.   I wonder whether he could bring the
P.R.A. to my Parliamentary "At Home" on Wednesday fortnight?'

Next day, at ten-thirty, we started on our drive.
Our team has been considered the best in Sussex.
Charles is an excellent, though somewhat anxious—
or, might I say better, somewhat careful?—whip.
He finds the management of two leaders and two
wheelers fills his hands for the moment, both literally
and figuratively, leaving very little time for general
conversation.   Lady Belleisle of Beacon bloomed
beside him on the box (her bloom is perennial, and
applied by her maid) ; Dr. Polperro occupied the
seat just behind with myself and Amelia.   The
Doctor talked most of the time to Lady Vandrift :
his discourse was of picture-galleries, which Amelia
detests, but in which she thinks it incumbent upon
her, as Sir Charles's wife, to affect now and then a
cultivated interest.   *Noblesse oblige;* and the walls
of Castle Seldon, our place in Ross-shire, are almost
covered now with Leaders and with Orchardsons.
This result was first arrived at by a singular accident.
Sir Charles wanted a leader—for his coach, you
understand—and told an artistic friend so.   The

artistic friend brought him a Leader next week with
a capital L; and Sir Charles was so taken aback
that he felt ashamed to confess the error. So he
was turned unawares into a patron of painting.

Dr. Polperro, in spite of his too pronouncedly
artistic talk, proved on closer view a most agreeable
companion. He diversified his art cleverly with
anecdotes and scandals; he told us exactly which
famous painters had married their cooks, and which
had only married their models; and otherwise
showed himself a most diverting talker. Among
other things, however, he happened to mention once
that he had recently discovered a genuine Rembrandt
—a quite undoubted Rembrandt, which had remained
for years in the keeping of a certain obscure Dutch
family. It had always been allowed to be a masterpiece of the painter, but it had seldom been seen
for the last half-century save by a few intimate
acquaintances. It was a portrait of one Maria
Vanrenen of Haarlem, and he had bought it of her
descendants at Gouda, in Holland.

I saw Charles prick up his ears, though he took
no open notice. This Maria Vanrenen, as it
happened, was a remote collateral ancestress of the
Vandrifts, before they emigrated to the Cape in
1780; and the existence of the portrait, though not
its whereabouts, was well known in the family.
Isabel had often mentioned it. If it was to be had
at anything like a reasonable price, it would be a
splendid thing for the boys (Sir Charles, I ought to

say, has two sons at Eton) to possess an undoubted portrait of an ancestress by Rembrandt.

Dr. Polperro talked a good deal after that about this valuable find. He had tried to sell it at first to the National Gallery ; but though the Directors admired the work immensely, and admitted its genuineness, they regretted that the funds at their disposal this year did not permit them to acquire so important a canvas at a proper figure. South Kensington again was too poor ; but the Doctor was in treaty at present with the Louvre and with Berlin. Still, it was a pity a fine work of art like that, once brought into the country, should be allowed to go out of it. Some patriotic patron of the fine arts ought to buy it for his own house, or else munificently present it to the nation.

All the time Charles said nothing. But I could feel him cogitating. He even looked behind him once, near a difficult corner (while the guard was actually engaged in tootling his horn to let passers-by know that the coach was coming), and gave Amelia a warning glance to say nothing committing, which had at once the requisite effect of sealing her mouth for the moment. It is a very unusual thing for Charles to look back while driving. I gathered from his doing so that he was inordinately anxious to possess this Rembrandt.

When we arrived at Lewes we put up our horses at the inn, and Charles ordered a lunch on his wonted scale of princely magnificence. Meanwhile we wandered, two and two, about the town and castle. I annexed Lady Belleisle, who is at least amusing. Charles drew me aside before starting. 'Look here, Sey,' he said, 'we must be *very* careful. This man, Polperro, is a chance acquaintance. There's nothing an astute rogue can take one in over more easily than an Old Master. If the Rembrandt is genuine I ought to have it ; if it really represents Maria Vanrenen, it's a duty I owe to the boys to buy it. But I've been done twice lately, and I won't be done a third time. We must go to work cautiously.'

'You are right,' I answered. 'No more seers and curates !'

'If this man's an impostor,' Charles went on— 'and in spite of what he says about the National Gallery and so forth, we know nothing of him—the story he tells is just the sort of one such a fellow would trump up in a moment to deceive me. He could easily learn who I was—I'm a well-known figure ; he knew I was in Brighton, and he may have been sitting on that glass seat on Sunday on purpose to entrap me.'

'He introduced your name,' I said, 'and the moment he found out who I was he plunged into talk with me.'

'Yes,' Charles continued. 'He may have learned about the portrait of Maria Vanrenen, which my grandmother always said was preserved at Gouda ; and, indeed, I myself have often mentioned it, as you

doubtless remember.   If so, what more natural, say,
for a rogue than to begin talking about the portrait
in that innocent way to Amelia ?   If he wants a
Rembrandt, I believe they can be turned out to
order to any amount in Birmingham.   The moral of
all which is, it behoves us to be careful.'

'Right you are,' I answered ; 'and I am keeping
my eye upon him.'

We drove back by another road, overshadowed
by beech-trees in autumnal gold.   It was a delightful excursion.   Dr. Polperro's heart was elated by
lunch and the excellent dry Monopole.   He talked
amazingly.   I never heard a man with a greater or
more varied flow of anecdote.   He had been everywhere and knew all about everybody.   Amelia
booked him at once for her 'At Home' on
Wednesday week, and he promised to introduce
her to several artistic and literary celebrities.

That evening, however, about half-past seven,
Charles and I strolled out together on the King's
Road for a blow before dinner.   We dine at eight.
The air was delicious.   We passed a small new
hotel, very smart and exclusive, with a big bow
window.   There, in evening dress, lights burning and
blind up, sat our friend, Dr. Polperro, with a lady
facing him, young, graceful, and pretty.   A bottle of
champagne stood open before him.   He was helping
himself plentifully to hot-house grapes, and full of
good humour.   It was clear he and the lady were
occupied in the intense enjoyment of some capital

joke ; for they looked queerly at one another, and burst now and again into merry peals of laughter.

I drew back. So did Sir Charles. One idea passed at once through both our minds. I murmured, 'Colonel Clay!' He answered, '*And* Madame Picardet!'

THERE SAT OUR FRIEND, DR. POLPERRO.

They were not in the least like the Reverend Richard and Mrs. Brabazon. But that clinched the matter. Nor did I see a sign of the aquiline nose of the Mexican Seer. Still, I had learnt by then to discount appearances. If these were indeed the famous sharper and his wife or accomplice, we must be very careful. We were forewarned this time. Supposing he had the audacity to try a third trick of the sort upon us we had him under our thumbs. Only, we must take steps to prevent his dexterously slipping through our fingers.

' He can wriggle like an eel,' said the Commissary at Nice. We both recalled those words, and laid our plans deep to prevent the man's wriggling away from us on this third occasion.

' I tell you what it is, Sey,' my brother-in-law said, with impressive slowness. ' This time we must deliberately lay ourselves out to be swindled. We must propose of our own accord to buy the picture, making him guarantee it in writing as a genuine Rembrandt, and taking care to tie him down by most stringent conditions. But we must seem at the same time to be unsuspicious and innocent as babes ; we must swallow whole whatever lies he tells us ; pay his price—nominally—by cheque for the portrait ; and then, arrest him the moment the bargain is complete, with the proofs of his guilt then and there upon him. Of course, what he'll try to do will be to vanish into thin air at once, as he did at Nice and Paris ; but, this time, we'll have the police in waiting and everything ready. We'll avoid precipitancy, but we'll avoid delay too. We must hold our hands off till he's actually accepted and pocketed the money ; and then, we must nab him instantly, and walk him off to the local Bow Street. That's my plan of campaign. Meanwhile, we should appear all trustful innocence and confiding guilelessness.'

In pursuance of this well-laid scheme, we called

next day on Dr. Polperro at his hotel, and were
introduced to his wife, a dainty little woman, in
whom we affected not to recognise that arch Madame
Picardet or that simple White Heather.   The Doctor
talked charmingly (as usual) about art—what a well-
informed rascal he was, to be sure!—and Sir Charles
expressed some interest in the supposed Rembrandt.
Our new friend was delighted ; we could see by his
well-suppressed eagerness of tone that he knew us
at once for probable purchasers.   He would run up
to town next day, he said, and bring down the
portrait.   And in effect, when Charles and I took
our wonted places in the Pullman next morning, on
our way up to the half-yearly meeting of Cloetedorp
Golcondas, there was our Doctor, leaning back in his
arm-chair as if the car belonged to him.   Charles
gave me an expressive look.   'Does it in style,' he
whispered, 'doesn't he ?   Takes it out of my five
thousand ; or discounts the amount he means to
chouse me of with his spurious Rembrandt.'

Arrived in town, we went to work at once.   We
set a private detective from Marvillier's to watch our
friend ; and from him we learned that the so-called
Doctor dropped in for a picture that day at a dealer's
in the West-end (I suppress the name, having a
judicious fear of the law of libel ever before my
eyes), a dealer who was known to be mixed up
before then in several shady or disreputable transactions.   Though, to be sure, my experience has been
that picture dealers are—picture dealers.   Horses

rank first in my mind as begetters and producers of unscrupulous agents, but pictures run them a very good second.   Anyhow, we found out that our distinguished art-critic picked up his Rembrandt at this dealer's shop, and came down with it in his care the same night to Brighton.

IN HIS JUDGMENT, IT WAS NOT A REMBRANDT AT ALL.

In order not to act precipitately, and so ruin our plans, we induced Dr. Polperro (what a cleverly chosen name!) to bring the Rembrandt round to the Métropole for our inspection, and to leave it with us while we got the opinion of an expert from London.

The expert came down, and gave us a full report upon the alleged Old Master.   In his judgment, it

was not a Rembrandt at all, but a cunningly-painted
and well-begrimed modern Dutch imitation. Moreover, he showed us by documentary evidence that
the real portrait of Maria Vanrenen had, as a matter
of fact, been brought to England five years before,
and sold to Sir J. H. Tomlinson, the well-known
connoisseur, for eight thousand pounds. Dr. Polperro's
picture was, therefore, at best either a replica by Rembrandt; or else, more probably, a copy by a pupil;
or, most likely of all, a mere modern forgery.

We were thus well prepared to fasten our charge
of criminal conspiracy upon the self-styled Doctor.
But in order to make assurance still more certain,
we threw out vague hints to him that the portrait of
Maria Vanrenen might really be elsewhere, and even
suggested in his hearing that it might not improbably
have got into the hands of that omnivorous collector,
Sir J. H. Tomlinson. But the vendor was proof
against all such attempts to decry his goods. He
had the effrontery to brush away the documentary
evidence, and to declare that Sir J. H. Tomlinson
(one of the most learned and astute picture-buyers
in England) had been smartly imposed upon by a
needy Dutch artist with a talent for forgery. The
real Maria Vanrenen, he declared and swore, was
the one he offered us. 'Success has turned the
man's head,' Charles said to me, well pleased. 'He
thinks we will swallow any obvious lie he chooses to
palm off upon us. But the bucket has come once too
often to the well. This time we checkmate him.' It

was a mixed metaphor, I admit ; but Sir Charles's tropes are not always entirely superior to criticism.

So we pretended to believe our man, and accepted his assurances.   Next came the question of price. This was warmly debated, for form's sake only. Sir J. H. Tomlinson had paid eight thousand for his genuine Maria.   The Doctor demanded ten thousand for his spurious one.   There was really no reason why we should higgle and dispute, for Charles meant merely to give his cheque for the sum and then arrest the fellow ; but, still, we thought it best for the avoidance of suspicion to make a show of resistance ; and we at last beat him down to nine thousand guineas. For this amount he was to give us a written warranty that the work he sold us was a genuine Rembrandt, that it represented Maria Vanrenen of Haarlem, and that he had bought it direct, without doubt or question, from that good lady's descendants at Gouda, in Holland.

It was capitally done.   We arranged the thing to perfection.   We had a constable in waiting in our rooms at the Métropole, and we settled that Dr. Polperro was to call at the hotel at a certain fixed hour to sign the warranty and receive his money. A regular agreement on sound stamped paper was drawn out between us.   At the appointed time the 'party of the first part' came, having already given us over possession of the portrait.   Charles drew a cheque for the amount agreed upon, and signed it. Then he handed it to the Doctor.   Polperro just clutched at it.   Meanwhile, I took up my post by the door, while two men in plain clothes, detectives from the police-station, stood as men-servants and watched the windows. We feared lest the impostor, once he had got the cheque, should dodge us somehow, as he had already done at Nice and in Paris. The moment he had pocketed his money with a smile of triumph, I advanced to him rapidly. I had in my possession a pair of handcuffs. Before he knew what was happening, I had slipped them on his wrists and secured them dexterously, while the constable stepped foward. 'We have got you this time!' I cried. 'We know who you are, Dr. Polperro. You are—Colonel Clay, *alias* Señor Antonio Herrera, *alias* the Reverend Richard Peploe Brabazon.'

I never saw any man so astonished in my life! He was utterly flabbergasted. Charles thought he must have expected to get clear away at once, and that this prompt action on our part had taken the fellow so much by surprise as to simply unman him. He gazed about him as if he hardly realised what was happening.

'Are these two raving maniacs?' he asked at last, 'or what do they mean by this nonsensical gibberish about Antonio Herrera?'

The constable laid his hand on the prisoner's shoulder.

'It's all right, my man,' he said. 'We've got warrants out against you. I arrest you, Edward Polperro, *alias* the Reverend Richard Peploe Brabazon, on a charge of obtaining money under false pretences from Sir Charles Vandrift, K.C.M.G.,

M.P., on his sworn information, now here subscribed
to.' For Charles had had the thing drawn out in
readiness beforehand.

Our prisoner drew himself up. ' Look here,

IT'S ALL RIGHT, MY MAN, HE SAID.

officer,' he said, in an offended tone, ' there's some
mistake here in this matter. I have never given an
alias at any time in my life. How do you know
this is really Sir Charles Vandrift? It may be a
case of bullying personation. My belief is, though,
they're a pair of escaped lunatics.'

' We'll see about that to-morrow,' the constable said, collaring him. ' At present you've got to go off with me quietly to the station, where these gentlemen will enter up the charge against you.'

They carried him off, protesting. Charles and I signed the charge-sheet ; and the officer locked him up to await his examination next day before the magistrate.

We were half afraid even now the fellow would manage somehow to get out on bail and give us the slip in spite of everything ; and, indeed, he protested in the most violent manner against the treatment to which we were subjecting ' a gentleman in his position.' But Charles took care to tell the police it was all right ; that he was a dangerous and peculiarly slippery criminal, and that on no account must they let him go on any pretext whatever, till he had been properly examined before the magistrates.

We learned at the hotel that night, curiously enough, that there really *was* a Dr. Polperro, a distinguished art critic, whose name, we didn't doubt, our impostor had been assuming.

Next morning, when we reached the court, an inspector met us with a very long face. ' Look here, gentlemen,' he said, ' I'm afraid you've com-mitted a very serious blunder. You've made a precious bad mess of it. You've got yourselves into a scrape ; and, what's worse, you've got us into one also. You were a deal too smart with your sworn information. We've made inquiries about this gentleman, and we find the account he gives of himself is perfectly correct. His name *is* Polperro ; he's a well-known art critic and collector of pictures, employed abroad by the National Gallery. He was formerly an official in the South Kensington Museum, and he's a C.B. and LL.D., very highly respected. You've made a sad mistake, that's where it is ; and you'll probably have to answer a charge of false imprisonment, in which I'm afraid you have also involved our own department.'

Charles gasped with horror. ' You haven't let him out,' he cried, ' on those absurd representations ? You haven't let him slip through your hands as you did that murderer fellow ? '

' Let him slip through our hands ? ' the inspector cried. ' I only wish he would. There's no chance of that, unfortunately. He's in the court there, this moment, breathing out fire and slaughter against you both ; and we're here to protect you if he should happen to fall upon you. He's been locked up all night on your mistaken affidavits, and, naturally enough, he's mad with anger.'

' If you haven't let him go, I'm satisfied,' Charles answered. ' He's a fox for cunning. Where is he ? Let me see him.'

We went into the court. There we saw our prisoner conversing amicably, in the most excited way, with the magistrate (who, it seems, was a personal friend of his) ; and Charles at once went

up and spoke to them. Dr. Polperro turned round
and glared at him through his *pince-nez*.

'The only possible explanation of this person's
extraordinary and incredible conduct,' he said, 'is,
that he must be mad—and his secretary equally so.
He made my acquaintance, unasked, on a glass seat
on the King's Road ; invited me to go on his coach
to Lewes ; volunteered to buy a valuable picture of
me ; and then, at the last moment, unaccountably
gave me in charge on this silly and preposterous
trumped-up accusation. I demand a summons for
false imprisonment.'

Suddenly it began to dawn upon us that the
tables were turned. By degrees it came out that we
had made a mistake. Dr. Polperro was really the
person he represented himself to be, and had been
always. His picture, we found out, was the real
Maria Vanrenen, and a genuine Rembrandt, which he
had merely deposited for cleaning and restoring at
the suspicious dealer's. Sir J. H. Tomlinson had been
imposed upon and cheated by a cunning Dutchman ;
his picture, though also an undoubted Rembrandt,
was *not* the Maria, and was an inferior specimen in
bad preservation. The authority we had consulted
turned out to be an ignorant, self-sufficient quack.
The Maria, moreover, was valued by other experts at
no more than five or six thousand guineas. Charles
wanted to cry off his bargain, but Dr. Polperro
naturally wouldn't hear of it. The agreement was a
legally binding instrument, and what passed in

Charles's mind at the moment had nothing to do with the written contract. Our adversary only consented to forego the action for false imprisonment on condition that Charles inserted a printed apology in the *Times*, and paid him five hundred pounds compensation for damage to character. So that was the end of our well-planned attempt to arrest the swindler.

Not quite the end, however ; for, of course, after this, the whole affair got by degrees into the papers. Dr. Polperro, who was a familiar person in literary and artistic society, as it turned out, brought an action against the so-called expert who had declared against the genuineness of his alleged Rembrandt, and convicted him of the grossest ignorance and misstatement. Then paragraphs got about. The *World* showed us up in a sarcastic article ; and *Truth*, which has always been terribly severe upon Sir Charles and all the other South Africans, had a pungent set of verses on ' High Art in Kimberley.' By this means, as we suppose, the affair became known to Colonel Clay himself ; for a week or two later my brother-in-law received a cheerful little note on scented paper from our persistent sharper. It was couched in these terms :—

' Oh, you innocent infant !

' Bless your ingenuous little heart ! And did it believe, then, it had positively caught the redoubtable colonel ? And had it ready a nice little pinch of salt to put upon his tail ? And is it true its

respected name is Sir Simple Simon? How heartily
we have laughed, White Heather and I, at your
neat little ruses! It would pay you, by the way,

A CHEERFUL LITTLE NOTE.

to take White Heather into your house for six
months to instruct you in the agreeable sport of
amateur detectives. Your charming *naïveté* quite

moves our envy. So you actually imagined a man of my brains would condescend to anything so flat and stale as the silly and threadbare Old Master deception! And this in the so-called nineteenth century! *O sancta simplicitas!* When again shall such infantile transparency be mine? When, ah, when? But never mind, dear friend. Though you didn't catch me, we shall meet before long at some delightful Philippi.

'Yours, with the profoundest respect and gratitude,

'ANTONIO HERRERA,
'Otherwise RICHARD PEPLOE BRABAZON.'

Charles laid down the letter with a deep-drawn sigh. 'Sey, my boy,' he mused aloud, 'no fortune on earth—not even mine—can go on standing it. These perpetual drains begin really to terrify me. I foresee the end. I shall die in a workhouse. What with the money he robs me of when he *is* Colonel Clay, and the money I waste upon him when he *isn't* Colonel Clay, the man is beginning to tell upon my nervous system. I shall withdraw altogether from this worrying life. I shall retire from a scheming and polluted world to some untainted spot in the fresh, pure mountains.'

'You *must* need rest and change,' I said, 'when you talk like that. Let us try the Tyrol.'

IV

THE EPISODE OF THE TYROLEAN CASTLE

WE went to Meran. The place was practically
decided for us by Amelia's French maid, who really
acts on such occasions as our guide and courier.

She is *such* a clever girl, is Amelia's French
maid. Whenever we are going anywhere, Amelia
generally asks (and accepts) her advice as to choice
of hotels and furnished villas. Césarine has been
all over the Continent in her time; and, being
Alsatian by birth, she of course speaks German as
well as she speaks French, while her long residence
with Amelia has made her at last almost equally at
home in our native English. She is a treasure, that
girl; so neat and dexterous, and not above dabbling
in anything on earth she may be asked to turn her
hand to. She walks the world with a needle-case
in one hand and an etna in the other. She can
cook an omelette on occasion, or drive a Norwegian
cariole; she can sew, and knit, and make dresses,
and cure a cold, and do anything else on earth you
ask her. Her salads are the most savoury I ever
tasted; while as for her coffee (which she prepares

for us in the train on long journeys), there isn't a *chef de cuisine* at a West-end club to be named in the same day with her.

So, when Amelia said, in her imperious way, 'Césarine, we want to go to the Tyrol—now—at once—in mid-October ; where do you advise us to put up?'—Césarine answered, like a shot, 'The Erzherzog Johann, of course, at Meran, for the autumn, madame.'

'Is he . . . an archduke?' Amelia asked, a little staggered at such apparent familiarity with Imperial personages.

'*Ma foi !* no, madame.   He is an hotel—as you would say in England, the " Victoria " or the " Prince of Wales's "—the most comfortable hotel in all South Tyrol ; and at this time of year, naturally, you must go beyond the Alps ; it begins already to be cold at Innsbruck.'

So to Meran we went ; and a prettier or more picturesque place, I confess, I have seldom set eyes on.   A rushing torrent ; high hills and mountain peaks ; terraced vineyard slopes ; old walls and towers ; quaint, arcaded streets ; a craggy waterfall ; a promenade after the fashion of a German Spa ; and when you lift your eyes from the ground, jagged summits of Dolomites : it was a combination such as I had never before beheld ; a Rhine town plumped down among green Alpine heights, and threaded by the cool colonnades of Italy.

I approved Césarine's choice ; and I was

particularly glad she had pronounced for an hotel,
where all is plain sailing, instead of advising a
furnished villa, the arrangements for which would
naturally have fallen in large part upon the shoulders
of the wretched secretary.   As in any case I have

MERCI, MONSIEUR !

to do three hours' work a day, I feel that such
additions to my normal burden may well be spared
me.   I tipped Césarine half a sovereign, in fact, for
her judicious choice.   Césarine glanced at it on her
palm in her mysterious, curious, half-smiling way,
and pocketed it at once with a 'Merci, monsieur !'

that had a touch of contempt in it. I always fancy
Césarine has large ideas of her own on the subject of
tipping, and thinks very small beer of the modest
sums a mere secretary can alone afford to bestow
upon her.

The great peculiarity of Meran is the number of
schlosses (I believe my plural is strictly irregular,
but very convenient to English ears) which you can
see in every direction from its outskirts. A statistical
eye, it is supposed, can count no fewer than forty of
these picturesque, ramshackled old castles from a
point on the Küchelberg. For myself, I hate
statistics (except as an element in financial prospectuses), and I really don't know how many ruinous
piles Isabel and Amelia counted under Césarine's
guidance; but I remember that most of them were
quaint and beautiful, and that their variety of
architecture seemed positively bewildering. One
would be square, with funny little turrets stuck out
at each angle; while another would rejoice in a big
round keep, and spread on either side long, ivy-
clad walls and delightful bastions. Charles was
immensely taken with them. He loves the picturesque, and has a poet hidden in that financial soul
of his. (Very effectually hidden, though, I am ready
to grant you.) From the moment he came he felt
at once he would love to possess a castle of his own
among these romantic mountains. 'Seldon!' he
exclaimed contemptuously. 'They call Seldon a
castle! But you and I know very well, Sey, it

was built in 1860, with sham antique stones, for
Macpherson of Seldon, at market rates, by Cubitt
and Co., worshipful contractors of London. Macpherson charged me for that sham antiquity a
preposterous price, at which one ought to procure a
real ancestral mansion. Now, *these* castles are real.
They are hoary with antiquity. Schloss Tyrol is
Romanesque—tenth or eleventh century.' (He had
been reading it up in *Baedeker*.) 'That's the sort
of place for *me!*—tenth or eleventh century. I
could live here, remote from stocks and shares, for
ever ; and in these sequestered glens, recollect, Sey,
my boy, there are no Colonel Clays, and no arch
Madame Picardets !'

As a matter of fact, he could have lived there six
weeks, and then tired for Park Lane, Monte Carlo,
Brighton.

As for Amelia, strange to say, she was equally
taken with this new fad of Charles's. As a rule she
hates everywhere on earth save London, except
during the time when no respectable person can be
seen in town, and when modest blinds shade the
scandalised face of Mayfair and Belgravia. She
bores herself to death even at Seldon Castle, Ross-
shire, and yawns all day long in Paris or Vienna.
She is a confirmed Cockney. Yet, for some occult
reason, my amiable sister-in-law fell in love with
South Tyrol. She wanted to vegetate in that lush
vegetation. The grapes were being picked ; pump-
kins hung over the walls ; Virginia creeper draped

the quaint gray schlosses with crimson cloaks ; and
everything was as beautiful as a dream of Burne-
Jones's. (I know I am quite right in mentioning
Burne-Jones, especially in connection with Romanesque architecture, because I heard him highly praised
on that very ground by our friend and enemy, Dr.
Edward Polperro.) So perhaps it was excusable
that Amelia should fall in love with it all, under the
circumstances ; besides, she is largely influenced by
what Césarine says, and Césarine declares there is no
climate in Europe like Meran in winter. I do not
agree with her. The sun sets behind the hills at
three in the afternoon, and a nasty warm wind blows
moist over the snow in January and February.

However, Amelia set Césarine to inquire of the
people at the hotel about the market price of tumble-
down ruins, and the number of such eligible family
mausoleums just then for sale in the immediate
neighbourhood. Césarine returned with a full, true,
and particular list, adorned with flowers of rhetoric
which would have delighted the soul of good old
John Robins. They were all picturesque, all
Romanesque, all richly ivy-clad, all commodious,
all historical, and all the property of high well-born
Grafs and very honourable Freiherrs. Most of them
had been the scene of celebrated tournaments ; several
of them had witnessed the gorgeous marriages of
Holy Roman Emperors ; and every one of them was
provided with some choice and selected first-class
murders. Ghosts could be arranged for or not, as

desired ; and armorial bearings could be thrown in
with the moat for a moderate extra remuneration.

The two we liked best of all these tempting piles
were Schloss Planta and Schloss Lebenstein. We
drove past both, and even I myself, I confess, was

CÉSARINE RETURNED WITH A FULL, TRUE, AND PARTICULAR LIST.

distinctly taken with them. (Besides, when a big
purchase like this is on the stocks, a poor beggar of
a secretary has always a chance of exerting his
influence and earning for himself some modest commission.) Schloss Planta was the most striking
externally, I should say, with its Rhine-like towers,

and its great gnarled ivy-stems, that looked as if
they antedated the House of Hapsburg ; but Lebenstein was said to be better preserved within, and more
fitted in every way for modern occupation. Its
staircase has been photographed by 7000 amateurs.

We got tickets to view. The invaluable Césarine
procured them for us. Armed with these, we drove
off one fine afternoon, meaning to go to Planta, by
Césarine's recommendation. Half-way there, however, we changed our minds, as it was such a lovely
day, and went on up the long, slow hill to Lebenstein.
I must say the drive through the grounds was simply
charming. The castle stands perched (say rather
poised, like St. Michael the archangel in Italian
pictures) on a solitary stack or crag of rock, looking
down on every side upon its own rich vineyards.
Chestnuts line the glens ; the valley of the Etsch
spreads below like a picture.

The vineyards alone make a splendid estate, by
the way ; they produce a delicious red wine, which
is exported to Bordeaux, and there bottled and sold
as a vintage claret under the name of Château
Monnivet. Charles revelled in the idea of growing
his own wines.

'Here we could sit,' he cried to Amelia, 'in the
most literal sense, under our own vine and fig-tree.
Delicious retirement ! For my part, I'm sick and
tired of the hubbub of Threadneedle Street.'

We knocked at the door—for there was really no
bell, but a ponderous, old-fashioned, wrought-iron

knocker. So deliciously mediæval! The late Graf Von Lebenstein had recently died, we knew; and his son, the present Count, a young man of means, having inherited from his mother's family a still more ancient and splendid schloss in the Salzburg district, desired to sell this outlying estate in order to afford himself a yacht, after the manner that is now becoming increasingly fashionable with the noblemen and gentlemen in Germany and Austria.

The door was opened for us by a high well-born menial, attired in a very ancient and honourable livery. Nice antique hall; suits of ancestral armour, trophies of Tyrolese hunters, coats of arms of ancient counts—the very thing to take Amelia's aristocratic and romantic fancy. The whole to be sold exactly as it stood; ancestors to be included at a valuation.

We went through the reception-rooms. They were lofty, charming, and with glorious views, all the more glorious for being framed by those graceful Romanesque windows, with their slender pillars and quaint, round-topped arches. Sir Charles had made his mind up. 'I must and will have it!' he cried. 'This is the place for me. Seldon! Pah, Seldon is a modern abomination.'

Could we see the high well-born Count? The liveried servant (somewhat haughtily) would inquire of his Serenity. Sir Charles sent up his card, and also Lady Vandrift's. These foreigners know title spells money in England.

He was right in his surmise. Two minutes later

the Count entered with our cards in his hands.   A
good-looking young man, with the characteristic
Tyrolese long black moustache, dressed in a gentlemanly variant on the costume of the country.   His
air was a jäger's ; the usual blackcock's plume stuck
jauntily in the side of the conical hat (which he held
in his hand), after the universal Austrian fashion.

He waved us to seats.   We sat down.   He spoke
to us in French ; his English, he remarked, with a
pleasant smile, being a *négligeable* quantity.   We
might speak it, he went on ; he could understand
pretty well ; but he preferred to answer, if we would
allow him, in French or German.

' French,' Charles replied, and the negotiation
continued thenceforth in that language,   It is the
only one, save English and his ancestral Dutch, with
which my brother-in-law possesses even a nodding
acquaintance.

We praised the beautiful scene.   The Count's
face lighted up with patriotic pride.   Yes ; it was
beautiful, beautiful, his own green Tyrol.   He was
proud of it and attached to it.   But he could endure
to sell this place, the home of his fathers, because he
had a finer in the Salzkammergut, and a *pied-à-terre*
near Innsbruck.   For Tyrol lacked just one joy—
the sea.   He was a passionate yachtsman.   For that
he had resolved to sell this estate ; after all, three
country houses, a ship, and a mansion in Vienna, are
more than one man can comfortably inhabit.

' Exactly,' Charles answered.   ' If I can come to

terms with you about this charming estate I shall sell my own castle in the Scotch Highlands.' And he tried to look like a proud Scotch chief who harangues his clansmen.

Then they got to business. The Count was a delightful man to do business with. His manners were perfect. While we were talking to him, a surly person, a steward or bailiff, or something of the sort, came into the room unexpectedly and addressed him in German, which none of us understand. We were impressed by the singular urbanity and benignity of the nobleman's demeanour towards this sullen dependant. He evidently explained to the fellow what sort of people we were, and remonstrated with him in a very gentle way for interrupting us. The steward understood, and clearly regretted his insolent air ; for after a few sentences he went out, and as he did so he bowed and made protestations of polite regard in his own language. The Count turned to us and smiled. ' Our people,' he said, ' are like your own Scotch peasants—kind-hearted, picturesque, free, musical, poetic, but wanting, *hélas*, in polish to strangers.' He was certainly an exception, if he described them aright ; for he made us feel at home from the moment we entered.

He named his price in frank terms. His lawyers at Meran held the needful documents, and would arrange the negotiations in detail with us. It was a stiff sum, I must say—an extremely stiff sum ; but no doubt he was charging us a fancy price for a fancy

castle. 'He will come down in time,' Charles said.
'The sum first named in all these transactions is
invariably a feeler. They know I'm a millionaire ;
and people always imagine millionaires are positively
made of money.'

I may add that people always imagine it must be
easier to squeeze money out of millionaires than out
of other people—which is the reverse of the truth, or
how could they ever have amassed their millions ?
Instead of oozing gold as a tree oozes gum, they
mop it up like blotting-paper, and seldom give it
out again.

We drove back from this first interview none the
less very well satisfied. The price was too high ; but
preliminaries were arranged, and for the rest, the Count
desired us to discuss all details with his lawyers
in the chief street, Unter den Lauben. We inquired
about these lawyers, and found they were most
respectable and respected men ; they had done the
family business on either side for seven generations.

They showed us plans and title-deeds. Everything quite *en règle*. Till we came to the price
there was no hitch of any sort.

As to price, however, the lawyers were obdurate.
They stuck out for the Count's first sum to the utter-
most florin. It was a very big estimate. We talked
and shilly-shallied till Sir Charles grew angry. He
lost his temper at last.

'They know I'm a millionaire, Sey,' he said, 'and
they're playing the old game of trying to diddle me.

But I won't be diddled. Except Colonel Clay, no man has ever yet succeeded in bleeding me. And shall I let myself be bled as if I were a chamois among these innocent mountains? Perish the thought!' Then he reflected a little in silence. ' Sey,' he mused on, at last, ' the question is, *are* they innocent? Do you know, I begin to believe there is no such thing left as pristine innocence anywhere.

AS TO PRICE, THE LAWYERS WERE OBDURATE.

This Tyrolese Count knows the value of a pound as distinctly as if he hung out in Capel Court or Kimberley.'

Things dragged on in this way, inconclusively, for a week or two. *We* bid down ; the lawyers stuck to it. Sir Charles grew half sick of the whole silly business. For my own part, I felt sure if the high well-born Count didn't quicken his pace, my respected relative would shortly have had enough of the Tyrol altogether, and be proof against the most lovely of crag-crowning castles. But the Count didn't see it. He came to call on us at our hotel— a rare honour for a stranger with these haughty and exclusive Tyrolese nobles—and even entered un-announced in the most friendly manner. But when it came to £ s. d., he was absolute adamant. Not one kreutzer would he abate from his original proposal.

'You misunderstand,' he said, with pride. 'We Tyrolese gentlemen are not shopkeepers or merchants, We do not higgle. If we say a thing we stick to it. Were you an Austrian, I should feel insulted by your ill-advised attempt to beat down my price. But as you belong to a great commercial nation——' he broke off with a snort and shrugged his shoulders compassionately.

We saw him several times driving in and out of the schloss, and every time he waved his hand at us gracefully. But when we tried to bargain, it was always the same thing : he retired behind the shelter of his Tyrolese nobility. We might take it or leave it. 'Twas still Schloss Lebenstein.

The lawyers were as bad. We tried all we knew, and got no forrarder.

At last Charles gave up the attempt in disgust. He was tiring, as I expected. 'It's the prettiest place I ever saw in my life,' he said ; 'but, hang it all, Sey, I *won't* be imposed upon.'

So he made up his mind, it being now December,

to return to London.   We met the Count next day,
and stopped his carriage, and told him so.   Charles
thought this would have the immediate effect of
bringing the man to reason.   But he only lifted his
hat, with the blackcock's feather, and smiled a bland
smile.   ' The Archduke Karl is inquiring about it,'
he answered, and drove on without parley.

Charles used some strong words, which I will not
transcribe (I am a family man), and returned to
England.

For the next two months we heard little from
Amelia save her regret that the Count wouldn't sell
us Schloss Lebenstein.   Its pinnacles had fairly
pierced her heart.   Strange to say, she was absolutely
infatuated about the castle.   She rather wanted the
place while she was there, and thought she could
get it ; now she thought she couldn't, her soul (if
she has one) was wildly set upon it.   Moreover,
Césarine further inflamed her desire by gently hinting
a fact which she had picked up at the courier's *table
d'hôte* at the hotel—that the Count had been far
from anxious to sell his ancestral and historical
estate to a South African diamond king.   He
thought the honour of the family demanded, at least,
that he should secure a wealthy buyer of good
ancient lineage.

One morning in February, however, Amelia
returned from the Row all smiles and tremors.
(She had been ordered horse-exercise to correct the
increasing excessiveness of her figure.)

'Who do you think I saw riding in the Park ? '
she inquired. 'Why, the Count of Lebenstein.'
'No !' Charles exclaimed, incredulous.
'Yes,' Amelia answered.
'Must be mistaken,' Charles cried.

But Amelia stuck to it. More than that, she
sent out emissaries to inquire diligently from the
London lawyers, whose name had been mentioned
to us by the ancestral firm in Unter den Lauben as
their English agents, as to the whereabouts of our
friend ; and her emissaries learned in effect that the
Count was in town and stopping at Morley's.

'I see through it,' Charles exclaimed. 'He finds
he's made a mistake ; and now he's come over here
to reopen negotiations.'

I was all for waiting prudently till the Count
made the first move. 'Don't let him see your
eagerness,' I said. But Amelia's ardour could not
now be restrained. She insisted that Charles should
call on the Graf as a mere return of his politeness
in the Tyrol.

He was as charming as ever. He talked to us
with delight about the quaintness of London. He
would be ravished to dine next evening with Sir
Charles. He desired his respectful salutations meanwhile to Miladi Vandrift and Madame Ventvorth.

He dined with us, almost *en famille*. Amelia's
cook did wonders. In the billiard-room, about midnight, Charles reopened the subject. The Count
was really touched. It pleased him that still, amid

the distractions of the City of Five Million Souls, we should remember with affection his beloved Lebenstein.

'Come to my lawyers,' he said, 'to-morrow, and I will talk it all over with you.'

We went—a most respectable firm in Southampton Row; old family solicitors. They had done business for years for the late Count, who had inherited from his grandmother estates in Ireland; and they were glad to be honoured with the confidence of his successor. Glad, too, to make the acquaintance of a prince of finance like Sir Charles Vandrift. Anxious (rubbing their hands) to arrange matters satisfactorily all round for everybody. (Two capital families with which to be mixed up, you see.)

Sir Charles named a price, and referred them to his solicitors. The Count named a higher, but still a little come-down, and left the matter to be settled between the lawyers. He was a soldier and a gentleman, he said, with a Tyrolese toss of his highborn head; he would abandon details to men of business.

As I was really anxious to oblige Amelia, I met the Count accidentally next day on the steps of Morley's. (Accidentally, that is to say, so far as he was concerned, though I had been hanging about in Trafalgar Square for half an hour to see him.) I explained, in guarded terms, that I had a great deal of influence in my way with Sir Charles; and that a word from me—— I broke off. He stared at me blankly.

'Commission?' he inquired, at last, with a queer little smile.

'Well, not exactly commission,' I answered,

COMMISSION? HE INQUIRED.

wincing. 'Still, a friendly word, you know. One good turn deserves another.'

He looked at me from head to foot with a curious scrutiny. For one moment I feared the Tyrolese nobleman in him was going to raise its foot and take active measures. But the next, I saw that Sir

Charles was right after all, and that pristine
innocence has removed from this planet to other
quarters.

He named his lowest price. ' M. Ventvorth,' he
said, ' I am a Tyrolese *seigneur ;* I do not dabble,
myself, in commissions and percentages. But if your
influence with Sir Charles—we understand each other,
do we not ?—as between gentlemen—a little friendly
present—no money, of course—but the equivalent
of say 5 per cent in jewellery, on whatever sum above
his bid to-day you induce him to offer—eh ?—*c'est
convenu ?* '

' Ten per cent is more usual,' I murmured.

He was the Austrian hussar again. ' Five,
monsieur—or nothing ! '

I bowed and withdrew. ' Well, five then,' I
answered, ' just to oblige your Serenity.'

A secretary, after all, can do a great deal. When
it came to the scratch, I had but little difficulty in
persuading Sir Charles, with Amelia's aid, backed
up on either side by Isabel and Césarine, to accede
to the Count's more reasonable proposal. The
Southampton Row people had possession of certain
facts as to the value of the wines in the Bordeaux
market which clinched the matter. In a week or
two all was settled ; Charles and I met the Count
by appointment in Southampton Row, and saw him
sign, seal, and deliver the title-deeds of Schloss
Lebenstein. My brother-in-law paid the purchase-
money into the Count's own hands, by cheque,

crossed on a first-class London firm where the Count kept an account to his high well-born order.   Then he went away with the proud knowledge that he was owner of Schloss Lebenstein.   And what to me was more important still, I received next morning by post a cheque for the five per cent, unfortunately drawn, by some misapprehension, to my order on the self-same bankers, and with the Count's signature. He explained in the accompanying note that the matter being now quite satisfactorily concluded, he saw no reason of delicacy why the amount he had promised should not be paid to me forthwith direct in money.

I cashed the cheque at once, and said nothing about the affair, not even to Isabel.   My experience is that women are not to be trusted with intricate matters of commission and brokerage.

Though it was now late in March, and the House was sitting, Charles insisted that we must all run over at once to take possession of our magnificent Tyrolese castle.   Amelia was almost equally burning with eagerness.   She gave herself the airs of a Countess already.   We took the Orient Express as far as Munich ; then the Brenner to Meran, and put up for the night at the Erzherzog Johann.   Though we had telegraphed our arrival, and expected some fuss, there was no demonstration.   Next morning we drove out in state to the schloss, to enter into enjoyment of our vines and fig-trees.

We were met at the door by the surly steward.

'I shall dismiss that man,' Charles muttered, as Lord of Lebenstein. 'He's too sour-looking for my taste. Never saw such a brute. Not a smile of welcome!'

He mounted the steps. The surly man stepped forward and murmured a few morose words in

WE WERE MET AT THE DOOR BY
THE SURLY STEWARD.

German. Charles brushed him aside and strode on. Then there followed a curious scene of mutual misunderstanding. The surly man called lustily for his servants to eject us. It was some time before we began to catch at the truth. The surly man was the *real* Graf von Lebenstein.

And the Count with the moustache? It dawned

upon us now.   Colonel Clay again !   More audacious
than ever !

Bit by bit it all came out.   He had ridden
behind us the first day we viewed the place, and,
giving himself out to the servants as one of our
party, had joined us in the reception-room.   We
asked the real Count why he had spoken to the
intruder.   The Count explained in French that the
man with the moustache had introduced my brother-
in-law as the great South African millionaire, while
he described himself as our courier and interpreter.
As such he had had frequent interviews with the
real Graf and his lawyers in Meran, and had driven
almost daily across to the castle.   The owner of the
estate had named one price from the first, and had
stuck to it manfully.   He stuck to it still ; and if
Sir Charles chose to buy Schloss Lebenstein over
again he was welcome to have it.   How the London
lawyers had been duped the Count had not really
the slightest idea.   He regretted the incident, and
(coldly) wished us a very good morning.

There was nothing for it but to return as best we
might to the Erzherzog Johann, crestfallen, and
telegraph particulars to the police in London.

Charles and I ran across post-haste to England
to track down the villain.   At Southampton Row
we found the legal firm by no means penitent ; on
the contrary, they were indignant at the way we
had deceived them.   An impostor had written to
them on Lebenstein paper from Meran to say that

he was coming to London to negotiate the sale of
the schloss and surrounding property with the
famous millionaire, Sir Charles Vandrift; and Sir
Charles had demonstratively recognised him at sight
as the real Count von Lebenstein. The firm had
never seen the present Graf at all, and had swallowed
the impostor whole, so to speak, on the strength of
Sir Charles's obvious recognition. He had brought
over as documents some most excellent forgeries—
facsimiles of the originals—which, as our courier
and interpreter, he had every opportunity of examining and inspecting at the Meran lawyers.' It was a
deeply-laid plot, and it had succeeded to a marvel.
Yet, all of it depended upon the one small fact that
we had accepted the man with the long moustache
in the hall of the schloss as the Count von Lebenstein on his own representation.

He held our cards in his hands when he came in;
and the servant had *not* given them to him, but to
the genuine Count. That was the one unsolved
mystery in the whole adventure.

By the evening's post two letters arrived for us
at Sir Charles's house : one for myself, and one for
my employer. Sir Charles's ran thus :—

'HIGH WELL-BORN INCOMPETENCE,—

'I only just pulled through ! A very small slip
nearly lost me everything. I believed you were
going to Schloss Planta that day, not to Schloss
Lebenstein. You changed your mind *en route*. That
might have spoiled all. Happily I perceived it, rode

up by the short cut, and arrived somewhat hurriedly
and hotly at the gate before you.   Then I introduced
myself.   I had one more bad moment when the
rival claimant to my name and title intruded into
the room.   But fortune favours the brave : your
utter ignorance of German saved me.   The rest was
pap.   It went by itself almost.

'Allow me, now, as some small return for your
various welcome cheques, to offer you a useful and
valuable present—a German dictionary, grammar,
and phrase-book !

'I kiss your hand.

'No longer

'VON LEBENSTEIN.'

The other note was to me.   It was as follows :—
'DEAR GOOD MR. VENTVORTH,—

'Ha, ha, ha ; just a *W* misplaced sufficed to take
you in, then !   And I risked the *TH*, though anybody with a head on his shoulders would surely
have known our *TH* is by far more difficult than
our *W* for foreigners !   However, all's well that ends
well ; and now I've got you.   The Lord has delivered
you into my hands, dear friend—on your own
initiative.   I hold my cheque, endorsed by you, and
cashed at my banker's, as a hostage, so to speak,
for your future good behaviour.   If ever you recognise me, and betray me to that solemn old ass, your
employer, remember, I expose it, and you with it to
him.   So now we understand each other.   I had

not thought of this little dodge; it was you who
suggested it. However, I jumped at it. Was it
not well worth my while paying you that slight
commission in return for a guarantee of your future
silence? Your mouth is now closed. And cheap
too at the price.—Yours, dear Comrade, in the great
confraternity of rogues,

'CUTHBERT CLAY, *Colonel.*'

Charles laid his note down, and grizzled. 'What's
yours, Sey?' he asked.

'From a lady,' I answered.

He gazed at me suspiciously. 'Oh, I thought it
was the same hand,' he said. His eye looked through
me.

'No,' I answered. 'Mrs. Mortimer's.' But I
confess I trembled.

He paused a moment. 'You made all inquiries
at this fellow's bank?' he went on, after a deep sigh.

'Oh, yes,' I put in quickly. (I had taken good
care about that, you may be sure, lest he should
spot the commission.) 'They say the self-styled
Count von Lebenstein was introduced to them by
the Southampton Row folks, and drew, as usual, on
the Lebenstein account: so they were quite unsuspicious. A rascal who goes about the world on
that scale, you know, and arrives with such credentials as theirs and yours, naturally imposes on anybody. The bank didn't even require to have him
formally identified. The firm was enough. He

came to pay money in, not to draw it out.   And he withdrew his balance just two days later, saying he was in a hurry to get back to Vienna.'

Would he ask for items?   I confess I felt it was an awkward moment.   Charles, however, was too full of regrets to bother about the account.   He

TWO LETTERS.

leaned back in his easy chair, stuck his hands in his pockets, held his legs straight out on the fender before him, and looked the very picture of hopeless despondency.

'Sey,' he began, after a minute or two, poking the fire, reflectively, 'what a genius that man has! 'Pon my soul, I admire him.   I sometimes wish——' He broke off and hesitated.

'Yes, Charles?' I answered.

'I sometimes wish . . . we had got him on the Board of the Cloetedorp Golcondas. Mag—nificent combinations he would make in the City!'

I rose from my seat and stared solemnly at my misguided brother-in-law.

'Charles,' I said, 'you are beside yourself. Too much Colonel Clay has told upon your clear and splendid intellect. There are certain remarks which, however true they may be, no self-respecting financier should permit himself to make, even in the privacy of his own room, to his most intimate friend and trusted adviser.'

Charles fairly broke down. 'You are right, Sey,' he sobbed out. 'Quite right. Forgive this outburst. At moments of emotion the truth will sometimes out, in spite of everything.'

I respected his feebleness. I did not even make it a fitting occasion to ask for a trifling increase of salary.

V

THE EPISODE OF THE DRAWN GAME

THE twelfth of August saw us, as usual, at Seldon Castle, Ross-shire. It is part of Charles's restless, roving temperament that, on the morning of the eleventh, wet or fine, he must set out from London, whether the House is sitting or not, in defiance of the most urgent three-line whips; and at dawn on the twelfth he must be at work on his moors, shooting down the young birds with might and main, at the earliest possible legal moment.

He goes on like Saul, slaying his thousands, or, like David, his tens of thousands, with all the guns in the house to help him, till the keepers warn him he has killed as many grouse as they consider desirable; and then, having done his duty, as he thinks, in this respect, he retires precipitately with flying colours to Brighton, Nice, Monte Carlo, or elsewhere. He must be always 'on the trek'; when he is buried, I believe he will not be able to rest quiet in his grave: his ghost will walk the world to terrify old ladies.

'At Seldon, at least,' he said to me, with a sigh,

as he stepped into his Pullman, 'I shall be safe from that impostor!'

And indeed, as soon as he had begun to tire a little of counting up his hundreds of brace per *diem*, he found a trifling piece of financial work cut ready to his hand, which amply distracted his mind for the moment from Colonel Clay, his accomplices, and his villainies.

Sir Charles, I ought to say, had secured during that summer a very advantageous option in a part of Africa on the Transvaal frontier, rumoured to be auriferous. Now, whether it was auriferous or not before, the mere fact that Charles had secured some claim on it naturally made it so ; for no man had ever the genuine Midas-touch to a greater degree than Charles Vandrift : whatever he handles turns at once to gold, if not to diamonds. Therefore, as soon as my brother-in-law had obtained this option from the native vendor (a most respected chief, by name Montsioa), and promoted a company of his own to develop it, his great rival in that region, Lord Craig-Ellachie (formerly Sir David Alexander Granton), immediately secured a similar option of an adjacent track, the larger part of which had pretty much the same geological conditions as that covered by Sir Charles's right of pre-emption.

We were not wholly disappointed, as it turned out, in the result. A month or two later, while we were still at Seldon, we received a long and encouraging letter from our prospectors on the spot, who had been hunting over the ground in search of gold-reefs. They reported that they had found a good auriferous vein in a corner of the tract, approachable by adit-levels ; but, unfortunately, only a few yards of the lode lay within the limits of Sir Charles's area.   The remainder ran on at once into what was locally known as Craig-Ellachie's section.

However, our prospectors had been canny, they said ; though young Mr. Granton was prospecting at the same time, in the self-same ridge, not very far from them, his miners had failed to discover the auriferous quartz ; so our men had held their tongues about it, wisely leaving it for Charles to govern himself accordingly.

'Can you dispute the boundary?' I asked.

'Impossible,' Charles answered.   'You see, the limit is a meridian of longitude.   There's no getting over that.   Can't pretend to deny it.   No buying over the sun !   No bribing the instruments !   Besides, we drew the line ourselves.   We've only one way out of it, Sey.   Amalgamate !   Amalgamate !'

Charles is a marvellous man !   The very voice in which he murmured that blessed word 'Amalgamate!' was in itself a poem.

'Capital !' I answered.   'Say nothing about it, and join forces with Craig-Ellachie.'

Charles closed one eye pensively.

That very same evening came a telegram in cipher from our chief engineer on the territory of the option :   'Young Granton has somehow given

us the slip and gone home. We suspect he knows
all. But we have not divulged the secret to anybody.'

'Seymour,' my brother-in-law said impressively,
'there is no time to be lost. I must write this
evening to Sir David—I mean to My Lord. Do
you happen to know where he is stopping at
present ? '

'The *Morning Post* announced two or three days
ago that he was at Glen-Ellachie,' I answered.

'Then I'll ask him to come over and thrash the
matter out with me,' my brother-in-law went on. 'A
very rich reef, they say. I must have my finger
in it ! '

We adjourned into the study, where Sir Charles
drafted, I must admit, a most judicious letter to the
rival capitalist. He pointed out that the mineral
resources of the country were probably great, but as
yet uncertain. That the expense of crushing and
milling might be almost prohibitive. That access to
fuel was costly, and its conveyance difficult. That
water was scarce, and commanded by our section.
That two rival companies, if they happened to hit
upon ore, might cut one another's throats by erecting
two sets of furnaces or pumping plants, and bringing
two separate streams to the spot, where one would
answer. In short—to employ the golden word—
that amalgamation might prove better in the end
than competition ; and that he advised, at least, a
conference on the subject.

I wrote it out fair for him, and Sir Charles, with the air of a Cromwell, signed it.

'This is important, Sey,' he said. 'It had better be registered, for fear of falling into improper hands. Don't give it to Dobson ; let Césarine take it over to Fowlis in the dog-cart.'

It is the drawback of Seldon that we are twelve miles from a railway station, though we look out on one of the loveliest firths in Scotland.

Césarine took it as directed —an invaluable servant, that girl! Meanwhile, we learned from the *Morning Post* next day that young Mr. Granton had stolen a march upon us. He had arrived from Africa by the same mail with our agent's letter, and had joined his father at once at Glen-Ellachie.

Two days later we received a most polite reply from the opposing interest. It ran after this fashion :—

CÉSARINE TOOK IT AS DIRECTED.

'CRAIG-ELLACHIE LODGE,
'GLEN-ELLACHIE, INVERNESS-SHIRE.

'DEAR SIR CHARLES VANDRIFT — Thanks for

yours of the 20th.   In reply, I can only say I fully
reciprocate your amiable desire that nothing adverse
to either of our companies should happen in South
Africa.   With regard to your suggestion that we
should meet in person, to discuss the basis of a
possible amalgamation, I can only say my house is
at present full of guests—as is doubtless your own
—and I should therefore find it practically impossible to leave Glen-Ellachie.   Fortunately, however, my son David is now at home on a brief
holiday from Kimberley ; and it will give him great
pleasure to come over and hear what you have to
say in favour of an arrangement which certainly, on
some grounds, seems to me desirable in the interests
of both our concessions alike.   He will arrive to-
morrow afternoon at Seldon, and he is authorised,
in every respect, to negotiate with full powers on
behalf of myself and the other directors.   With
kindest regards to your wife and sons, I remain,
dear Sir Charles, yours faithfully,

                              ' CRAIG-ELLACHIE.'

'Cunning old fox ! ' Sir Charles exclaimed, with
a sniff.   'What's he up to now, I wonder ?   Seems
almost as anxious to amalgamate as we ourselves
are, Sey.'   A sudden thought struck him.   'Do you
know,' he cried, looking up, 'I really believe the
same thing must have happened to *both* our exploring
parties.   *They* must have found a reef that goes
under. *our* ground, and the wicked old rascal wants
to cheat us out of it ! '

'As we want to cheat him,' I ventured to interpose.

Charles looked at me fixedly. 'Well, if so, we're
both in luck,' he murmured, after a pause ; 'though
we can only get to know the whereabouts of *their*
find by joining hands with them and showing them
ours. Still, it's good business either way. But I
shall be cautious—cautious.'

'What a nuisance!' Amelia cried, when we told
her of the incident. 'I suppose I shall have to put
the man up for the night—a nasty, raw-boned, half-
baked Scotchman, you may be certain.'

On Wednesday afternoon, about three, young
Granton arrived. He was a pleasant-featured, red-
haired, sandy-whiskered youth, not unlike his father ;
but, strange to say, he dropped in to call, instead of
bringing his luggage.

'Why, you're not going back to Glen-Ellachie
to-night, surely?' Charles exclaimed, in amazement.
'Lady Vandrift will be *so* disappointed! Besides,
this business can't be arranged between two trains,
do you think, Mr. Granton?'

Young Granton smiled. He had an agreeable
smile—canny, yet open.

'Oh no,' he said frankly. 'I didn't mean to go
back. I've put up at the inn. I have my wife with
me, you know—and, I wasn't invited.'

Amelia was of opinion, when we told her this
episode, that David Granton wouldn't stop at Seldon
because he was an Honourable. Isabel was of

opinion he wouldn't stop because he had married an unpresentable young woman somewhere out in South Africa. Charles was of opinion that, as representative of the hostile interest, he put up at the inn, because it might tie his hands in some way to be the guest of the chairman of the rival company. And *I* was of opinion that he had heard of the castle, and knew it well by report as the dullest country-house to stay at in Scotland.

However that may be, young Granton insisted on remaining at the Cromarty Arms, though he told us his wife would be delighted to receive a call from Lady Vandrift and Mrs. Wentworth. So we all returned with him to bring the Honourable Mrs. Granton up to tea at the Castle.

She was a nice little thing, very shy and timid, but by no means unpresentable, and an evident lady. She giggled at the end of every sentence ; and she was endowed with a slight squint, which somehow seemed to point all her feeble sallies. She knew little outside South Africa ; but of that she talked prettily ; and she won all our hearts, in spite of the cast in her eye, by her unaffected simplicity.

Next morning Charles and I had a regular debate with young Granton about the rival options. Our talk was of cyanide processes, reverberatories, pennyweights, water-jackets. But it dawned upon us soon that, in spite of his red hair and his innocent manners, our friend, the Honourable David Granton, knew a thing or two. Gradually and gracefully he

let us see that Lord Craig-Ellachie had sent him for
the benefit of the company, but that *he* had come
for the benefit of the Honourable David Granton.

'I'm a younger son, Sir Charles,' he said ; 'and
therefore I have to feather my nest for myself.   I
know the ground.   My father will be guided

SHE WAS ENDOWED WITH A SLIGHT SQUINT.

implicitly by what I advise in the matter.   We are
men of the world.   Now, let's be business-like.
You want to amalgamate.   You wouldn't do that,
of course, if you didn't know of something to the
advantage of my father's company—say, a lode on
our land—which you hope to secure for yourself by
amalgamation.   Very well ; *I* can make or mar

your project. If you choose to render it worth my
while, I'll induce my father and his directors to
amalgamate. If you don't, I won't. That's the
long and the short of it!'

Charles looked at him admiringly.

'Young man,' he said, 'you're deep, very deep—
for your age. Is this candour—or deception? Do
you mean what you say? Or do you know some
reason why it suits your father's book to amalgamate
as well as it suits mine? And are you trying to
keep it from me?' He fingered his chin. 'If I
only knew that,' he went on, 'I should know how to
deal with you.'

Young Granton smiled again. 'You're a financier,
Sir Charles,' he answered. 'I wonder, at your time
of life, you should pause to ask another financier
whether he's trying to fill his own pocket—or his
father's. Whatever is my father's goes to his eldest
son—and *I* am his youngest.'

'You are right as to general principles,' Sir
Charles replied, quite affectionately. 'Most sound and
sensible. But how do I know you haven't bargained
already in the same way with your father? You may
have settled with *him*, and be trying to diddle me.'

The young man assumed a most candid air.
'Look here,' he said, leaning forward. 'I offer you
this chance. Take it or leave it. *Do* you wish to
purchase my aid for this amalgamation by a
moderate commission on the net value of my father's
option to yourself—which I know approximately?'

'Say five per cent,' I suggested, in a tentative voice, just to justify my presence.

He looked me through and through. '*Ten* is more usual,' he answered, in a peculiar tone and with a peculiar glance.

Great heavens, how I winced! I knew what his words meant. They were the very words I had said myself to Colonel Clay, as the Count von Lebenstein,

TEN IS MORE USUAL.

about the purchase-money of the schloss—and in the very same accent. I saw through it all now. That beastly cheque! This was Colonel Clay; and he was trying to buy up my silence and assistance by the threat of exposure!

My blood ran cold. I didn't know how to answer him. What happened at the rest of that interview I really couldn't tell you. My brain reeled round. I heard just faint echoes of 'fuel'

and 'reduction works.'   What on earth was I to do?
If I told Charles my suspicion—for it was only a
suspicion—the fellow might turn upon me and dis-
close the cheque, which would suffice to ruin me.
If I didn't, I ran a risk of being considered by
Charles an accomplice and a confederate.

The interview was long.   I hardly know how I
struggled through it.   At the end young Granton
went off, well satisfied, if it was young Granton ; and
Amelia invited him and his wife up to dinner at the
castle.

Whatever else they were, they were capital
company.   They stopped for three days more at
the Cromarty Arms.   And Charles debated and discussed incessantly.   He couldn't quite make up
his mind what to do in the affair ; and *I* certainly
couldn't help him.   I never was placed in such a
fix in my life.   I did my best to preserve a strict
neutrality.

Young Granton, it turned out, was a most
agreeable person ; and so, in her way, was that
timid, unpretending South African wife of his.
She was naïvely surprised Amelia had never met
her mamma at Durban.   They both talked delight-
fully, and had lots of good stories—mostly with
points that told against the Craig-Ellachie people.
Moreover, the Honourable David was a splendid
swimmer.   He went out in a boat with us, and
dived like a seal.   He was burning to teach Charles
and myself to swim, when we told him we could

neither of us take a single stroke ; he said it was an accomplishment incumbent upon every true Englishman. But Charles hates the water ; while, as for myself, I detest every known form of muscular exercise.

However, we consented that he should row us on the Firth, and made an appointment one day with himself and his wife for four the next evening.

That night Charles came to me with a very grave face in my own bedroom. "Sey,' he said, under his breath, ' have you observed ?   Have you watched ? Have you any suspicions ? '

I trembled violently.   I felt all was up. ' Suspicions of whom ? ' I asked.   ' Not surely of Simpson ? ' (he was Sir Charles's valet).

My respected brother-in-law looked at me contemptuously.

' Sey,' he said, ' are you trying to take me in ? No, *not* of Simpson : of these two young folks. My own belief is—they're Colonel Clay and Madame Picardet.'

' Impossible ! ' I cried.

He nodded.   ' I'm sure of it.'

' How do you know ? '

' Instinctively.'

I seized his arm.   ' Charles,' I said, imploring him, ' do nothing rash.   Remember how you exposed yourself to the ridicule of fools over Dr. Polperro ! '

' I've thought of that,' he answered, ' and I mean to ca' caller.' (When in Scotland as laird of Seldon,

Charles loves both to dress and to speak the part thoroughly.) 'First thing to-morrow I shall telegraph over to inquire at Glen-Ellachie; I shall find out whether this is really young Granton or not; meanwhile, I shall keep my eye close upon the fellow.'

A GROOM WAS DISPATCHED WITH
A TELEGRAM.

Early next morning, accordingly, a groom was dispatched with a telegram to Lord Craig-Ellachie. He was to ride over to Fowlis, send it off at once, and wait for the answer. At the same time, as it was probable Lord Craig-Ellachie would have started

for the moors before the telegram reached the Lodge,
I did not myself expect to see the reply arrive much
before seven or eight that evening. Meanwhile, as
it was far from certain we had not the real David
Granton to deal with, it was necessary to be polite
to our friendly rivals.   Our experience in the
Polperro incident had shown us both that too
much zeal may be more dangerous than too little.
Nevertheless, taught by previous misfortunes, we
kept watching our man pretty close, determined that
on this occasion, at least, he should neither do us nor
yet escape us.

About four o'clock the red-haired young man
and his pretty little wife came up to call for us.
She looked so charming and squinted so enchantingly,
one could hardly believe she was not as simple and
innocent as she seemed to be. She tripped down
to the Seldon boat-house, with Charles by her side,
giggling and squinting her best, and then helped
her husband to get the skiff ready. As she did so,
Charles sidled up to me. ' Sey,' he whispered, ' I'm
an old hand, and I'm not readily taken in.   I've
been talking to that girl, and upon my soul I think
she's all right. She's a charming little lady.   We
may be mistaken after all, of course, about young
Granton.   In any case, it's well for the present to
be courteous.   A most important option! If it's
really he, we must do nothing to annoy him or let
him see we suspect him.'

I had noticed, indeed, that Mrs. Granton had

made herself most agreeable to Charles from the very beginning. And as to one thing he was right. In her timid, shrinking way she was undeniably charming. That cast in her eye was all pure piquancy.

We rowed out on to the Firth, or, to be more strictly correct, the two Grantons rowed while Charles and I sat and leaned back in the stern on the luxurious cushions. They rowed fast and well. In a very few minutes they had rounded the point and got clear out of sight of the Cockneyfied towers and false battlements of Seldon.

Mrs. Granton pulled stroke. Even as she rowed she kept up a brisk undercurrent of timid chaff with Sir Charles, giggling all the while, half forward, half shy, like a school-girl who flirts with a man old enough to be her grandfather.

Sir Charles was flattered. He is susceptible to the pleasures of female attention, especially from the young, the simple, and the innocent. The wiles of women of the world he knows too well ; but a pretty little *ingénue* can twist him round her finger. They rowed on and on, till they drew abreast of Seamew's island. It is a jagged stack or skerry, well out to sea, very wild and precipitous on the landward side, but shelving gently outward ; perhaps an acre in extent, with steep gray cliffs, covered at that time with crimson masses of red valerian. Mrs. Granton rowed up close to it. ' Oh, what lovely flowers ! ' she cried, throwing her head back and gazing at them. 'I wish I could get some! Let's land here and pick them. Sir Charles, you shall gather me a nice bunch for my sitting-room.'

Charles rose to it innocently, like a trout to a fly.

'By all means, my dear child, I—I have a passion for flowers;' which was a flower of speech itself, but it served its purpose.

They rowed us round to the far side, where is the easiest landing-place. It struck me as odd at the moment that they seemed to know it. Then young Granton jumped lightly ashore ; Mrs. Granton skipped after him. I confess it made me feel rather ashamed to see how clumsily Charles and I followed them, treading gingerly on the thwarts for fear of upsetting the boat, while the artless young thing just flew over the gunwale. So like White Heather! However, we got ashore at last in safety, and began to climb the rocks as well as we were able in search of the valerian.

Judge of our astonishment when next moment those two young people bounded back into the boat, pushed off with a peal of merry laughter, and left us there staring at them !

They rowed away, about twenty yards, into deep water. Then the man turned, and waved his hand at us gracefully. 'Good-bye !' he said, 'good-bye ! Hope you'll pick a nice bunch ! We're off to London !'

'Off !' Charles exclaimed, turning pale. 'Off !

What do you mean ?   You don't surely mean to say you're going to leave us here ? '

The young man raised his cap with perfect politeness, while Mrs. Granton smiled, nodded, and kissed her pretty hand to us. ' Yes,' he answered ; ' for the present. We retire from the game. The fact of it is, it's a trifle too thin : this is a *coup manqué.'*

' A *what ?* ' Charles exclaimed, perspiring visibly.

' A *coup manqué,*' the young man replied, with a compassionate smile. ' A failure, don't you know ; a bad shot ; a fiasco. I learn from my scouts that you sent a telegram by special messenger to Lord Craig-Ellachie this morning. That shows you suspect me. Now, it is a principle of my system never to go on for one move with a game when I find myself suspected. The slightest symptom of distrust, and—I back out immediately. My plans can only be worked to satisfaction when there is perfect confidence on the part of my patient. It is a well-known rule of the medical profession. I *never* try to bleed a man who struggles. So now we're off.   Ta-ta !   Good luck to you ! '

He was not much more than twenty yards away, and could talk to us quite easily. But the water was deep ; the islet rose sheer from I'm sure I don't know how many fathoms of sea ; and we could neither of us swim. Charles stretched out his arms imploringly. ' For Heaven's sake,' he cried, ' don't tell me you really mean to leave us here.'

He looked so comical in his distress and terror
that Mrs. Granton—Madame Picardet—whatever I
am to call her—laughed melodiously in her prettiest
way at the sight of him. 'Dear Sir Charles,' she
called out, 'pray don't be afraid! It's only a short

TA-TA!

and temporary imprisonment. We will send men
to take you off. Dear David and I only need just
time enough to get well ashore and make—oh!—
a few slight alterations in our personal appearance.'
And she indicated with her hand, laughing, dear
David's red wig and false sandy whiskers, as we felt

convinced they must be now. She looked at them and tittered. Her manner at this moment was anything but shy. In fact, I will venture to say, it was that of a bold and brazen-faced hoyden.

'Then you *are* Colonel Clay!' Sir Charles cried, mopping his brow with his handkerchief.

'If you choose to call me so,' the young man answered politely. 'I'm sure it's most kind of you to supply me with a commission in Her Majesty's service. However, time presses, and we want to push off. Don't alarm yourselves unnecessarily. I will send a boat to take you away from this rock at the earliest possible moment consistent with my personal safety and my dear companion's.' He laid his hand on his heart and struck a sentimental attitude. 'I have received too many unwilling kindnesses at your hands, Sir Charles,' he continued, 'not to feel how wrong it would be of me to inconvenience you for nothing. Rest assured that you shall be rescued by midnight at latest. Fortunately, the weather just at present is warm, and I see no chance of rain; so you will suffer, if at all, from nothing worse than the pangs of temporary hunger.'

Mrs. Granton, no longer squinting—'twas a mere trick she had assumed—rose up in the boat and stretched out a rug to us. 'Catch!' she cried, in a merry voice, and flung it at us, doubled. It fell at our feet; she was a capital thrower.

'Now, you dear Sir Charles,' she went on, 'take

that to keep you warm! You know I am really quite fond of you. You're not half a bad old boy when one takes you the right way. You have a human side to you. Why, I often wear that sweetly pretty brooch you gave me at Nice, when I was Madame Picardet! And I'm sure your goodness to me at Lucerne, when I was the little curate's wife, is a thing to remember. 'We're so glad to have seen you in your lovely Scotch home you were always so proud of! *Don't* be frightened, please. We wouldn't hurt you for worlds. We *are* so sorry we have to take this inhospitable means of evading you. But dear David—I *must* call him dear David still—instinctively felt that you were beginning to suspect us; and he can't bear mistrust. He *is* so sensitive! The moment people mistrust him, he *must* break off with them at once. This was the only way to get you both off our hands while we make the needful little arrangements to depart; and we've been driven to avail ourselves of it. However, I will give you my word of honour, as a lady, you shall be fetched away to-night. If dear David doesn't do it, why, I'll do it myself.' And she blew another kiss to us.

Charles was half beside himself, divided between alternate terror and anger. 'Oh, we shall die here!' he exclaimed. 'Nobody'd ever dream of coming to this rock to search for me.'

'What a pity you didn't let me teach you to swim!' Colonel Clay interposed. 'It is a noble exercise, and very useful indeed in such special emergencies! Well, ta-ta! I'm off! You nearly scored one this time; but, by putting you here for the moment, and keeping you till we're gone, I

CHARLES WAS HALF BESIDE HIMSELF.

venture to say I've redressed the board, and I think we may count it a drawn game, mayn't we? The match stands at *three*, *love*—with some thousands in pocket?'

'You're a murderer, sir!' Charles shrieked out. 'We shall starve or die here!'

Colonel Clay on his side was all sweet reason-
ableness. ' Now, my dear sir,' he expostulated, one
hand held palm outward, ' *do* you think it probable
I would kill the goose that lays the golden eggs,
with so little compunction? No, no, Sir Charles
Vandrift ; I know too well how much you are worth
to me. I return you on my income-tax paper as
five thousand a year, clear profit of my profession.
Suppose you were to die ! I might be compelled to
find some new and far less lucrative source of
plunder. Your heirs, executors, or assignees might
not suit my purpose. The fact of it is, sir, your
temperament and mine are exactly adapted one to
the other. *I* understand *you;* and *you* do not
understand *me*—which is often the basis of the
firmest friendships. I can catch you just where
you are trying to catch other people. Your very
smartness assists me ; for I admit you *are* smart.
As a regular financier, I allow, I couldn't hold a
candle to you. But in my humbler walk of life I
know just how to utilise you. I lead you on,
where you think you are going to gain some
advantage over others ; and by dexterously playing
upon your love of a good bargain, your innate
desire to best somebody else—I succeed in besting
you. There, sir, you have the philosophy of our
mutual relations.'

He bowed and raised his cap. Charles looked
at him and cowered. Yes, genius as he is, he
positively cowered. ' And do you mean to say,'

he burst out, 'you intend to go on so bleeding me?'

The Colonel smiled a bland smile. ' Sir Charles Vandrift,' he answered, ' I called you just now the goose that lays the golden eggs. You may have thought the metaphor a rude one. But you *are* a goose, you know, in certain relations. Smartest man on the Stock Exchange, I readily admit; easiest fool to bamboozle in the open country that ever I met with. You fail in one thing—the perspicacity of simplicity. For that reason, among others, I have chosen to fasten upon you. Regard me, my dear sir, as a microbe of millionaires, a parasite upon capitalists. You know the old rhyme :

Great fleas have little fleas upon their backs to bite 'em,
And these again have lesser fleas, and so *ad infinitum !*

Well, that's just how I view myself. *You* are a capitalist and a millionaire. In *your* large way you prey upon society. *You* deal in Corners, Options, Concessions, Syndicates. You drain the world dry of its blood and its money. You possess, like the mosquito, a beautiful instrument of suction— Founders' Shares — with which you absorb the surplus wealth of the community. In *my* smaller way, again, *I* relieve you in turn of a portion of the plunder. I am a Robin Hood of my age ; and, looking upon *you* as an exceptionally bad form of millionaire—as well as an exceptionally easy form

of pigeon for a man of my type and talents to pluck
—I have, so to speak, taken up my abode upon
you.'

Charles looked at him and groaned.

The young man continued, in a tone of gentle
badinage. ' I love the plot-interest of the game,' he
said, ' and so does dear Jessie here. We both of us
adore it. As long as I find such good pickings upon
you, I certainly am not going to turn away from
so valuable a carcass, in order to batten myself, at
considerable trouble, upon minor capitalists, out of
whom it is difficult to extract a few hundreds. It
may have puzzled you to guess why I fix upon you
so persistently. Now you know, and understand.
When a fluke finds a sheep that suits him, that fluke
lives upon him. You are my host : I am your
parasite. This *coup* has failed. But don't flatter
yourself for a moment it will be the last one.'

' Why do you insult me by telling me all this ? '
Sir Charles cried, writhing.

The Colonel waved his hand. It was small and
white. ' Because I *love* the game,' he answered, with
a relish ; ' and also, because the more prepared
you are beforehand, the greater credit and amusement is there in besting you. Well, now, ta-ta once
more ! I am wasting valuable time. I might be
cheating somebody. I must be off at once. . . .
Take care of yourself, Wentworth. But I know
you *will*. You always do. Ten per cent *is* more
usual ! '

He rowed away and left us.   As the boat began
to disappear round the corner of the island, White
Heather—so she looked—stood up in the stern and
shouted aloud through her pretty hands to us.   ' By-
bye, dear Sir Charles ! ' she cried.   ' Do wrap the rug
around you !   I'll send the men to fetch you as soon

I CLIMBED TO THE TOP OF THE CLIFF.

as ever I possibly can.   And thank you so much for
those lovely flowers ! '

The boat rounded the crags.   We were alone on
the island.   Charles flung himself on the bare rock
in a wild access of despondency.   He is accustomed
to luxury, and cannot get on without his padded
cushions.   As for myself, I climbed with some

difficulty to the top of the cliff, landward, and tried
to make signals of distress with my handkerchief to
some passer-by on the mainland.   All in vain.
Charles had dismissed the crofters on the estate ;
and, as the shooting-party that day was in an
opposite direction, not a soul was near to whom we
could call for succour.

I climbed down again to Charles.   The evening
came on slowly.   Cries of sea-birds rang weird upon
the water.   Puffins and cormorants circled round
our heads in the gray of twilight.   Charles suggested
that they might even swoop down upon us and bite
us.   They did not, however, but their flapping wings
added none the less a painful touch of eeriness to
our hunger and solitude.   Charles was horribly
depressed.   For myself, I will confess I felt so much
relieved at the fact that Colonel Clay had not
openly betrayed me in the matter of the commission,
as to be comparatively comfortable.

We crouched on the hard crag.   About eleven
o'clock we heard human voices.   ' Boat ahoy ! ' I
shouted.   An answering shout aroused us to action.
We rushed down to the landing-place and cooee'd
for the men, to show them where we were.   They
came up at once in Sir Charles's own boat.   They
were fishermen from Niggarey, on the shore of the
Firth opposite.

A lady and gentleman had sent them, they said,
to return the boat and call for us on the island ;
their description corresponded to the two supposed

Grantons. They rowed us home almost in silence to Seldon. It was half-past twelve by the gatehouse clock when we reached the castle. Men had been sent along the coast each way to seek us. Amelia had gone to bed, much alarmed for our safety. Isabel was sitting up. It was too late, of course, to do much that night in the way of apprehending the miscreants, though Charles insisted upon dispatching a groom, with a telegram for the police at Inverness, to Fowlis.

Nothing came of it all. A message awaited us from Lord Craig-Ellachie, to be sure, saying that his son had not left Glen-Ellachie Lodge ; while research the next day and later showed that our correspondent had never even received our letter. An empty envelope alone had arrived at the house, and the postal authorities had been engaged meanwhile, with their usual lightning speed, in 'investigating the matter.' Césarine had posted the letter herself at Fowlis, and brought back the receipt ; so the only conclusion we could draw was this—Colonel Clay must be in league with somebody at the post-office. As for Lord Craig-Ellachie's reply, that was a simple forgery ; though, oddly enough, it was written on Glen-Ellachie paper.

However, by the time Charles had eaten a couple of grouse, and drunk a bottle of his excellent Rudesheimer, his spirits and valour revived exceedingly. Doubtless he inherits from his Boer ancestry a tendency towards courage of the Batavian description. He was in capital feather.

'After all, Sey,' he said, leaning back in his chair, 'this time we score one.   He has *not* done us brown ; we have at least detected him.   To detect him in time is half-way to catching him.   Only the remoteness of our position at Seldon Castle saved him from capture.   Next set-to, I feel sure, we will not merely spot him, we will also nab him.   I only wish he would try on such a rig in London.'

HIS SPIRITS REVIVED.

But the oddest part of it all was this, that from the moment those two people landed at Niggarey, and told the fishermen there were some gentlemen stranded on the Seamew's island, all trace of them vanished.   At no station along the line could we gain any news of them.   Their maid had left the inn the same morning with their luggage, and we tracked her to Inverness ; but there the trail stopped short, no spoor lay farther. It was a most singular and insoluble mystery.

Charles lived in hopes of catching his man in London.

But for my part, I felt there was a show of reason in one last taunt which the rascal flung back at us as the boat receded : ' Sir Charles Vandrift, we are a pair of rogues. The law protects *you*. It persecutes *me*. That's all the difference.'

VI

THE EPISODE OF THE GERMAN PROFESSOR

THAT winter in town my respected brother-in-law had little time on his hands to bother himself about trifles like Colonel Clay. A thunderclap burst upon him. He saw his chief interest in South Africa threatened by a serious, an unexpected, and a crushing danger.

Charles does a little in gold, and a little in land ; but his principal operations have always lain in the direction of diamonds. Only once in my life, indeed, have I seen him pay the slightest attention to poetry, and that was when I happened one day to recite the lines :—

> Full many a gem of purest ray serene
> The dark, unfathomed caves of ocean bear.

He rubbed his hands at once and murmured enthusiastically, ' I never thought of that. We might get up an Atlantic Exploration Syndicate, Limited.' So attached is he to diamonds. You may gather, therefore, what a shock it was to that gigantic brain to learn that science was rapidly reaching a point where his favourite gems might become all at once a mere drug in the market. Depreciation is the one bugbear that perpetually torments Sir Charles's soul ; that winter he stood within measurable distance of so appalling a calamity.

It happened after this manner.

We were strolling along Piccadilly towards Charles's club one afternoon—he is a prominent member of the Crœsus, in Pall Mall—when, near Burlington House, whom should we happen to knock up against but Sir Adolphus Cordery, the famous mineralogist, and leading spirit of the Royal Society ! He nodded to us pleasantly. ' Halloa, Vandrift,' he cried, in his peculiarly loud and piercing voice ; ' you're the very man I wanted to meet to-day. Good morning, Wentworth. Well, how about diamonds now, Sir Gorgius ? You'll have to sing small. It's all up with you Midases. Heard about this marvellous new discovery of Schleiermacher's? It's calculated to make you diamond kings squirm like an eel in a frying-pan.'

I could see Charles wriggle inside his clothes. He was most uncomfortable. That a man like Cordery should say such things, in so loud a voice, on no matter how little foundation, openly in Piccadilly, was enough in itself to make a sensitive barometer such as Cloetedorp Golcondas go down a point or two.

' Hush, hush ! ' Charles said solemnly, in that

awed tone of voice which he always assumes when
Money is blasphemed against. '*Please* don't talk
quite so loud! All London can hear you.'

Sir Adolphus ran his arm through Charles's most
amicably. There's nothing Charles hates like having
his arm taken.

'Come along with me to the Athenæum,' he went
on, in the same stentorian voice, 'and I'll tell you
all about it. Most interesting discovery. Makes
diamonds cheap as dirt. Calculated to supersede
South Africa altogether.'

Charles allowed himself to be dragged along.
There was nothing else possible. Sir Adolphus
continued, in a somewhat lower key, induced upon
him by Charles's mute look of protest. It was a
disquieting story. He told it with gleeful unction.
It seems that Professor Schleiermacher, of Jena, 'the
greatest living authority on the chemistry of gems,'
he said, had lately invented, or claimed to have invented, a system for artificially producing diamonds,
which had yielded most surprising and unexception-
able results.

Charles's lip curled slightly. 'Oh, I know the
sort of thing,' he said. 'I've heard of it before.
Very inferior stones, quite small and worthless, produced at immense cost, and even then not worth
looking at. I'm an old bird, you know, Cordery;
not to be caught with chaff. Tell me a better one!'

Sir Adolphus produced a small cut gem from his
pocket. 'How's that for the first water?' he in-

quired, passing it across, with a broad smile, to the sceptic. 'Made under my own eyes — and quite inexpensively!'

Charles examined it close, stopping short against the railings in St. Jámes's Square to look at it with his pocket-lens. There was no denying the truth. It was a capital small gem of the finest quality.

'Made under your own eyes?' he exclaimed, still incredulous. 'Where, my dear sir?—at Jena?'

The answer was a thunderbolt from a blue sky. 'No, here in London; last night as ever was; before myself and Dr. Gray; and about to be exhibited by the President himself at a meeting of Fellows of the Royal Society.'

Charles drew a long breath. 'This nonsense must be stopped,' he said firmly—'it must be nipped in the bud. It won't do, my dear friend; we can't have such tampering with important Interests.'

'How do you mean?' Cordery asked, astonished.

Charles gazed at him steadily. I could see by the furtive gleam in my brother-in-law's eye he was distinctly frightened. 'Where *is* the fellow?' he asked. 'Did he come himself, or send over a deputy?'

'Here in London,' Sir Adolphus replied. 'He's staying at my house; and he says he'll be glad to show his experiments to anybody scientifically interested in diamonds. We propose to have a demonstration of the process to-night at Lancaster Gate. Will you drop in and see it?'

Would he 'drop in' and see it?   'Drop in' at
such a function!   Could he possibly stop away?
Charles clutched the enemy's arm with a nervous

THIS NONSENSE MUST BE STOPPED, HE SAID.

grip.   'Look here, Cordery,' he said, quivering;
'this is a question affecting very important Interests.
Don't do anything rash.   Don't do anything foolish.
Remember that Shares may rise or fall on this.'

He said 'Shares' in a tone of profound respect that I can hardly even indicate. It was the crucial word in the creed of his religion.

'I should think it very probable,' Sir Adolphus replied, with the callous indifference of the mere man of science to financial suffering.

Sir Charles was bland, but peremptory. 'Now, observe,' he said, 'a grave responsibility rests on your shoulders. The Market depends upon you. You must not ask in any number of outsiders.to witness these experiments. Have a few mineralogists and experts, if you like ; but also take care to invite representatives of the menaced Interests. I will come myself—I'm engaged to dine out, but I can contract an indisposition ; and I should advise you to ask Mosenheimer, and, say, young Phipson. They would stand for the mines, as you and the mineralogists would stand for science. Above all, don't blab ; for Heaven's sake, let there be no premature gossip. Tell Schleiermacher not to go gassing and boasting of his success all over London.'

'We are keeping the matter a profound secret, at Schleiermacher's own request,' Cordery answered, more seriously.

'Which is why,' Charles said, in his severest tone, 'you bawled it out at the very top of your voice in Piccadilly !'

However, before nightfall, everything was arranged to Charles's satisfaction ; and off we went to Lancaster Gate, with a profound expectation that the German professor would do nothing worth seeing.

He was a remarkable-looking man, once tall, I should say, from his long, thin build, but now bowed and bent with long devotion to study and leaning over a crucible. His hair, prematurely white, hung down upon his forehead, but his eye was keen and his mouth sagacious. He shook hands cordially with the men of science, whom he seemed to know of old, whilst he bowed somewhat distantly to the South African interest. Then he began to talk, in very German-English, helping out the sense now and again, where his vocabulary failed him, by waving his rather dirty and chemical-stained hands demonstratively about him. His nails were a sight, but his fingers, I must say, had the delicate shape of a man's accustomed to minute manipulation. He plunged at once into the thick of the matter, telling us briefly in his equally thick accent that he 'now brobosed by his new brocess to make for us some goot and sadisfactory tiamonds.'

He brought out his apparatus, and explained— or, as he said, 'eggsblained'—his novel method. 'Tiamonds,' he said, 'were nozzing but pure crystalline carbon. He knew how to crystallise it—zat was all ze secret.' The men of science examined the pots and pans carefully. Then he put in a certain number of raw materials, and went to work with ostentatious openness. There were three distinct processes, and he made two stones by each simul-

taneously. The remarkable part of his methods, he
said, was their rapidity and their cheapness. In
three-quarters of an hour (and he smiled sardoni-
cally) he could produce a diamond worth at current
prices two hundred pounds sterling. 'As you shall
now see me berform,' he remarked, 'viz zis simple
abbaradus.'

THE SCIENTIFIC MEN CRANED THEIR NECKS IN THEIR EAGERNESS.

The materials fizzed and fumed. The Professor
stirred them. An unpleasant smell like burnt
feathers pervaded the room. The scientific men
craned their necks in their eagerness, and looked
over one another; Vane-Vivian, in particular, was
all attention. After three-quarters of an hour, the
Professor, still smiling, began to empty the ap-

paratus. He removed a large quantity of dust or powder, which he succinctly described as 'by-broducts,' and then took between finger and thumb from the midst of each pan a small white pebble, not water-worn apparently, but slightly rough and wart-like on the surface.

From one pair of the pannikins he produced two such stones, and held them up before us triumph-antly. 'Zese,' he said, 'are genuine tiamonds, manufactured at a gost of fourteen shillings and siggspence abiece!' Then he tried the second pair. 'Zese,' he said, still more gleefully, 'are broduced at a gost of eleffen and ninebence!' Finally, he came to the third pair, which he positively brandished before our astonished eyes. 'And zese,' he cried, transported, 'haff gost me no more zan tree and eightbence!'

They were handed round for inspection. Rough and uncut as they stood, it was, of course, impossible to judge of their value. But one thing was certain. The men of science had been watching close at the first, and were sure Herr Schleiermacher had not put the stones in; they were keen at the withdrawal, and were equally sure he had taken them honestly out of the pannikins.

'I vill now disdribute zem,' the Professor re-marked in a casual tone, as if diamonds were peas, looking round at the company. And he singled out my brother-in-law. 'One to Sir Charles!' he said, handing it; 'one to Mr. Mosenheimer; one to Mr. Phibson—as representing the tiamond interest. Zen, one each to Sir Atolphus, to Dr. Gray, to Mr. Fane-Fiffian, as representing science. You will haff zem cut and rebort upon zem in due gourse. We meet again at zis blace ze day afder do-morrow.'

Charles gazed at him reproachfully. The profoundest chords of his moral nature were stirred. 'Professor,' he said, in a voice of solemn warning, '*are* you aware that, *if* you have succeeded, you have destroyed the value of thousands of pounds' worth of precious property?'

The Professor shrugged his shoulders. 'Fot is dat to me?' he inquired, with a curious glance of contempt. 'I am not a financier! I am a man of science. I seek to know; I do not seek to make a fortune.'

'Shocking!' Charles exclaimed. 'Shocking! I never before in my life beheld so strange an instance of complete insensibility to the claims of others!'

We separated early. The men of science were coarsely jubilant. The diamond interest exhibited a corresponding depression. If this news were true, they foresaw a slump. Every eye grew dim. It was a terrible business.

Charles walked homeward with the Professor. He sounded him gently as to the sum required, should need arise, to purchase his secrecy. Already Sir Adolphus had bound us all down to temporary silence—as if that were necessary; but Charles wished to know how much Schleiermacher would take to suppress his discovery. The German was immovable.

'No, no!' he replied, with positive petulance. 'You do not unterstant. I do not buy and sell. Zis is a chemical fact. We must bublish it for the sake off its seoretical falue. I do not care for wealse. I haff no time to waste in making money.'

'What an awful picture of a misspent life!' Charles observed to me afterwards.

And, indeed, the man seemed to care for nothing on earth but the abstract question—not whether he could make good diamonds or not, but whether he could or could not produce a crystalline form of pure carbon!

On the appointed night Charles went back to Lancaster Gate, as I could not fail to remark, with a strange air of complete and painful preoccupation. Never before in his life had I seen him so anxious.

The diamonds were produced, with one surface of each slightly scored by the cutters, so as to show the water. Then a curious result disclosed itself. Strange to say, each of the three diamonds given to the three diamond kings turned out to be a most inferior and valueless stone ; while each of the three intrusted to the care of the scientific investigators turned out to be a fine gem of the purest quality.

I confess it was a sufficiently suspicious conjunction. The three representatives of the diamond interest gazed at each other with inquiring side-glances. Then their eyes fell suddenly : they avoided one another. Had each independently substituted a weak and inferior natural stone for Professor

Schleiermacher's manufactured pebbles? It almost seemed so. For a moment, I admit, I was half inclined to suppose it. But next second I changed my mind. Could a man of Sir Charles Vandrift's integrity and high principle stoop for lucre's sake to so mean an expedient?—not to mention the fact that, even if he did, and if Mosenheimer did likewise, the stones submitted to the scientific men would have amply sufficed to establish the reality and success of the experiments!

Still, I must say, Charles looked guiltily across at Mosenheimer, and Mosenheimer at Phipson, while three more uncomfortable or unhappy-faced men could hardly have been found at that precise minute in the City of Westminster.

Then Sir Adolphus spoke—or, rather, he orated. He said, in his loud and grating voice, we had that evening, and on a previous evening, been present at the conception and birth of an Epoch in the History of Science. Professor Schleiermacher was one of those men of whom his native Saxony might well be proud ; while as a Briton he must say he regretted somewhat that this discovery, like so many others, should have been 'Made in Germany.' However, Professor Schleiermacher was a specimen of that noble type of scientific men to whom gold was merely the rare metal Au, and diamonds merely the element C in the scarcest of its manifold allotropic embodiments. The Professor did not seek to make money out of his discovery. He rose above the

sordid greed of capitalists.   Content with the glory
of having traced the element C to its crystalline
origin, he asked no more than the approval of
science.   However, out of deference to the wishes of
those financial gentlemen who were oddly concerned

THREE UNCOMFORTABLE, UNHAPPY-
FACED MEN.

in maintaining the present price of C in its crystalline
form—in other words, the diamond interest—they
had arranged that the secret should be strictly
guarded and kept for the present ; not one of the
few persons admitted to the experiments would
publicly divulge the truth about them.   This secrecy

would be maintained till he himself, and a small
committee of the Royal Society, should have time to
investigate and verify for themselves the Professor's
beautiful and ingenious processes—an investigation
and verification which the learned Professor himself
both desired and suggested. (Schleiermacher nodded
approval.) When that was done, if the process stood
the test, further concealment would be absolutely
futile. The price of diamonds must fall at once
below that of paste, and any protest on the part of
the financial world would, of course, be useless. The
laws of Nature were superior to millionaires. Meanwhile, in deference to the opinion of Sir Charles
Vandrift, whose acquaintance with that fascinating
side of the subject nobody could deny, they had
consented to send no notices to the Press, and to
abstain from saying anything about this beautiful
and simple process in public. He dwelt with horrid
gusto on that epithet ' beautiful.' And now, in the
name of British mineralogy, he must congratulate
Professor Schleiermacher, our distinguished guest, on
his truly brilliant and crystalline contribution to our
knowledge of brilliants and of crystalline science.

Everybody applauded. It was an awkward
moment. Sir Charles bit his lip. Mosenheimer
looked glum. Young Phipson dropped an expression which I will not transcribe. (I understand this
work may circulate among families.) And after a
solemn promise of death-like secrecy, the meeting
separated.

I noticed that my brother-in-law somewhat ostentatiously avoided Mosenheimer at the door ; and that Phipson jumped quickly into his own carriage. ' Home ! ' Charles cried gloomily to the coachman as we took our seats in the brougham. And all the way to Mayfair he leaned back in his seat, with close-set lips, never uttering a syllable.

Before he retired to rest, however, in the privacy of the billiard-room, I ventured to ask him : ' Charles, will you unload Golcondas to-morrow ? ' Which, I need hardly explain, is the slang of the Stock Exchange for getting rid of undesirable securities. It struck me as probable that, in the event of the invention turning out a reality, Cloetedorp A's might become unsaleable within the next few weeks or so.

He eyed me sternly. ' Wentworth,' he said, ' you're a fool ! ' (Except on occasions when he is *very* angry, my respected connection *never* calls me ' Wentworth ' ; the familiar abbreviation, ' Sey '— derived from Seymour—is his usual mode of address to me in private.) ' *Is* it likely I would unload, and wreck the confidence of the public in the Cloetedorp Company at such a moment ? As a director—as Chairman—would it be just or right of me ? I ask you, sir, *could* I reconcile it to my conscience ? '

' Charles,' I answered, ' you are right. Your conduct is noble. You will not save your own personal interests at the expense of those who have put their trust in you. Such probity is, alas ! very rare in

finance!' And I sighed involuntarily; for I had
lost in Liberators.

At the same time I thought to myself, '*I* am not
a director. No trust is reposed in *me*. *I* have to
think first of dear Isabel and the baby. Before the
crash comes *I* will sell out to-morrow the few shares
I hold, through Charles's kindness, in the Cloetedorp
Golcondas.'

With his marvellous business instinct, Charles
seemed to divine my thought, for he turned round
to me sharply. 'Look here, Sey,' he remarked, in
an acidulous tone, 'recollect, you're my brother-in-
law. You are also my secretary. The eyes of
London will be upon us to-morrow. If *you* were to
sell out, and operators got to know of it, they'd
suspect there was something up, and the company
would suffer for it. Of course, you can do what you
like with your own property. I can't interfere with
that. I do not dictate to you. But as Chairman of
the Golcondas, I am bound to see that the interests
of widows and orphans whose All is invested with
me should not suffer at this crisis.' His voice
seemed to falter. 'Therefore, though I don't like to
threaten,' he went on, 'I am bound to give you
warning: *if* you sell out those shares of yours,
openly or secretly, you are no longer my secretary;
you receive forthwith six months' salary in lieu of
notice, and——you leave me instantly.'

'Very well, Charles,' I answered, in a submissive
voice; though I debated with myself for a moment

whether it would be best to stick to the ready money
and quit the sinking ship, or to hold fast by my
friend, and back Charles's luck against the Professor's
science.   After a short, sharp struggle within my
own mind, I am proud to say, friendship and
gratitude won.   I felt sure that, whether diamonds
went up or down, Charles Vandrift was the sort of
man who would come to the top in the end in spite
of everything.   And I decided to stand by him!

I slept little that night, however.   My mind was
a whirlwind.   At breakfast Charles also looked
haggard and moody.   He ordered the carriage early,
and drove straight into the City.

There was a block in Cheapside.   Charles,
impatient and nervous, jumped out and walked.   I
walked beside him.   Near Wood Street a man we
knew casually stopped us.

' I think I ought to mention to you,' he said,
confidentially, ' that I have it on the very best
authority that Schleiermacher, of Jena——'

' Thank you,' Charles said, crustily, ' I know that
tale, and—there's not a word of truth in it.'

He brushed on in haste.   A yard or two farther
a broker paused in front of us.

' Halloa, Sir Charles!' he called out, in a bantering tone.   ' What's all this about diamonds?   Where
are Cloetedorps to-day?   Is it Golconda, or Queer
Street?'

Charles drew himself up very stiff.   ' I fail to
understand you,' he answered, with dignity.

'Why, you were there yourself,' the man cried.
'Last night at Sir Adolphus's! Oh yes, it's all
over the place ; Schleiermacher of Jena has succeeded
in making the most perfect diamonds—for sixpence
apiece—as good as real—and South Africa's ancient
history. In less than six weeks Kimberley, they
say, will be a howling desert. Every costermonger
in Whitechapel will wear genuine Koh-i-noors for
buttons on his coat ; every girl in Bermondsey will
sport a *rivière* like Lady Vandrift's to her favourite
music-hall. There's a slump in Golcondas. Sly,
sly, I can see ; but *we* know all about it !'

Charles moved on, disgusted. The man's manners
were atrocious. Near the Bank we ran up against a
most respectable jobber.

'Ah, Sir Charles,' he said ; 'you here? Well,
this is strange news, isn't it? For my part, I advise
you not to take it too seriously. Your stock will go
down, of course, like lead this morning. But it'll
rise to-morrow, mark my words, and fluctuate every
hour till the discovery's proved or disproved for
certain. There's a fine time coming for operators, I
feel sure. Reports this way and that. Rumours,
rumours, rumours. And nobody will know which
way to believe till Sir Adolphus has tested it.'

We moved on towards the House. Black care
was seated on Sir Charles's shoulders. As we drew
nearer and nearer, everybody was discussing the one
fact of the moment. The seal of secrecy had proved
more potent than publication on the housetops.

Some people told us of the exciting news in confidential whispers ; some proclaimed it aloud in vulgar exultation. The general opinion was that Cloetedorps were doomed, and that the sooner a man cleared out the less was he likely to lose by it.

Charles strode on like a general ; but it was a Napoleon brazening out his retreat from Moscow. His mien was resolute. He disappeared at last into the precincts of an office, waving me back, not to follow. After a long consultation he came out and rejoined me.

All day long the City rang with Golcondas, Golcondas. Everybody murmured, 'Slump, slump in Golcondas.' The brokers had more business to do than they could manage ; though, to be sure, almost every one was a seller and no one a buyer. But Charles stood firm as a rock, and so did his brokers. 'I don't want to sell,' he said, doggedly. 'The whole thing is trumped up. It's a mere piece of jugglery. For my own part, I believe Professor Schleiermacher is deceived, or else is deceiving us. In another week the bubble will have burst, and prices will restore themselves.' His brokers, Finglemores, had only one answer to all inquiries : 'Sir Charles has every confidence in the stability of Golcondas, and doesn't wish to sell or to increase the panic.'

All the world said he was splendid, splendid ! There he stationed himself on 'Change like some granite stack against which the waves roll and break

themselves in vain.   He took no notice of the slump,
but ostentatiously bought up a few shares here and
there so as to restore public confidence.

'I would buy more,' he said, freely, 'and make
my fortune ; only, as I was one of those who
happened to spend last night at Sir Adolphus's,
people might think I had helped to spread the
rumour and produce the slump, in order to buy in
at panic rates for my own advantage.   A chairman,
like Cæsar's wife, should be above suspicion.   So I
shall only buy up just enough, now and again, to let
people see I, at least, have no doubt as to the firm
future of Cloetedorps.'

He went home that night, more harassed and ill
than I have ever seen him.   Next day was as bad.
The slump continued, with varying episodes.   Now,
a rumour would surge up that Sir Adolphus had
declared the whole affair a sham, and prices would
steady a little ; now, another would break out that
the diamonds were actually being put upon the
market in Berlin by the cart-load, and timid old
ladies would wire down to their brokers to realise
off-hand at whatever hazard.   It was an awful day.
I shall never forget it.

The morning after, as if by miracle, things righted
themselves of a sudden.   While we were wondering
what it meant, Charles received a telegram from Sir
Adolphus Cordery :—

'The man is a fraud.   Not Schleiermacher at all.
Just had a wire from Jena saying the Professor

knows nothing about him.   Sorry unintentionally
to have caused you trouble.   Come round and see
me.'

CHARLES WAS BESIDE HIMSELF WITH ANGER.

'Sorry unintentionally to have caused you trouble.'
Charles was beside himself with anger.   Sir Adolphus
had upset the share-market for forty-eight mortal

hours, half-ruined a round dozen of wealthy operators,
convulsed the City, upheaved the House, and now
—he apologised for it as one might apologise for
being late ten minutes for dinner! Charles jumped
into a hansom and rushed round to see him. How
had he dared to introduce the impostor to solid men
as Professor Schleiermacher? Sir Adolphus shrugged
his shoulders. The fellow had come and introduced
himself as the great Jena chemist; he had long
white hair, and a stoop in the shoulders. What
reason had *he* for doubting his word? (I reflected
to myself that on much the same grounds Charles
in turn had accepted the Honourable David Granton
and Graf von Lebenstein.) Besides, what object
could the creature have for this extraordinary
deception? Charles knew only too well. It was
clear it was done to disturb the diamond market,
and we realised, too late, that the man who had done
it was—Colonel Clay, in 'another of his manifold
allotropic embodiments!' Charles had had his wish,
and had met his enemy once more in London!

We could see the whole plot. Colonel Clay was
polymorphic, like the element carbon! Doubtless,
with his extraordinary sleight of hand, he had
substituted real diamonds for the shapeless mass that
came out of the apparatus, in the interval between
handing the pebbles round for inspection, and
distributing them piecemeal to the men of science
and representatives of the diamond interest. We
all watched him closely, of course, when he opened

the crucibles ; but when once we had satisfied ourselves that *something* came out, our doubts were set at rest, and we forgot to watch whether he distributed those somethings or not to the recipients. Conjurers always depend upon such momentary distractions or lapses of attention. As usual, too, the Professor had disappeared into space the moment his trick was once well performed. He vanished like smoke, as the Count and Seer had vanished before, and was never again heard of.

Charles went home more angry than I have ever beheld him. I couldn't imagine why. He seemed as deeply hipped as if he had lost his thousands. I endeavoured to console him. 'After all,' I said, 'though Golcondas have suffered a temporary loss, it's a comfort to think that you should have stood so firm, and not only stemmed the tide, but also prevented yourself from losing anything at all of your own through panic. I'm sorry, of course, for the widows and orphans ; but if Colonel Clay has rigged the market, at least it isn't *you* who lose by it this time.'

Charles withered me with a fierce scowl of undisguised contempt. 'Wentworth,' he said once more, 'you are a fool !' Then he relapsed into silence.

'But you declined to sell out,' I said.

He gazed at me fixedly. 'Is it likely,' he asked at last, 'I would tell *you* if I meant to sell out ? or that I'd sell out openly through Finglemore, my usual broker? Why, all the world would have known, and Golcondas would have been finished. As it is, I don't desire to tell an ass like you exactly how much I've lost. But I *did* sell out, and some unknown operator bought in at once, and closed for ready money, and has sold again this morning; and after all that has happened, it will be impossible to track him. He didn't wait for the account: he settled up instantly. And he sold in like manner. I know now what has been done, and how cleverly it has all been disguised and covered; but the most I'm going to tell you to-day is just this—it's by far the biggest haul Colonel Clay has made out of me. He could retire on it if he liked. My one hope is, it may satisfy him for life; but, then, no man has ever had enough of making money.'

' *You* sold out!' I exclaimed. ' *You*, the Chairman of the company! *You* deserted the ship! And how about your trust? How about the widows and orphans confided to you?'

Charles rose and faced me. 'Seymour Wentworth,' he said, in his most solemn voice, ' you have lived with me for years and had every advantage. You have seen high finance. Yet you ask me that question! It's my belief you will never, never understand business!'

VII

THE EPISODE OF THE ARREST OF THE COLONEL

HOW much precisely Charles dropped over the slump
in Cloetedorps I never quite knew.   But the incident
left him dejected, limp, and dispirited.

'Hang it all, Sey,' he said to me in the smoking-
room, a few evenings later.   'This Colonel Clay is
enough to vex the patience of Job—and Job had
large losses, too, if I recollect aright, from the
Chaldeans and other big operators of the period.'

'Three thousand camels,' I murmured, recalling
my dear mother's lessons ; 'all at one fell swoop ;
not to mention five hundred yoke of oxen, carried
off by the Sabeans, then a leading firm of speculative
cattle-dealers !'

'Ah, well,' Charles meditated aloud, shaking the
ash from his cheroot into a Japanese tray—fine
antique bronze-work.   'There were big transactions
in live-stock even then !   Still, Job or no Job, the
man is too much for me.'

'The difficulty is,' I assented, 'you never know
where to have him.'

'Yes,' Charles mused ; 'if he were always the

same, like Horniman's tea or a good brand of whisky, it would be easier, of course; you'd stand some chance of spotting him.   But when a man turns up smiling every time in a different disguise, which fits him like a skin, and always apparently with the best credentials, why, hang it all, Sey, there's no wrestling with him anyhow.'

'Who could have come to us, for example, better vouched,' I acquiesced, 'than the Honourable David?'

'Exactly so,' Charles murmured.   'I invited him myself, for my own advantage.   And he arrived with all the prestige of the Glen-Ellachie connection.'

'Or the Professor?' I went on.   'Introduced to us by the leading mineralogist of England.'

I had touched a sore point.   Charles winced and remained silent.

'Then, women again,' he resumed, after a painful pause.   'I must meet in society many charming women.   I can't everywhere and always be on my guard against every dear soul of them.   Yet the moment I relax my attention for one day—or even when I don't relax it—I am bamboozled and led a dance by that arch Mme. Picardet, or that transparently simple little minx, Mrs. Granton. She's the cleverest girl I ever met in my life, that hussy, whatever we're to call her.   She's a different person each time; and each time, hang it all, I lose my heart afresh to that different person.'

I glanced round to make sure Amelia was well out of earshot.

'No, Sey,' my respected connection went on, after another long pause, sipping his coffee pensively, 'I feel I must be aided in this superhuman task by

I AM BAMBOOZLED AND LED A DANCE.

a professional unraveller of cunning disguises. I shall go to Marvillier's to-morrow—fortunate man, Marvillier—and ask him to supply me with a really good 'tec, who will stop in the house and keep an

eye upon every living soul that comes near me. He
shall scan each nose, each eye, each wig, each whisker.
He shall be my watchful half, my unsleeping self; it
shall be his business to suspect all living men, all
breathing women. The Archbishop of Canterbury
shall not escape for a moment his watchful regard ;
he will take care that royal princesses don't collar
the spoons or walk off with the jewel-cases. He
must see possible Colonel Clays in the guard of
every train and the parson of every parish ; he must
detect the off-chance of a Mme. Picardet in every
young girl that takes tea with Amelia, every fat old
lady that comes to call upon Isabel. Yes, I have
made my mind up. I shall go to-morrow and
secure such a man at once at Marvillier's.'

'If you please, Sir Charles,' Césarine interposed,
pushing her head through the portière, 'her ladyship
says, will you and Mr. Wentworth remember that
she goes out with you both this evening to Lady
Carisbrooke's ? '

'Bless my soul,' Charles cried, 'so she does!
And it's now past ten! The carriage will be at the
door for us in another five minutes ! '

Next morning, accordingly, Charles drove round
to Marvillier's. The famous detective listened to
his story with glistening eyes ; then he rubbed his
hands and purred. 'Colonel Clay!' he said ;
'Colonel Clay! That's a very tough customer!
The police of Europe are on the look-out for Colonel
Clay. He is wanted in London, in Paris, in Berlin.

It is *le Colonel Caoutchouc* here, *le Colonel Caoutchouc*
there ; till one begins to ask, at last, *is* there *any*
Colonel Caoutchouc, or is it a convenient class name
invented by the Force to
cover a gang of undis-
covered sharpers ? How-
ever, Sir Charles, we will
do our best.   I will set on
the track without delay
the best and cleverest detective in England.'

'The very man I want,'
Charles said. ' What name,
Marvillier ? '

The principal smiled.
'Whatever name you like,'
he said. 'He isn't particular.
Medhurst he's called at
home. *We* call him Joe.
I'll send him round to
your house this afternoon
for certain.'

'Oh no,' Charles said
promptly, ' you won't ; or
Colonel Clay himself will

MEDHURST.

come instead of him.   I've been sold too often.
No casual strangers !   I'll wait here and see him.'

' But he isn't in,' Marvillier objected.

Charles was firm as a rock. ' Then send and
fetch him.'

In half an hour, sure enough, the detective arrived. He was an odd-looking small man, with hair cut short and standing straight up all over his head, like a Parisian waiter. He had quick, sharp eyes, very much like a ferret's ; his nose was depressed, his lips thin and bloodless. A scar marked his left cheek—made by a sword-cut, he said, when engaged one day in arresting a desperate French smuggler, disguised as an officer of Chasseurs d'Afrique. His mien was resolute. Altogether, a quainter or 'cuter little man it has never yet been my lot to set eyes on. He walked in with a brisk step, eyed Charles up and down, and then, without much formality, asked for what he was wanted.

This is Sir Charles Vandrift, the great diamond king,' Marvillier said, introducing us.

' So I see,' the man answered.

' Then you know me ? ' Charles asked.

' I wouldn't be worth much,' the detective replied, ' if I didn't know everybody. And *you're* easy enough to know ; why, every boy in the street knows you.'

' Plain spoken ! ' Charles remarked.

' As you like it, sir,' the man answered in a respectful tone. ' I endeavour to suit my dress and behaviour on every occasion to the taste of my employers.'

' Your name ? ' Charles asked, smiling.

' Joseph Medhurst, at your service. What sort of work ? Stolen diamonds ? Illicit diamond-buying ? '

'No,' Charles answered, fixing him with his eye. 'Quite another kind of job. You've heard of Colonel Clay?'

Medhurst nodded. 'Why, certainly,' he said; and, for the first time, I detected a lingering trace of American accent. 'It's my business to know about him.'

'Well, I want you to catch him,' Charles went on.

Medhurst drew a long breath. 'Isn't that rather a large order?' he murmured, surprised.

Charles explained to him exactly the sort of services he required. Medhurst promised to comply. 'If the man comes near you, I'll spot him,' he said, after a moment's pause. 'I can promise you that much. I'll pierce any disguise. I should know in a minute whether he's got up or not. I'm death on wigs, false moustaches, artificial complexions. I'll engage to bring the rogue to book if I see him. You may set your mind at rest, that, while *I'm* about you, Colonel Clay can do nothing without my instantly spotting him.'

'He'll do it,' Marvillier put in. 'He'll do it, if he says it. He's my very best hand. Never knew any man like him for unravelling and unmasking the cleverest disguises.'

'Then he'll suit me,' Charles answered, 'for *I* never knew any man like Colonel Clay for assuming and maintaining them.'

It was arranged accordingly that Medhurst should take up his residence in the house for the

present, and should be described to the servants as
assistant secretary.   He came that very day, with a

CÉSARINE TOOK A VIOLENT DISLIKE TO HIM.

marvellously small portmanteau. But from the
moment he arrived, we noticed that Césarine took a
violent dislike to him.

Medhurst was a most efficient detective. Charles and I told him all we knew about the various shapes in which Colonel Clay had 'materialised,' and he gave us in turn many valuable criticisms and suggestions. Why, when we began to suspect the Honourable David Granton, had we not, as if by accident, tried to knock his red wig off? Why, when the Reverend Richard Peploe Brabazon first discussed the question of the paste diamonds, had we not looked to see if any of Amelia's unique gems were missing? Why, when Professor Schleiermacher made his bow to assembled science at Lancaster Gate, had we not strictly inquired how far he was personally known beforehand to Sir Adolphus Cordery and the other mineralogists? He supplied us also with several good hints about false hair and make-up; such as that Schleiermacher was probably much shorter than he looked, but by imitating a stoop with padding at his back he had produced the illusion of a tall bent man, though in reality no bigger than the little curate or the Graf von Lebenstein. High heels did the rest; while the scientific keenness we noted in his face was doubtless brought about by a trifle of wax at the end of the nose, giving a peculiar tilt that is extremely effective. In short, I must frankly admit, Medhurst made us feel ashamed of ourselves. Sharp as Charles is, we realised at once he was nowhere in observation beside the trained and experienced senses of this professional detective.

The worst of it all was, while Medhurst was with us, by some curious fatality, Colonel Clay stopped away from us. Now and again, to be sure, we ran up against somebody whom Medhurst suspected ; but after a short investigation (conducted, I may say, with admirable cleverness), the spy always showed us the doubtful person was really some innocent and well-known character, whose antecedents and surroundings he elucidated most wonderfully. He was a perfect marvel, too, in his faculty of suspicion. He suspected everybody. If an old friend dropped in to talk business with Charles, we found out afterwards that Medhurst had lain concealed all the time behind the curtain, and had taken short-hand notes of the whole conversation, as well as snap-shot photographs of the supposed sharper, by means of a kodak. If a fat old lady came to call upon Amelia, Medhurst was sure to be lurking under the ottoman in the drawing-room, and carefully observing, with all his eyes, whether or not she was really Mme. Picardet, padded. When Lady Tresco brought her four plain daughters to an ' At Home ' one night, Medhurst, in evening dress, disguised as a waiter, followed them each round the room with obtrusive ices, to satisfy himself just how much of their complexion was real, and how much was patent rouge and Bloom of Ninon. He doubted whether Simpson, Sir Charles's valet, was not Colonel Clay in plain clothes ; and he had half an idea that Césarine herself was our saucy White Heather in an alternative avatar. We pointed out to him in vain that Simpson had often been present in the very same room with David Granton, and that Césarine had dressed Mrs. Brabazon's hair at Lucerne : this partially satisfied him, but only partially. He remarked that Simpson might double both parts with somebody else unknown ; and that as for Césarine, she might well have a twin sister who took her place when she was Mme. Picardet.

Still, in spite of all his care—or because of all his care—Colonel Clay stopped away for whole weeks together. An explanation occurred to us. Was it possible he knew we were guarded and watched ? Was he afraid of measuring swords with this trained detective ?

If so, how had he found it out ? I had an inkling, myself—but, under all the circumstances, I did not mention it to Charles. It was clear that Césarine intensely disliked this new addition to the Vandrift household. She would not stop in the room where the detective was, or show him common politeness. She spoke of him always as 'that odious man, Medhurst.' Could she have guessed, what none of the other servants knew, that the man was a spy in search of the Colonel ? I was inclined to believe it. And then it dawned upon me that Césarine had known all about the diamonds and their story ; that it was Césarine who took us to see Schloss Lebenstein ; that it was Césarine who posted the letter to Lord Craig-

Ellachie! If Césarine was in league with Colonel Clay, as I was half inclined to surmise, what more natural than her obvious dislike to the detective who was there to catch her principal? What more simple for her than to warn her fellow-conspirator of the danger that awaited him if he approached this man Medhurst?

However, I was too much frightened by the episode of the cheque to say anything of my nascent suspicions to Charles. I waited rather to see how events would shape themselves.

After a while Medhurst's vigilance grew positively annoying. More than once he came to Charles with reports and shorthand notes distinctly distasteful to my excellent brother-in-law. 'The fellow is getting to know too much about us,' Charles said to me one day. 'Why, Sey, he spies out everything. Would you believe it, when I had that confidential interview with Brookfield the other day, about the new issue of Golcondas, the man was under the easy-chair, though I searched the room beforehand to make sure he wasn't there ; and he came to me afterwards with full notes of the conversation, to assure me he thought Brookfield—whom I've known for ten years—was too tall by half an inch to be one of Colonel Clay's impersonations.'

'Oh, but, Sir Charles,' Medhurst cried, emerging suddenly from the bookcase, 'you must never look upon *any one* as above suspicion merely because you've known him for ten years or thereabouts.

Colonel Clay may have approached you at various times under many disguises. He may have built up this thing gradually. Besides, as to my knowing too much, why, of course, a detective always learns

MEDHURST SUDDENLY EMERGED FROM THE BOOKCASE.

many things about his employer's family which he is not supposed to know ; but professional honour and professional etiquette, as with doctors and lawyers, compel him to lock them up as absolute secrets in his own bosom. You need never be afraid

I will divulge one jot of them. If I did, my occupation would be gone, and my reputation shattered.'

Charles looked at him, appalled. 'Do you dare to say,' he burst out, 'you've been listening to my talk with my brother-in-law and secretary?'

'Why, of course,' Medhurst answered. 'It's my business to listen, and to suspect everybody. If you push me to say so, how do I know Colonel Clay is not—Mr. Wentworth?'

Charles withered him with a look. 'In future, Medhurst,' he said, 'you must never conceal yourself in a room where I am without my leave and knowledge.'

Medhurst bowed politely. 'Oh, as you will, Sir Charles,' he answered; 'that's *quite* at your own wish. Though how can I act as an efficient detective, any way, if you insist upon tying my hands like that, beforehand?'

Again I detected a faint American flavour.

After that rebuff, however, Medhurst seemed put upon his mettle. He redoubled his vigilance in every direction. 'It's not my fault,' he said plaintively, one day, 'if my reputation's so good that, while I'm near you, this rogue won't approach you. If I can't *catch* him, at least I keep him away from coming near you!'

A few days later, however, he brought Charles some photographs. These he produced with evident pride. The first he showed us was a vignette of a little parson. 'Who's that, then?' he inquired, much pleased.

We gazed at it, open-eyed. One word rose to our lips simultaneously : 'Brabazon !'

'And how's this for high?' he asked again, producing another—the photograph of a gay young dog in a Tyrolese costume.

We murmured, 'Von Lebenstein !'

'*And* this?' he continued, showing us the portrait of a lady with a most fetching squint.

We answered with one voice, 'Little Mrs. Granton !'

Medhurst was naturally proud of this excellent exploit. He replaced them in his pocket-book with an air of just triumph.

'How did you get them?' Charles asked.

Medhurst's look was mysterious. 'Sir Charles,' he answered, drawing himself up, 'I must ask you to trust me awhile in this matter. Remember, there are people whom you decline to suspect. *I* have learned that it is always those very people who are most dangerous to capitalists. If I were to give you the names now, you would refuse to believe me. Therefore, I hold them over discreetly for the moment. One thing, however, I say. I *know* to a certainty where Colonel Clay is at this present speaking. But I will lay my plans deep, and I hope before long to secure him. You shall be present when I do so ; and I shall make him confess his personality openly. More than that you cannot reasonably ask. I shall leave it to *you*, then, whether or not you wish to arrest him.'

Charles was considerably puzzled, not to say piqued, by this curious reticence ; he begged hard for names ; but Medhurst was adamant. 'No, no,' he replied ; 'we detectives have our own just pride in our profession. If I told you now, you would probably spoil all by some premature action. You are too open and impulsive ! I will mention this alone : Colonel Clay will be shortly in Paris, and before long will begin from that city a fresh attempt at defrauding you, which he is now hatching. Mark my words, and see whether or not I have been kept well informed of the fellow's movements !'

He was perfectly correct. Two days later, as it turned out, Charles received a 'confidential' letter from Paris, purporting to come from the head of a second-rate financial house with which he had had dealings over the Craig-Ellachie Amalgamation—by this time, I ought to have said, an accomplished union. It was a letter of small importance in itself —a mere matter of detail ; but it paved the way, so Medhurst thought, to some later development of more serious character. Here once more the man's singular foresight was justified. For, in another week, we received a second communication, ·containing other proposals of a delicate financial character, which would have involved the transference of some two thousand pounds to the head of the Parisian firm at an address given. Both these letters Med-

hurst cleverly compared with those written to
Charles before, in the names of Colonel Clay and of
Graf von Lebenstein. At first sight, it is true, the
differences between the two seemed quite enormous :
the Paris hand was broad and black, large and bold;
while the earlier manuscript was small, neat, thin,
and gentlemanly. Still, when Medhurst pointed out
to us certain persistent twists in the formation of his
capitals, and certain curious peculiarities in the
relative length of his t's, his l's, his b's, and his h's,
we could see for ourselves he was right ; both
were the work of one hand, writing in the one case
with a sharp-pointed nib, very small, and in the
other with a quill, very large and freely.

This discovery was *most* important. We stood
now within measurable distance of catching Colonel
Clay, and bringing forgery and fraud home to him
without hope of evasion.

To make all sure, however, Medhurst communicated with the Paris police, and showed us their
answers. Meanwhile, Charles continued to write to
the head of the firm, who had given a private address
in the Rue Jean Jacques, alleging, I must say, a
most clever reason why the negotiations at this stage
should be confidentially conducted. But one never
expected from Colonel Clay anything less than consummate cleverness. In the end, it was arranged
that we three were to go over to Paris together, that
Medhurst was to undertake, under the guise of being
Sir Charles, to pay the two thousand pounds to the

pretended financier, and that Charles and I, waiting with the police outside the door, should, at a given signal, rush in with our forces and secure the criminal.

We went over accordingly, and spent the night

THE DISCOVERY WAS MOST IMPORTANT.

at the Grand, as is Charles's custom. The Bristol, which I prefer, he finds too quiet. Early next morning we took a *fiacre* and drove to the Rue Jean Jacques. Medhurst had arranged everything in advance with the Paris police, three of whom, in plain clothes, were waiting at the foot of the staircase to assist us. Charles had further provided himself with two thousand pounds, in notes of the Bank of France, in order that the payment might be duly made, and no doubt arise as to the crime having been perpetrated as well as meditated—in the former case, the penalty would be fifteen years; in the latter, three only. He was in very high spirits. The fact that we had tracked the rascal to earth at last, and were within an hour of apprehending him, was in itself enough to raise his courage greatly. We found, as we expected, that the number given in the Rue Jean Jacques was that of an hotel, not a private residence. Medhurst went in first, and inquired of the landlord whether our man was at home, at the same time informing him of the nature of our errand, and giving him to understand that if we effected the capture by his friendly aid, Sir Charles would see that the expenses incurred on the swindler's bill were met in full, as the price of his assistance. The landlord bowed; he expressed his deep regret, as M. le Colonel—so we heard him call him—was a most amiable person, much liked by the household; but justice, of course, must have its way; and, with a regretful sigh, he undertook to assist us.

The police remained below, but Charles and Medhurst were each provided with a pair of handcuffs. Remembering the Polperro case, however, we determined to use them with the greatest caution. We would only put them on in case of violent

resistance. We crept up to the door where the
miscreant was housed. Charles handed the notes
in an open envelope to Medhurst, who seized them

BREATHLESS EXPECTATION.

hastily and held them in his hands in readiness for
action. We had a sign concerted. Whenever he
sneezed—which he could do in the most natural

manner—we were to open the door, rush in, and secure the criminal!

He was gone for some minutes. Charles and I waited outside in breathless expectation. Then Medhurst sneezed. We flung the door open at once, and burst in upon the creature.

Medhurst rose as we did so. He pointed with his finger. '*This* is Colonel Clay!' he said; 'keep him well in charge while I go down to the door for the police to arrest him!'

A gentlemanly man, about middle height, with a grizzled beard and a well-assumed military aspect, rose at the same moment. The envelope in which Charles had placed the notes lay on the table before him. He clutched it nervously. 'I am at a loss, gentlemen,' he said, in an excited voice, 'to account for this interruption.' He spoke with a tremor, yet with all the politeness to which we were accustomed in the little curate and the Honourable David.

'No nonsense!' Charles exclaimed, in his authoritative way. 'We know who you are. We have found you out this time. You are Colonel Clay. If you attempt to resist—take care—I will handcuff you!'

The military gentleman gave a start. 'Yes, I *am* Colonel Clay,' he answered. 'On what charge do you arrest me?'

Charles was bursting with wrath. The fellow's coolness seemed never to desert him. 'You *are* Colonel Clay!' he muttered. 'You have the un-

speakable effrontery to stand there and admit
it ? '

'Certainly,' the Colonel answered, growing hot in
turn. 'I have done nothing to be ashamed of.
What do you mean by this conduct?   How dare
you talk of arresting me ? '

Charles laid his hand on the man's shoulder.
'Come, come, my friend,' he said. 'That sort of
bluff won't go down with us.   You know very well
on what charge I arrest you ; and here are the
police to give effect to it.'

He called out 'Entrez !'   The police entered the
room.   Charles explained as well as he could in
most doubtful Parisian what they were next to do.
The Colonel drew himself up in an indignant attitude.
He turned and addressed them in excellent French.

'I am an officer in the service of her Britannic
Majesty,' he said. 'On what ground do you venture
to interfere with me, messieurs ? '

The chief policeman explained.   The Colonel
turned to Charles. ' *Your* name, sir ? ' he inquired.

'You know it very well,' Charles answered. 'I
am Sir Charles Vandrift ; and, in spite of your clever
disguise, I can instantly recognise you.   I know
your eyes and ears.   I can see the same man who
cheated me at Nice, and who insulted me on the
island.'

'*You* Sir Charles Vandrift !' the rogue cried.
'No, no, sir, you are a madman !'   He looked round
at the police. 'Take care what you do !' he cried.

'This is a raving maniac.   I had business just now
with Sir Charles Vandrift, who quitted the room as
these gentlemen entered.   This person is mad, and
you, monsieur, I doubt not,' bowing to me, 'you are,
of course, his keeper.'

'Do not let him deceive you,' I cried to the police,
beginning to fear that with his usual incredible
cleverness the fellow would even now manage to slip
through our fingers.   'Arrest him, as you are told.
We will take the responsibility.'   Though I trembled
when I thought of that cheque he held of mine.

The chief of our three policemen came forward
and laid his hand on the culprit's shoulder.   'I
advise you, M. le Colonel,' he said, in an official voice,
'to come with us quietly for the present.   Before the
juge d'instruction we can enter at length into all these
questions.'

The Colonel, very indignant still—and acting the
part marvellously—yielded and went along with
them.

'Where's Medhurst?' Charles inquired, glancing
round as we reached the door.   'I wish he had
stopped with us.'

'You are looking for monsieur your friend?' the
landlord inquired, with a side bow to the Colonel.
'He has gone away in a *fiacre*.   He asked me to
give this note to you.'

He handed us a twisted note.   Charles opened
and read it.   'Invaluable man!' he cried.   'Just
hear what he says, Sey: " Having secured Colonel

Clay, I am off now again on the track of Mme.
Picardet. She was lodging in the same house. She
has just driven away ; I know to what place ; and
I am after her to arrest her. In blind haste, MED-
HURST." That's smartness, *if* you like. Though
poor little woman, I think he might have left her.'

'Does a Mme. Picardet stop here ?' I inquired
of the landlord, thinking it possible she might have
assumed again the same old alias.

He nodded assent. ' *Oui, oui, oui,*' he answered.
' She has just driven off, and monsieur your friend
has gone posting after her.'

'Splendid man !' Charles cried. 'Marvillier was
quite right. He is the prince of detectives !'

We hailed a couple of *fiacres,* and drove off, in
two detachments, to the *juge d'instruction.* There
Colonel Clay continued to brazen it out, and asserted
that he was an officer in the Indian Army, home on
six months' leave, and spending some weeks in Paris.
He even declared he was known at the Embassy,
where he had a cousin an *attaché ;* and he asked
that this gentleman should be sent for at once from
our Ambassador's to identify him. The *juge d'instruction* insisted that this must be done ; and Charles
waited in very bad humour for the foolish formality.
It really seemed as if, after all, when we had actually
caught and arrested our man, he was going by some
cunning device to escape us.

After a delay of more than an hour, during which
Colonel Clay fretted and fumed quite as much as we

did, the *attaché* arrived.   To our horror and astonishment, he proceeded to salute the prisoner most
affectionately.

'Halloa, Algy!' he cried, grasping his hand;
'what's up?   What do these ruffians want with
you?'

It began to dawn upon us, then, what Medhurst

HE ACCUSES ME OF FORGERY, FRAUD, AND THEFT.

had meant by 'suspecting everybody': the real
Colonel Clay was no common adventurer, but a
gentleman of birth and high connections!

The Colonel glared at us.   'This fellow declares
he's Sir Charles Vandrift,' he said sulkily.   'Though,
in fact, there are two of them.   And he accuses me
of forgery, fraud, and theft, Bertie.'

The *attaché* stared hard at us.   'This *is* Sir
Charles Vandrift,' he replied, after a moment.   'I

remember hearing him make a speech once at a City
dinner. And what charge have you to prefer, Sir
Charles, against my cousin?'

'Your cousin?' Charles cried. 'This is Colonel
Clay, the notorious sharper!'

The *attaché* smiled a gentlemanly and superior
smile. 'This is Colonel Clay,' he answered, 'of the
Bengal Staff Corps.'

It began to strike us there was something wrong
somewhere.

'But he has cheated me, all the same,' Charles
said—'at Nice two years ago, and many times since;
and this very day he has tricked me out of two
thousand pounds in French bank-notes, which he
has now about him!'

The Colonel was speechless. But the *attaché*
laughed. 'What he has done to-day I don't know,'
he said; 'but if it's as apocryphal as what you say
he did two years ago, you've a thundering bad case,
sir; for he was then in India, and I was out there,
visiting him.'

'Where are the two thousand pounds?' Charles
cried. 'Why, you've got them in your hand! You're
holding the envelope!'

The Colonel produced it. 'This envelope,' he
said, 'was left with me by the man with short stiff
hair, who came just before you, and who announced
himself as Sir Charles Vandrift. He said he was
interested in tea in Assam, and wanted me to join
the board of directors of some bogus company.

These are his papers, I believe,' and he handed them to his cousin.

'Well, I'm glad the notes are safe, anyhow,' Charles murmured, in a tone of relief, beginning to smell a rat. 'Will you kindly return them to me?'

The *attaché* turned out the contents of the envelope. They proved to be prospectuses of bubble companies of the moment, of no importance.

'Medhurst must have put them there,' I cried, 'and decamped with the cash.'

Charles gave a groan of horror. 'And Medhurst is Colonel Clay!' he exclaimed, clapping his hand to his forehead.

'I beg your pardon, sir,' the Colonel interposed. 'I have but one personality, and no aliases.'

It took quite half an hour to explain this imbroglio. But as soon as all was explained, in French and English, to the satisfaction of ourselves and the *juge d'instruction*, the real Colonel shook hands with us in a most forgiving way, and informed us that he had more than once wondered, when he gave his name at shops in Paris, why it was often received with such grave suspicion. We instructed the police that the true culprit was Medhurst, whom they had seen with their own eyes, and whom we urged them to pursue with all expedition. Meanwhile, Charles and I, accompanied by the Colonel and the *attaché* —'to see the fun out,' as they said—called at the Bank of France for the purpose of stopping the notes immediately. It was too late, however. They had been presented at once, and cashed in gold, by a pleasant little lady in an American costume, who was afterwards identified by the hotel-keeper (from our description) as his lodger, Mme. Picardet. It was clear she had taken rooms in the same hotel, to be near the Indian Colonel ; and it was *she* who had received and sent the letters. As for our foe, he had vanished into space, as always.

Two days later we received the usual insulting communication on a sheet of Charles's own dainty note. Last time he wrote it was on Craig-Ellachie paper : this time, like the wanton lapwing, he had got himself another crest.

'MOST PERSPICACIOUS OF MILLIONAIRES !— Said I not well, as Medhurst, that you must distrust everybody ? And the one man you never dreamt of distrusting was—Medhurst. Yet see how truthful I was ! I told you I knew where Colonel Clay was living—and I *did* know, exactly. I promised to take you to Colonel Clay's rooms, and to get him arrested for you—and I kept my promise. I even exceeded your expectations ; for I gave you *two* Colonel Clays instead of one—and you took the wrong man—that is to say, the real one. This was a neat little trick ; but it cost me some trouble.

'First, I found out there *was* a real Colonel Clay, in the Indian Army. I also found out he chanced to be coming home on leave this season. I might have made more out of him, no doubt ; but I dis-

liked annoying him, and preferred to give myself
the fun of this peculiar mystification. I therefore
waited for him to reach Paris, where the police
arrangements suited me better than in London.
While I was looking about, and delaying operations
for his return, I happened to hear you wanted a
detective. So I offered myself as out of work to my
old employer, Marvillier, from whom I have had
many good jobs in the past ; and there you get, in
short, the kernel of the Colonel.

'Naturally, after this, I can never go back as a
detective to Marvillier's. But, on the large scale on
which I have learned to work since I first had the
pleasure of making your delightful acquaintance, this
matters little. To say the truth, I begin to feel
detective work a cut or two below me. I am now a
gentleman of means and leisure. Besides, the extra
knowledge of your movements which I have acquired
in your house has helped still further to give me
various holds upon you. So the fluke will be true
to his own pet lamb. To vary the metaphor, you
are not fully shorn yet.

'Remember me most kindly to your charming
family, give Wentworth my love, and tell Mlle.
Césarine I owe her a grudge which I shall never
forget. She clearly suspected me. You are much
too rich, dear Charles ; I relieve your plethora. I
bleed you financially. Therefore I consider myself
—Your sincerest friend,

'CLAY-BRABAZON-MEDHURST,
'*Fellow of the Royal College of Surgeons.*'

Charles was threatened with apoplexy. This blow was severe. 'Whom can I trust,' he asked, plaintively, 'when the detectives themselves, whom I employ to guard me, turn out to be swindlers? Don't you remember that line in the Latin grammar —something about, "Who shall watch the watchers?" I think it used to run, "*Quis custodes custodiet ipsos?*"'

But I felt this episode had at least disproved my suspicions of poor Césarine.

VIII

THE EPISODE OF THE SELDON GOLD-MINE

ON our return to London, Charles and Marvillier had a difference of opinion on the subject of Medhurst.

Charles maintained that Marvillier ought to have known the man with the cropped hair was Colonel Clay, and ought never to have recommended him. Marvillier maintained that Charles had *seen* Colonel Clay half-a-dozen times, at least, to his own never; and that my respected brother-in-law had therefore nobody on earth but himself to blame if the rogue imposed upon him. The head detective had known Medhurst for ten years, he said, as a most respectable man, and even a ratepayer; he had always found him the cleverest of spies, as well he might be, indeed, on the familiar set-a-thief-to-catch-a-thief principle. However, the upshot of it all was, as usual—nothing. Marvillier was sorry to lose the services of so excellent a hand; but he had done the very best he could for Sir Charles, he declared; and if Sir Charles was not satisfied, why, he might catch his Colonel Clays for himself in future.

'So I will, Sey,' Charles remarked to me, as we

walked back from the office in the Strand by
Piccadilly. 'I won't trust any more to these private
detectives. It's my belief they're a pack of thieves
themselves, in league with the rascals they're set to
catch, and with no more sense of honour than a Zulu
diamond-hand.'

'Better try the police,' I suggested, by way of
being helpful. One must assume an interest in one's
employer's business.

But Charles shook his head. 'No, no,' he said ;
'I'm sick of all these fellows. I shall trust in
future to my own sagacity. We learn by experience,
Sey—and I've learned a thing or two. One of them
is this : It's not enough to suspect everybody ; you
must have no preconceptions. Divest yourself
entirely of every fixed idea if you wish to cope with
a rascal of this calibre. Don't jump at conclusions.
We should disbelieve everything, as well as distrust
everybody. That's the road to success ; and I mean
to pursue it.'

So, by way of pursuing it, Charles retired to
Seldon.

'The longer the man goes on, the worse he
grows,' he said to me one morning. 'He's just like
a tiger that has tasted blood. Every successful haul
seems only to make him more eager for another. I
fully expect now before long we shall see him down
here.'

About three weeks later, sure enough, my respected connection received a communication from

the abandoned swindler, with an Austrian stamp and a Vienna post-mark.

'MY DEAR VANDRIFT.—(After so long and so varied an acquaintance we may surely drop the absurd formalities of " Sir Charles " and "Colonel.") I write to ask you a delicate question. Can you kindly tell me exactly how much I have received from your various generous acts during the last three years? I have mislaid my account-book, and as this is the season for making the income tax return, I am anxious, as an honest and conscientious citizen, to set down my average profits out of you for the triennial period. For reasons which you will amply understand, I do not this time give my private address, in Paris or elsewhere ; but if you will kindly advertise the total amount, above the signature " Peter Simple," in the Agony Column of the *Times*, you will confer a great favour upon the Revenue Commissioners, and also upon your constant friend and companion,   CUTHBERT CLAY,

'*Practical Socialist.*'

' Mark my word, Sey,' Charles said, laying the letter down, ' in a week or less the man himself will follow. This is his cunning way of trying to make me think he's well out of the country and far away from Seldon. That means he's meditating another descent. But he told us too much last time, when he was Medhurst the detective. He gave us some hints about disguises and their unmasking that I

shall not forget.   This turn I shall be even with
him.'

On Saturday of that week, in effect, we were
walking along the road that leads into the village,
when we met a gentlemanly-looking man, in a
rough and rather happy-go-lucky brown tweed suit,
who had the air of a tourist.   He was middle-aged,
and of middle height; he wore a small leather
wallet suspended round his shoulder; and he was
peering about at the rocks in a suspicious manner.
Something in his gait attracted our attention.

'Good-morning,' he said, looking up as we
passed; and Charles muttered a somewhat surly
inarticulate, 'Good-morning.'

We went on without saying more.   'Well, *that's*
not Colonel Clay, anyhow,' I said, as we got out of
earshot.   'For he accosted us first; and you may
remember it's one of the Colonel's most marked
peculiarities that, like the model child, he never
speaks till he's spoken to—never begins an acquaintance.   He always waits till we make the first
advance; he doesn't go out of his way to cheat us;
he loiters about till we ask him to do it.'

'Seymour,' my brother-in-law responded, in a
severe tone, 'there you are, now, doing the very
thing I warned you not to do!   You're succumbing
to a preconception.   Avoid fixed ideas.   The probability is this man *is* Colonel Clay.   Strangers are
generally scarce at Seldon.   If he isn't Colonel
Clay, what's he here for, I'd like to know?   What

money is there to be made here in any other way?
I shall inquire about him.'

We dropped in at the Cromarty Arms, and
asked good Mrs. M'Lachlan if she could tell us
anything about the gentlemanly stranger. Mrs.
M'Lachlan replied that he was from London, she
believed, a pleasant gentleman enough ; and he had
his wife with him.

' Ha ! Young ? Pretty ? ' Charles inquired, with a
speaking glance at me.

' Weel, Sir Charles, she'll no be exactly what
you'd be ca'ing a bonny lass,' Mrs. M'Lachlan
replied ; ' but she's a guid body for a' that, an' a
fine braw woman.'

' Just what I should expect,' Charles murmured,
' He varies the programme. The fellow has tried
White Heather as the parson's wife, and as Madame
Picardet, and as squinting little Mrs. Granton, and
as Medhurst's accomplice ; and now, he has almost
exhausted the possibilities of a disguise for a really
young and pretty woman ; so he's playing her off
at last as the riper product—a handsome matron.
Clever, extremely clever ; but—we begin to see
through him.' And he chuckled to himself quietly.

Next day, on the hillside, we came upon our
stranger again, occupied as before in peering into
the rocks, and sounding them with a hammer.
Charles nudged me and whispered, ' I have it this
time. He's posing as a geologist.'

I took a good look at the man. By now, of

course, we had some experience of Colonel Clay in his various disguises; and I could observe that while the nose, the hair, and the beard were varied, the eyes and the build remained the same as ever. He was a trifle stouter, of course, being got up as a

PEERING AT THE ROCKS IN A SUSPICIOUS MANNER.

man of between forty and fifty; and his forehead was lined in a way which a less consummate artist than Colonel Clay could easily have imitated. But I felt we had at least some grounds for our identification; it would not do to dismiss the suggestion of Clayhood at once as a flight of fancy.

His wife was sitting near, upon a bare boss of rock, reading a volume of poems. Capital variant, that, a volume of poems! Exactly suited the selected type of a cultivated family. White Heather and Mrs. Granton never used to read poems. But that was characteristic of all Colonel Clay's impersonations, and Mrs. Clay's too—for I suppose I must call her so. They were not mere outer disguises; they were finished pieces of dramatic study. Those two people were an actor and actress, as well as a pair of rogues; and in both their *rôles* they were simply inimitable.

As a rule, Charles is by no means polite to casual trespassers on the Seldon estate; they get short shrift and a summary ejection. But on this occasion he had a reason for being courteous, and he approached the lady with a bow of recognition. 'Lovely day,' he said, 'isn't it? Such belts on the sea, and the heather smells sweet. You are stopping at the inn, I fancy?'

'Yes,' the lady answered, looking up at him with a charming smile. ('I know that smile,' Charles whispered to me. 'I have succumbed to it too often.') 'We're stopping at the inn, and my husband is doing a little geology on the hill here. I hope Sir Charles Vandrift won't come and catch us. He's so down upon trespassers. They tell us at the inn he's a regular Tartar.'

('Saucy minx as ever,' Charles murmured to me. 'She said it on purpose.') 'No, my dear madam,' he

continued, aloud ; 'you have been quite misinformed.
I am Sir Charles Vandrift ; and I am *not* a Tartar.
If your husband is a man of science I respect and
admire him. It is geology that has made me what
I am to-day.' And he drew himself up proudly. ' We

I HOPE SIR CHARLES WON'T COME AND CATCH US.

owe to it the present development of South African
mining.'

The lady blushed as one seldom sees a mature
woman blush——but exactly as I had seen Madame
Picardet and White Heather. ' Oh, I'm so sorry,'
she said, in a confused way that recalled Mrs.
Granton. ' Forgive my hasty speech. I——I didn't
know you.'

('She did,' Charles whispered. 'But let that pass.') 'Oh, don't think of it again; so many people disturb the birds, don't you know, that we're obliged in self-defence to warn trespassers some-times off our lovely mountains. But I do it with regret—with profound regret. I admire the—er— the beauties of Nature myself; and, therefore, I desire that all others should have the freest possible access to them—possible, that is to say, consistently with the superior claims of Property.'

'I see,' the lady replied, looking up at him quaintly. 'I admire your wish, though not your reservation. I've just been reading those sweet lines of Wordsworth's—

> And O, ye fountains, meadows, hills, and groves,
> Forebode not any severing of our loves.

I suppose you know them?' And she beamed on him pleasantly.

'Know them?' Charles answered. 'Know them! Oh, of course, I know them. They're old favourites of mine—in fact, I adore Wordsworth.' (I doubt whether Charles has ever in his life read a line of poetry, except Doss Chiderdoss in the *Sporting Times*.) He took the book and glanced at them. 'Ah, charm-ing, charming!' he said, in his most ecstatic tone. But his eyes were on the lady, and not on the poet.

I saw in a moment how things stood. No matter under what disguise that woman appeared to him, and whether he recognised her or not, Charles couldn't help falling a victim to Madame Picardet's attractions.

Here he actually suspected her ; yet, like a moth round a candle, he was trying his hardest to get his wings singed ! I almost despised him with his gigantic intellect ! The greatest men are the greatest fools, I verily believe, when there's a woman in question.

The husband strolled up by this time, and entered into conversation with us. According to his own account, his name was Forbes-Gaskell, and he was a Professor of Geology in one of those new-fangled northern colleges. He had come to Seldon rock-spying, he said, and found much to interest him. He was fond of fossils, but his special hobby was rocks and minerals. He knew a vast deal about cairngorms and agates and such-like pretty things, and showed Charles quartz and felspar and red cornelian, and I don't know what else, in the crags on the hillside. Charles pretended to listen to him with the deepest interest and even respect, never for a moment letting him guess he knew for what purpose this show of knowledge had been recently acquired. If we were ever to catch the man, we must not allow him to see we suspected him. So Charles played a dark game. He swallowed the geologist whole without question.

Most of that morning we spent with them on the hillside. Charles took them everywhere and showed them everything. He pretended to be polite to the scientific man, and he was really polite, most polite, to the poetical lady. Before lunch time we had become quite friends.

The Clays were always easy people to get on with ; and, bar their roguery, we could not deny they were delightful companions. Charles asked them in to lunch. They accepted willingly. He introduced them to Amelia with sundry raisings of his eyebrows and contortions of his mouth. 'Professor and Mrs. Forbes-Gaskell,' he said, half-dislocating his jaw with his violent efforts. 'They're stopping at the inn, dear. I've been showing them over the place, and they're good enough to say they'll drop in and take a share in our cold roast mutton ;' which was a frequent form of Charles's pleasantry.

Amelia sent them upstairs to wash their hands —which, in the Professor's case, was certainly desirable, for his fingers were grimed with earth and dust from the rocks he had been investigating. As soon as we were left alone Charles drew me into the library.

'Seymour,' he said, 'more than ever there is a need for us strictly to avoid preconceptions. We must not make up our minds that this man is Colonel Clay—nor, again, that he isn't. We must remember that we have been mistaken in *both* ways in the past, and must avoid our old errors. I shall hold myself in readiness for either event—and a policeman in readiness to arrest them, if necessary !'

'A capital plan,' I murmured. 'Still, if I may venture a suggestion, in what way are these two people endeavouring to entrap us? They have no scheme on hand—no schloss, no amalgamation.'

'Seymour,' my brother-in-law answered in his board-room style, 'you are a great deal too previous, as Medhurst used to say—I mean, Colonel Clay in his character as Medhurst. In the first place, these are early days ; our friends have not yet developed their intentions. We may find before long they have a property to sell, or a company to promote, or a concession to exploit in South Africa or elsewhere. Then again, in the second place, we don't always spot the exact nature of their plan until it has burst in our hands, so to speak, and revealed its true character. What could have seemed more transparent than Medhurst, the detective, till he ran away with our notes in the very moment of triumph ? What more innocent than White Heather and the little curate, till they landed us with a couple of Amelia's own gems as a splendid bargain ? I will not take it for granted *any* man is not Colonel Clay, merely because I don't happen to spot the particular scheme he is trying to work against me. The rogue has so many schemes, and some of them so well concealed, that up to the moment of the actual explosion you fail to detect the presence of moral dynamite. Therefore, I shall proceed as if there were dynamite everywhere. But in the third place —and this is *very* important—you mark my words, I believe I detect already the lines he will work upon. He's a geologist, he says, with a taste for minerals. Very good. You see if he doesn't try to persuade me before long he has found a coal mine,

whose locality he will disclose for a trifling consideration ; or else he will salt the Long Mountain with
emeralds, and claim a big share for helping to discover
them ; or else he will try something in the minera-
logical line to *do* me somehow.   I see it in the very
transparency of the fellow's face ; and I'm determined
this time neither to pay him one farthing on any
pretext, nor to let him escape me ! '

We went in to lunch.   The Professor and Mrs.
Forbes-Gaskell, all smiles, accompanied us.   I don't
know whether it was Charles's warning to take
nothing for granted that made me do so—but I
kept a close eye upon the suspected man all the
time we were at table.   It struck me there was
something very odd about his hair.   It didn't seem
quite the same colour all over.   The locks that hung
down behind, over the collar of his coat, were a trifle
lighter and a trifle grayer than the black mass that
covered the greater part of his head.   I examined
it carefully.   The more I did so, the more the
conviction grew upon me : he was wearing a wig.
There was no denying it !

A trifle less artistic, perhaps, than most of Colonel
Clay's get-ups ; but then, I reflected (on Charles's
principle of taking nothing for granted), we had
never before suspected Colonel Clay himself, except
in the one case of the Honourable David, whose red
hair and whiskers even Madame Picardet had admitted to be absurdly false by her action of pointing
at them and tittering irrepressibly.   It was possible

that in every case, if we had scrutinised our man closely, we should have found that the disguise betrayed itself at once (as Medhurst had suggested) to an acute observer.

The detective, in fact, had told us too much.   I remembered what he said to us about knocking off David Granton's red wig the moment we doubted him ; and I positively tried to help myself awkwardly to potato-chips, when the footman offered them, so as to hit the supposed wig with an apparently careless brush of my elbow.   But it was of no avail.   The fellow seemed to anticipate or suspect my intention, and dodged aside carefully, like one well accustomed to saving his disguise from all chance of such real or seeming accidents.

I was so full of my discovery that immediately after lunch I induced Isabel to take our new friends round the home garden and show them Charles's famous prize dahlias, while I proceeded myself to narrate to Charles and Amelia my observations and my frustrated experiment.

' It *is* a wig,' Amelia assented.   ' *I* spotted it at once.   A very good wig, too, and most artistically planted.   Men don't notice these things, though women do.   It is creditable to you, Seymour, to have succeeded in detecting it.'

Charles was less complimentary.   ' You fool,' he answered, with that unpleasant frankness which is much too common with him.   ' Supposing it *is*, why on earth should you try to knock it off and disclose

him ?   What good would it have done ?   If it *is* a
wig, and we spot it, that's all that we need.   We
are put on our guard ; we know with whom we have
now to deal.   But you can't take a man up on a
charge of wig-wearing.   The law doesn't interfere
with it.   Most respectable men may sometimes wear
wigs.   Why, I knew a promoter who did, and also
the director of fourteen companies !   What we have
to do next is, wait till he tries to cheat us, and then
-- pounce down upon him.   Sooner or later, you
may be sure, his plans will reveal themselves.'

So we concocted an excellent scheme to keep
them under constant observation, lest they should
slip away again, as they did from the island.   First
of all, Amelia was to ask them to come and stop at
the castle, on the ground that the rooms at the inn
were uncomfortably small.   We felt sure, however,
that, as on a previous occasion, they would refuse
the invitation, in order to be able to slink off un-
perceived, in case they should find themselves apparently suspected.   Should they decline, it was
arranged that Césarine should take a room at the
Cromarty Arms as long as they stopped there, and
report upon their movements ; while, during the day,
we would have the house watched by the head gillie's
son, a most intelligent young man, who could be
trusted, with true Scotch canniness, to say nothing
to anybody.

To our immense surprise, Mrs. Forbes-Gaskell
accepted the invitation with the utmost alacrity.

She was profuse in her thanks, indeed ; for she told us the Arms was an ill-kept house, and the cookery by no means agreed with her husband's liver. It was sweet of us to invite them ; such kindness to perfect strangers was quite unexpected. She should always say that nowhere on earth had she met with so cordial or friendly a reception as at Seldon Castle. But—she accepted, unreservedly.

'It *can't* be Colonel Clay,' I remarked to Charles. 'He would never have come here. Even as David Granton, with far more reason for coming, he wouldn't put himself in our power : he preferred the security and freedom of the Cromarty Arms.'

'Sey,' my brother-in-law said sententiously, 'you're incorrigible. You *will* persist in being the slave of prepossessions. He may have some good reason of his own for accepting. Wait till he shows his hand—and then, we shall understand everything.'

So for the next three weeks the Forbes-Gaskells formed part of the house-party at Seldon. I must say, Charles paid them most assiduous attention. He positively neglected his other guests in order to keep close to the two new-comers. Mrs. Forbes-Gaskell noticed the fact, and commented on it. 'You are really too good to us, Sir Charles,' she said. 'I'm afraid you allow us quite to monopolise you !'

But Charles, gallant as ever, replied with a smile, 'We have you with us for so short a time, you know !' Which made Mrs. Forbes-Gaskell blush again that delicious blush of hers.

During all this time the Professor went on calmly and persistently mineralogising. 'Wonderful character!' Charles said to me. 'He works out his parts so well! Could anything exceed the picture he gives one of scientific ardour?' And, indeed, he was at it, morning, noon, and night. 'Sooner or later,' Charles observed, 'something practical must come of it.'

Twice, meanwhile, little episodes occurred which are well worth notice. One day I was out with the Professor on the Long Mountain, watching him hammer at the rocks, and a little bored by his performance, when, to pass the time, I asked him what a particular small water-worn stone was. He looked at it and smiled. 'If there were a little more mica in it,' he said, 'it would be the characteristic gneiss of ice-borne boulders, hereabouts. But there isn't *quite* enough.' And he gazed at it curiously.

'Indeed,' I answered, 'it doesn't come up to sample, doesn't it?'

He gave me a meaning look. 'Ten per cent,' he murmured in a slow, strange voice; 'ten per cent is more usual.'

I trembled violently. Was he bent, then, upon ruining me? 'If you betray me——' I cried, and broke off.

'I beg your pardon,' he said. He was all pure innocence.

I reflected on what Charles had said about taking nothing for granted, and held my tongue prudently.

The other incident was this. Charles picked a
sprig of white heather on the hill one afternoon, after
a picnic lunch, I regret to say, when he had taken
perhaps a glass more champagne than was strictly
good for him. He was not exactly the worse for it,
but he was excited, good-humoured, reckless, and
lively. He brought the sprig to Mrs. Forbes-Gaskell,

TEN PER CENT, HE MURMURED, IS MORE USUAL.

and handed it to her, ogling a little. 'Sweets to the
sweet,' he murmured, and looked at her meaningly.
'White heather to White Heather.' Then he saw
what he had done, and checked himself instantly.

Mrs. Forbes-Gaskell coloured up in the usual
manner. 'I—I don't quite understand,' she faltered.

Charles scrambled out of it somehow. 'White
heather for luck,' he said, 'and—the man who is

privileged to give a piece of it to you is surely lucky.'

She smiled, none too well pleased. I somehow felt she suspected us of suspecting her.

However, as it turned out, nothing came, after all, of the untoward incident.

Next day Charles burst upon me, triumphant. 'Well, he has shown his hand!' he cried. 'I knew he would. He has come to me to-day with—what do you think?—a fragment of gold, in quartz, from the Long Mountain.'

'No!' I exclaimed.

'Yes,' Charles answered. 'He says there's a vein there with distinct specks of gold in it, which might be worth mining. When a man begins *that* way you know what he's driving at! And what's more, he's got up the subject beforehand; for he began saying to me there had long been gold in Suther-landshire—why not therefore in Ross-shire? And then he went at full into the comparative geology of the two regions.'

'This is serious,' I said. 'What will you do?'

'Wait and watch,' Charles answered; 'and the moment he develops a proposal for shares in the syndicate to work the mine, or a sum of money down as the price of his discovery—get in the police, and arrest him.'

For the next few days the Professor was more active and ardent than ever. He went peering about the rocks on every side with his hammer. He kept on bringing in little pieces of stone, with gold specks stuck in them, and talking learnedly of the 'probable cost of crushing and milling.' Charles had heard all that before ; in point of fact, he had assisted at the drafting of some dozens of prospectuses. So he took no notice, and waited for the man with the wig to develop his proposals. He knew they would come soon ; and he watched and waited. But, of course, to draw him on he pretended to be interested.

While we were all in this attitude of mind, attending on Providence and Colonel Clay, we happened to walk down by the shore one day, in the opposite direction from the Seamew's island. Suddenly we came upon the Professor linked arm-in-arm with— Sir Adolphus Cordery ! They were wrapped in deep talk, and appeared to be most amicable.

Now, naturally, relations had been a trifle strained between Sir Adolphus and the house of Vandrift since the incident of the Slump ; but under the present circumstances, and with such a matter at stake as the capture of Colonel Clay, it was necessary to overlook all such minor differences. So Charles managed to disengage the Professor from his friend, sent Amelia on with Forbes-Gaskell towards the castle, and stopped behind, himself, with Sir Adolphus and me, to clear up the question.

'Do you know this man, Cordery ? ' he asked, with some little suspicion.

'Know him ? Why, of course I do,' Sir Adolphus answered. 'He's Marmaduke Forbes-Gaskell, of the

Yorkshire College, a very distinguished man of science. First-rate mineralogist—perhaps the best (*but* one) in England.' Modesty forbade him to name the exception.

'But are you sure it's he?' Charles inquired, with growing doubt. 'Have you known him before? This isn't a second case of Schleiermachering me, is it?'

'Sure it's he?' Sir Adolphus echoed. 'Am I sure of myself? Why, I've known Marmy Gaskell ever since we were at Trinity together. Knew him before he married Miss Forbes of Glenluce, my wife's second cousin, and hyphened his name with hers, to keep the property in the family. Know them both most intimately. Came down here to the inn because I heard that Marmy was on the prowl among these hills, and I thought he had probably something good to prowl after—in the way of fossils.'

'But the man wears a wig!' Charles expostulated.

'Of course,' Cordery answered. 'He's as bald as a bat—in front at least—and he wears a wig to cover his baldness.'

'It's disgraceful,' Charles exclaimed; 'disgraceful —taking us in like that.' And he grew red as a turkey-cock.

Sir Adolphus has no delicacy. He burst out laughing.

'Oh, I see,' he cried out, simply bursting with amusement. 'You thought Forbes-Gaskell was

Colonel Clay in disguise! Oh, my stars, what a lovely one!'

'*You*, at least, have no right to laugh,' Charles responded, drawing himself up and growing still redder. 'You led me once into a similar scrape, and then backed out of it in a way unbecoming a

OH, MY STARS, WHAT A LOVELY ONE!

gentleman. Besides,' he went on, getting angrier at each word, 'this fellow, whoever he is, has been trying to cheat me on his own account. Colonel Clay or no Colonel Clay, he's been salting my rocks with gold-bearing quartz, and trying to lead me on into an absurd speculation!'

Sir Adolphus exploded. 'Oh, this is too good,'

he cried. 'I must go and tell Marmy!' And he rushed off to where Forbes-Gaskell was seated on a corner of rock with Amelia.

As for Charles and myself, we returned to the house. Half an hour later Forbes-Gaskell came back, too, in a towering temper.

'What is the meaning of this, sir?' he shouted out, as soon as he caught sight of Charles. 'I'm told you've invited my wife and myself here to your house in order to spy upon us, under the impression that I was Clay, the notorious swindler!'

'I thought you were,' Charles answered, equally angry. 'Perhaps you may be still! Anyhow, you're a rogue, and you tried to bamboozle me!'

Forbes-Gaskell, white with rage, turned to his trembling wife. 'Gertrude,' he said, 'pack up your box and come away from these people instantly. Their pretended hospitality has been a studied insult. They've put you and me in a most ridiculous position. We were told before we came here—and no doubt with truth—that Sir Charles Vandrift was the most close-fisted and tyrannical old curmudgeon in Scotland. We've been writing to all our friends to say ecstatically that he was, on the contrary, a most hospitable, generous, and large-hearted gentleman. And now we find out he's a disgusting cad, who asks strangers to his house from the meanest motives, and then insults his guests with gratuitous vituperation. It is well such people should hear the plain truth now and again in their lives; and it

therefore gives me the greatest pleasure to tell Sir
Charles Vandrift that he's a vulgar bounder of the
first water. Go and pack your box, Gertrude! I'll
run down to the Cromarty Arms, and order a cab
to carry us away at once from this inhospitable
sham castle.'

'You wear a wig, sir; you wear a wig,' Charles
exclaimed, half-choking with passion. For, indeed,
as Forbes-Gaskell spoke, and tossed his head angrily,
the nature of his hair-covering grew painfully
apparent. It was quite one-sided.

'I do, sir, that I may be able to shake it in the
face of a cad!' the Professor responded, tearing it
off to readjust it; and, suiting the action to the
word, he brandished it thrice in Charles's eyes; after
which he darted from the room, speechless with
indignation.

As soon as they were gone, and Charles had
recovered breath sufficiently to listen to rational
conversation, I ventured to observe, 'This comes of
being too sure! We made one mistake. We took
it for granted that because a man wears a wig, he
must be an impostor—which does not necessarily
follow. We forgot that not Colonel Clays alone
have false coverings to their heads, and that wigs
may sometimes be worn from motives of pure
personal vanity. In fact, we were again the slaves
of preconceptions.'

I looked at him pointedly. Charles rose before
he replied. 'Seymour Wentworth,' he said at last,

gazing down upon me with lofty scorn, 'your
moralising is ill-timed.   It appears to me you
entirely misunderstand the position and duties of a
private secretary!

HE BRANDISHED IT THRICE IN CHARLES'S EYES.

The oddest part of it all, however, was this—that
Charles, being convinced Forbes-Gaskell, though he
wasn't Colonel Clay, had been fraudulently salting
the rocks with gold, with intent to deceive, took

no further notice of the alleged discoveries. The consequence was that Forbes - Gaskell and Sir Adolphus went elsewhere with the secret; and it was not till after Charles had sold the Seldon Castle estate (which he did shortly afterward, the place having somehow grown strangely distasteful to him) that the present 'Seldon Eldorados, Limited,' were put upon the market by Lord Craig-Ellachie, who purchased the place from him. Forbes-Gaskell, as it happened, had reported to Craig-Ellachie that he had found a lode of high-grade ore on an estate unnamed, which he would particularise on promise of certain contingent claims to founder's shares; and the old lord jumped at it. Charles sold at grouse-moor prices; and the consequence is that the capital of the Eldorados is yielding at present very fair returns, even after allowing for expenses of promotion—while Charles has been done out of a good thing in gold-mines!

But, remembering 'the position and duties of a private secretary,' I refrained from pointing out to him at the time that this loss was due to a fixed idea—though as a matter of fact it depended upon Charles's strange preconception that the man with the wig, whoever he might be, was trying to diddle him.

IX

THE EPISODE OF THE JAPANNED DISPATCH-BOX

'SEY,' my brother-in-law said next spring, 'I'm sick and tired of London! Let's shoulder our wallets at once, and I will to some distant land, where no man doth me know.'

'Mars or Mercury?' I inquired; 'for, in our own particular planet, I'm afraid you'll find it just a trifle difficult for Sir Charles Vandrift to hide his light under a bushel.'

'Oh, I'll manage it,' Charles answered. 'What's the good of being a millionaire, I should like to know, if you're always obliged to "behave as sich"? I shall travel *incog.* I'm dog-tired of being dogged by these endless impostors.'

And, indeed, we had passed through a most painful winter. Colonel Clay had stopped away for some months, it is true, and for my own part, I will confess, since it wasn't *my* place to pay the piper, I rather missed the wonted excitement than otherwise. But Charles had grown horribly and morbidly suspicious. He carried out his principle of 'distrusting everybody and disbelieving everything,' till life was a burden to him. He spotted impossible Colonel Clays under a thousand disguises ; he was quite convinced he had frightened his enemy away at least a dozen times over, beneath the varying garb of a fat club waiter, a tall policeman, a washer-woman's boy, a solicitor's clerk, the Bank of England beadle, and the collector of water-rates. He saw him as constantly, and in as changeful forms, as mediæval saints used to see the devil. Amelia and I really began to fear for the stability of that splendid intellect ; we foresaw that unless the Colonel Clay nuisance could be abated somehow, Charles might sink by degrees to the mental level of a common or ordinary Stock-Exchange plunger.

So, when my brother-in-law announced his intention of going away *incog.* to parts unknown, on the succeeding Saturday, Amelia and I felt a flush of relief from long-continued tension. Especially Amelia—who was *not* going with him.

' For rest and quiet,' he said to us at breakfast, laying down the *Morning Post*, ' give *me* the deck of an Atlantic liner ! No letters ; no telegrams. No stocks ; no shares. No *Times ;* no *Saturday.* I'm sick of these papers ! '

' The *World* is too much with us,' I assented cheerfully. I regret to say, nobody appreciated the point of my quotation.

Charles took infinite pains, I must admit, to ensure perfect secrecy. He made me write and secure the best state-rooms—main deck, amidships—

under my own name, without mentioning his, in the *Etruria*, for New York, on her very next voyage. He spoke of his destination to nobody but Amelia ; and Amelia warned Césarine, under pains and penalties, on no account to betray it to the other servants.   Further to secure his *incog.*, Charles assumed the style and title of Mr. Peter Porter, and booked as such in the *Etruria* at Liverpool.

The day before starting, however, he went down with me to the City for an interview with his brokers in Adam's Court, Old Broad Street.   Finglemore, the senior partner, hastened, of course, to receive us. As we entered his private room a good-looking young man rose and lounged out.   ' Halloa, Finglemore,' Charles said, ' that's that scamp of a brother of yours !   I thought you had shipped him off years and years ago to China ? '

' So I did, Sir Charles,' Finglemore answered, rubbing his hands somewhat nervously.   ' But he never went there.   Being an idle young dog, with a taste for amusement, he got for the time no further than Paris.   Since then, he's hung about a bit, here, there, and everywhere, and done no particular good for himself or his family.   But about three or four years ago he somehow " struck ile " : he went to South Africa, poaching on your preserves ; and now he's back again — rich, married, and respectable. His wife, a nice little woman, has reformed him. Well, what can I do for you this morning ? '

Charles has large interests in America, in Santa

Fé and Topekas, and other big concerns ; and he insisted on taking out several documents and vouchers connected in various ways with his widespread ventures there.   He meant to go, he said, for com-

FINGLEMORE'S BROTHER.

plete rest and change, on a general tour of private inquiry—New York, Chicago, Colorado, the mining districts.   It was a millionaire's holiday.   So he took all these valuables in a black japanned dispatch-box, which he guarded like a child with absurd precautions. He never allowed that box out of his sight one moment ; and he gave me no peace as to its safety and integrity.   It was a perfect fetish. 'We must be cautious,' he said, 'Sey, cautious ! Especially in travelling.   Recollect how that little curate spirited the diamonds out of Amelia's jewel-case !   I shall not let this box out of my sight.   I shall stick to it myself, if we go to the bottom.'

We did *not* go to the bottom.   It is the proud boast of the Cunard Company that it has 'never lost a passenger's life' ; and the captain would not consent to send the *Etruria* to Davy Jones's locker, merely in order to give Charles a chance of sticking to his dispatch-box under trying circumstances.   On the contrary, we had a delightful and uneventful passage ; and we found our fellow-passengers most agreeable people.   Charles, as Mr. Peter Porter, being freed for the moment from his terror of Colonel Clay, would have felt really happy, I believe—had it not been for the dispatch-box.   He made friends from the first hour (quite after the fearless old fashion of the days before Colonel Clay had begun to embitter life for him) with a nice American doctor and his charming wife, on their way back to Kentucky. Dr. Elihu Quackenboss—that was his characteristic-ally American name—had been studying medicine for a year in Vienna, and was now returning to his native State with a brain close crammed with all the latest bacteriological and antiseptic discoveries.

His wife, a pretty and piquant little American, with a tip-tilted nose and the quaint sharpness of her countrywomen, amused Charles not a little. The funny way in which she would make room for him by her side on the bench on deck, and say, with a sweet smile, 'You sit right here, Mr. Porter; the sun's just elegant,' delighted and flattered him. He was proud to find out that female attention was not always due to his wealth and title; and that plain Mr. Porter could command on his merits the same amount of blandishments as Sir Charles Vandrift, the famous millionaire, on his South African celebrity.

During the whole of that voyage, it was Mrs. Quackenboss here, and Mrs. Quackenboss there, and Mrs. Quackenboss the other place, till, for Amelia's sake, I was glad she was not on board to witness it. Long before we sighted Sandy Hook, I will admit, I was fairly sick of Charles's two-stringed harp—Mrs. Quackenboss and the dispatch-box.

Mrs. Quackenboss, it turned out, was an amateur artist, and she painted Sir Charles, on calm days on deck, in all possible attitudes. She seemed to find him a most attractive model.

The doctor, too, was a precious clever fellow. He knew something of chemistry—and of most other subjects, including, as I gathered, the human character. For he talked to Charles about various ideas of his, with which he wished to 'liven up folks in Kentucky a bit,' on his return, till Charles conceived the highest possible regard for his intelligence and enterprise. 'That's a go-ahead fellow, Sey!' he remarked to me one day. 'Has the right sort of grit in him! Those Americans are the men. Wish I had a round hundred of them on my works in South Africa!'

That idea seemed to grow upon him. He was immensely taken with it. He had lately dismissed one of his chief superintendents at the Cloetedorp mine, and he seriously debated whether or not he should offer the post to the smart Kentuckian. For my own part, I am inclined to connect this fact with his expressed determination to visit his South African undertakings for three months yearly in future; and I am driven to suspect he felt life at Cloetedorp would be rendered much more tolerable by the agreeable society of a quaint and amusing American lady.

'If you offer it to him,' I said, 'remember, you must disclose your personality.'

'Not at all,' Charles answered. 'I can keep it dark for the present, till all is arranged for. I need only say I have interests in South Africa.'

So, one morning on deck, as we were approaching the Banks, he broached his scheme gently to the doctor and Mrs. Quackenboss. He remarked that he was connected with one of the biggest financial concerns in the Southern hemisphere; and that he would pay Elihu fifteen hundred a year to represent him at the diggings.

'What, dollars?' the lady said, smiling and

accentuating the tip-tilted nose a little more. 'Oh, Mr. Porter, it ain't good enough!'

'No, pounds, my dear madam,' Charles responded. 'Pounds sterling, you know. In United States currency, seven thousand five hundred.'

'I guess Elihu would just jump at it,' Mrs. Quackenboss replied, looking at him quizzically.

The doctor laughed. 'You make a good bid, sir,' he said, in his slow American way, emphasising all the most unimportant words: '*but* you overlook one element. I *am* a man of science, not a speculator. I *have* trained myself for medical work, *at* considerable cost, *in* the best schools of Europe, *and* I do not propose *to* fling away the results *of* much arduous labour *by* throwing myself out elastically *into* a new line of work *for* which my faculties *may* not perhaps equally adapt me.'

('How thoroughly American!' I murmured, in the background.)

Charles insisted; all in vain. Mrs. Quackenboss was impressed; but the doctor smiled always a sphinx-like smile, and reiterated his belief in the unfitness of mid-stream as an ideal place for swopping horses. The more he declined, and the better he talked, the more eager Charles became each day to secure him. And, as if on purpose to draw him on, the doctor each day gave more and more surprising proofs of his practical abilities. 'I *am* not a specialist,' he said. 'I just ketch the drift, appropriate the kernel, *and* let the rest slide.'

He could do anything, it really seemed, from
shoeing a mule to conducting a camp-meeting ; he
was a capital chemist, a very sound surgeon, a fair
judge of horseflesh, a first class euchre player, and a
pleasing baritone.   When occasion demanded he
could occupy a pulpit.   He had invented a cork-
screw which brought him in a small revenue ; and he
was now engaged in the translation of a Polish work

CHARLES INSISTED.

on the 'Application of Hydrocyanic Acid to the
Cure of Leprosy.'

Still, we reached New York without having got
any nearer our goal, as regarded Dr. Quackenboss.
He came to bid us good-bye at the quay, with that
sphinx-like smile still playing upon his features.
Charles clutched the dispatch-box with one hand, and
Mrs. Quackenboss's little palm with the other.

'*Don't* tell us,' he said, 'this is good-bye—for
ever !'   And his voice quite faltered.

'I guess so, Mr. Porter,' the pretty American replied, with a telling glance. 'What hotel do you patronise?'

'The Murray Hill,' Charles responded.

'Oh my, ain't that odd?' Mrs. Quackenboss echoed. 'The Murray Hill! Why, that's just where we're going too, Elihu!'

The upshot of which was that Charles persuaded them, before returning to Kentucky, to diverge for a few days with us to Lake George and Lake Champlain, where he hoped to over-persuade the recalcitrant doctor.

To Lake George therefore we went, and stopped at the excellent hotel at the terminus of the railway. We spent a good deal of our time on the light little steamers that ply between that point and the road to Ticonderoga. Somehow, the mountains mirrored in the deep green water reminded me of Lucerne; and Lucerne reminded me of the little curate. For the first time since we left England a vague terror seized me. *Could* Elihu Quackenboss be Colonel Clay again, still dogging our steps through the opposite continent?

I could not help mentioning my suspicion to Charles—who, strange to say, pooh-poohed it. He had been paying great court to Mrs. Quackenboss that day, and was absurdly elated because the little American had rapped his knuckles with her fan and called him 'a real silly.'

Next day, however, an odd thing occurred. We

strolled out together, all four of us, along the banks
of the lake, among woods just carpeted with strange,
triangular flowers—trilliums, Mrs. Quackenboss called
them—and lined with delicate ferns in the first green
of springtide.

I began to grow poetical. (I wrote verses in my
youth before I went to South Africa.) We threw
ourselves on the grass, near a small mountain stream
that descended among moss-clad boulders from the
steep woods above us. The Kentuckian flung himself at full length on the sward, just in front of
Charles. He had a strange head of hair, very thick
and shaggy. I don't know why, but, of a sudden, it
reminded me of the Mexican Seer, whom we had
learned to remember as Colonel Clay's first embodiment. At the same moment the same thought
seemed to run through Charles's head; for, strange
to say, with a quick impulse he leant forward and
examined it. I saw Mrs. Quackenboss draw back in
wonder. The hair looked too thick and close for
nature. It ended abruptly, I now remembered, with
a sharp line on the forehead. Could this, too, be a
wig? It seemed very probable.

Even as I thought that thought, Charles appeared
to form a sudden and resolute determination. With
one lightning swoop he seized the doctor's hair in
his powerful hand, and tried to lift it off bodily.
He had made a bad guess. Next instant the doctor
uttered a loud and terrified howl of pain, while
several of his hairs, root and all, came out of his

scalp in Charles's hand, leaving a few drops of blood on the skin of the head in the place they were torn from. There was no doubt at all it was not a wig, but the Kentuckian's natural hirsute covering.

The scene that ensued I am powerless to describe. My pen is unequal to it. The doctor arose, not so

HE SEIZED THE DOCTOR'S HAIR.

much angry as astonished, white and incredulous. 'What did you do that for, any way?' he asked, glaring fiercely at my brother-in-law. Charles was all abject apology. He began by profusely express-ing his regret, and offering to make any suitable reparation, monetary or otherwise. Then he revealed his whole hand. He admitted that he was Sir Charles Vandrift, the famous millionaire, and that he had suffered egregiously from the endless machinations of a certain Colonel Clay, a machiavellian rogue, who had hounded him relentlessly round the capitals of Europe. He described in graphic detail how the impostor got himself up with wigs and wax, so as to deceive even those who knew him intimately; and then he threw himself on Dr. Quackenboss's mercy, as a man who had been cruelly taken in so often that he could not help suspecting the best of men falsely. Mrs. Quackenboss admitted it was natural to have suspicions—'Especially,' she said, with candour, 'as you're not the first to observe the notable way Elihu's hair seems to originate from his forehead,' and she pulled it up to show us. But Elihu himself sulked on in the dumps : his dignity was offended. '*If* you wanted to know,' he said, 'you might as well have asked me. Assault *and* battery *is* not the right way to test whether *a* citizen's hair is primitive or acquired.'

'It was an impulse,' Charles pleaded ; 'an instinctive impulse !'

'Civilised man restrains his impulses,' the doctor answered. 'You *have* lived too long *in* South Africa, Mr. Porter—I mean, Sir Charles Vandrift, if that's the right way *to* address such a gentleman. You appear to *have* imbibed the habits *and* manners of the Kaffirs you lived among.'

For the next two days, I will really admit, Charles seemed more wretched than I could have believed it possible for him to be on somebody else's account. He positively grovelled. The fact was, he saw he had hurt Dr. Quackenboss's feelings, and—much to my surprise—he seemed truly grieved at it. If the doctor would have accepted a thousand pounds down to shake hands at once and forget the incident —in my opinion Charles would have gladly paid it. Indeed, he said as much in other words to the pretty American—for he could not insult her by offering her money. Mrs. Quackenboss did her best to make it up, for she was a kindly little creature, in spite of her roguishness ; but Elihu stood aloof. Charles urged him still to go out to South Africa, increasing his bait to two thousand a year ; yet the doctor was immovable. ' No, no,' he said ; ' I had half decided *to* accept your offer—*till* that unfortunate impulse ; but that settled the question. *As* an American citizen, I decline *to* become the representative *of* a British nobleman who takes such means *of* investigating questions which affect the hair and happiness *of* his fellow-creatures.'

I don't know whether Charles was most disappointed at missing the chance of so clever a superintendent for the mine at Cloetedorp, or elated at the novel description of himself as 'a British nobleman ; ' which is not precisely our English idea of a colonial knighthood.

Three days later, accordingly, the Quackenbosses left the Lakeside Hotel. We were bound on an expedition up the lake ourselves, when the pretty little woman burst in with a dash to tell us they were leaving. She was charmingly got up in the

neatest and completest of American travelling-
dresses. Charles held her hand affectionately. 'I'm
sorry it's good-bye,' he said. 'I have done my best
to secure your husband.'

'You couldn't have tried harder than I did,' the
little woman answered, and the tip-tilted nose looked

THE PRETTY LITTLE WOMAN BURST IN.

quite pathetic; 'for I just hate to be buried right
down there in Kentucky! However, Elihu is the
sort of man a woman can neither drive nor lead; so
we've got to put up with him.' And she smiled
upon us sweetly, and disappeared for ever.

Charles was disconsolate all that day. Next
morning he rose, and announced his intention of
setting out for the West on his tour of inspection.

He would recreate by revelling in Colorado silver lodes.

We packed our own portmanteaus, for Charles had not brought even Simpson with him, and then we prepared to set out by the morning train for Saratoga.

Up till almost the last moment Charles nursed his dispatch-box. But as the 'baggage-smashers' were taking down our luggage, and a chambermaid was lounging officiously about in search of a tip, he laid it down for a second or two on the centre table while he collected his other immediate impedimenta. He couldn't find his cigarette-case, and went back to the bedroom for it. I helped him hunt, but it had disappeared mysteriously. That moment lost him. When we had found the cigarette-case, and returned to the sitting-room—lo, and behold! the dispatch-box was missing! Charles questioned the servants, but none of them had noticed it. He searched round the room—not a trace of it anywhere.

'Why, I laid it down here just two minutes ago!' he cried. But it was not forthcoming.

'It'll turn up in time,' I said. 'Everything turns up in the end—including Mrs. Quackenboss's nose.'

'Seymour,' said my brother-in-law, 'your hilarity is inopportune.'

To say the truth, Charles was beside himself with anger. He took the elevator down to the

'Bureau,' as they call it, and complained to the
manager.   The manager, a sharp-faced New Yorker,
smiled as he remarked in a nonchalant way that
guests with valuables were required to leave them
in charge of the management, in which case they
were locked up in the safe and duly returned to the
depositor on leaving.   Charles declared somewhat
excitedly that he had been robbed, and demanded
that nobody should be allowed to leave the hotel
till the dispatch-box was discovered.   The manager,
quite cool, and obtrusively picking his teeth, responded that such tactics might be possible in an
hotel of the European size, putting up a couple of
hundred guests or so ; but that an American house,
with over a thousand visitors—many of whom came
and went daily—could not undertake such a quixotic
quest on behalf of a single foreign complainant.

That epithet, 'foreign,' stung Charles to the
quick.   No Englishman can admit that he is anywhere a foreigner.   'Do you know who I am, sir ? '
he asked, angrily.   'I am Sir Charles Vandrift, of
London—a member of the English Parliament.'

'You may be the Prince of Wales,' the man
answered, 'for all I care.   You'll get the same
treatment as anyone else, in America.   But if you're
Sir Charles Vandrift,' he went on, examining his
books, 'how does it come you've registered as Mr.
Peter Porter ? '

Charles grew red with embarrassment.   The
difficulty deepened.

The dispatch-box, always covered with a leather case, bore on its inner lid the name 'Sir Charles Vandrift, K.C.M.G.,' distinctly painted in the orthodox white letters. This was a painful *contretemps :* he had lost his precious documents ; he had given a false name ; and he had rendered the manager supremely careless whether or not he recovered his stolen property. Indeed, seeing he had registered as Porter, and now 'claimed' as Vandrift, the manager hinted in pretty plain language he very much doubted whether there had ever been a dispatch-box in the matter at all, or whether, if there were one, it had ever contained any valuable documents.

We spent a wretched morning. Charles went round the hotel, questioning everybody as to whether they had seen his dispatch-box. Most of the visitors resented the question as a personal imputation ; one fiery Virginian, indeed, wanted to settle the point then and there with a six-shooter. Charles telegraphed to New York to prevent the shares and coupons from being negotiated ; but his brokers telegraphed back that, though they had stopped the numbers as far as possible, they did so with reluctance, as they were not aware of Sir Charles Vandrift being now in the country. Charles declared he wouldn't leave the hotel till he recovered his property ; and for myself, I was inclined to suppose we would have to remain there accordingly for the term of our natural lives—and longer.

That night again we spent at the Lakeside Hotel.
In the small hours of the morning, as I lay awake
and meditated, a thought broke across me.   I was
so excited by it that I rose and rushed into my
brother-in-law's bedroom.   'Charles, Charles!' I
exclaimed, 'we have taken too much for granted
once more.   Perhaps Elihu Quackenboss carried off
your dispatch-box!'

A FIERY VIRGINIAN.

'You fool,' Charles answered, in his most un-
amiable manner (he applies that word to me with
increasing frequency); 'is *that* what you've waked
me up for? Why, the Quackenbosses left Lake
George on Tuesday morning, and I had the dispatch-
box in my own hands on Wednesday.'

'We have only their word for it,' I cried.
'Perhaps they stopped on—and walked off with it
afterwards!'

'We will inquire to-morrow,' Charles answered.

'But I confess I don't think it was worth waking me up for. I could stake my life on that little woman's integrity.'

We *did* inquire next morning—with this curious result: it turned out that, though the Quackenbosses had left the Lakeside Hotel on Tuesday, it was only for the neighbouring Washington House, which they quitted on Wednesday morning, taking the same train for Saratoga which Charles and I had intended to go by. Mrs. Quackenboss carried a small brown paper parcel in her hands—in which, under the circumstances, we had little difficulty in recognising Charles's dispatch-box, loosely enveloped.

Then I knew how it was done. The chamber-maid, loitering about the room for a tip, was—Mrs. Quackenboss! It needed but an apron to transform her pretty travelling-dress into a chambermaid's costume; and in any of those huge American hotels one chambermaid more or less would pass in the crowd without fear of challenge.

'We will follow them on to Saratoga,' Charles cried. 'Pay the bill at once, Seymour.'

'Certainly,' I answered. 'Will you give me some money?'

Charles clapped his hand to his pockets. 'All, all in the dispatch-box,' he murmured.

That tied us up another day, till we could get some ready cash from our agents in New York; for the manager, already most suspicious at the change of name and the accusation of theft, peremptorily refused to accept Charles's cheque, or anything else, as he phrased it, except 'hard money.' So we lingered on perforce at Lake George in ignoble inaction.

'Of course,' I observed to my brother-in-law that evening, 'Elihu Quackenboss was Colonel Clay.'

'I suppose so,' Charles murmured resignedly. 'Everybody I meet seems to be Colonel Clay nowadays—except when I believe they *are*, in which case they turn out to be harmless nobodies. But who would have thought it was he after I pulled his hair out? Or after he persisted in his trick, even when I suspected him—which, he told us at Seldon, was against his first principles?'

A light dawned upon me again. But, warned by previous ebullitions, I expressed myself this time with becoming timidity. 'Charles,' I suggested, 'may we not here again have been the slaves of a preconception? We thought Forbes - Gaskell was Colonel Clay—for no better reason than because he wore a wig. We thought Elihu Quackenboss wasn't Colonel Clay—for no better reason than because he didn't wear one. But how do we know he *ever* wears wigs? Isn't it possible, after all, that those hints he gave us about make-up, when he was Medhurst the detective, were framed on purpose, so as to mislead and deceive us? And isn't it possible what he said of his methods at the Seamew's island that day was similarly designed in order to hoodwink us?'

'That is so obvious, Sey,' my brother-in-law observed, in a most aggrieved tone, 'that I should have thought any secretary worth his salt would have arrived at it instantly.'

I abstained from remarking that Charles himself had not arrived at it even now, until I told him. I thought that to say so would serve no good purpose. So I merely went on : 'Well, it seems to me likely that when he came as Medhurst, with his hair cut short, he was really wearing his own natural crop, in its simplest form and of its native hue. By now it has had time to grow long and bushy. When he was David Granton, no doubt, he clipped it to an intermediate length, trimmed his beard and moustache, and dyed them all red, to a fine Scotch colour. As the Seer, again, he wore his hair much the same as Elihu's ; only, to suit the character, more combed and fluffy. As the little curate, he darkened it and plastered it down. As Von Lebenstein, he shaved close, but cultivated his moustache to its utmost dimensions, and dyed it black after the Tyrolese fashion. He need never have had a wig ; his own natural hair would throughout have been sufficient, allowing for intervals.'

'You're right, Sey,' my brother-in-law said, growing almost friendly. 'I will do you the justice to admit that's the nearest thing we have yet struck out to an idea for tracking him.'

On the Saturday morning a letter arrived which relieved us a little from our momentary tension. It was from our enemy himself—but most different in tone from his previous bantering communications :—

'Saratoga, Friday.

'SIR CHARLES VANDRIFT—Herewith I return your dispatch-box, intact, with the papers untouched. As you will readily observe, it has not even been opened.

'You will ask me the reason for this strange conduct. Let me be serious for once, and tell you truthfully.

'White Heather and I (for I will stick to Mr. Wentworth's judicious *sobriquet*) came over on the *Etruria* with you, intending, as usual, to make something out of you. We followed you to Lake George —for I had "forced a card," after my habitual plan, by inducing you to invite us, with the fixed intention of playing a particular trick upon you. It formed no part of our original game to steal your dispatch-box ; that I consider a simple and elementary trick unworthy the skill of a practised operator. We persisted in the preparations for our *coup*, till you pulled my hair out. Then, to my great surprise, I saw you exhibited a degree of regret and genuine compunction with which, till that moment, I could never have credited you. You thought you had hurt my feelings ; and you behaved more like a gentleman than I had previously known you to do. You not only apologised, but you also endeavoured voluntarily to make reparation. That produced an effect upon me. You may not believe it, but I desisted accordingly from the trick I had prepared for you.

' I might also have accepted your offer to go to South Africa, where I could soon have cleared out, having embezzled thousands. But, then, I should have been in a position of trust and responsibility— and I am not *quite* rogue enough to rob you under those conditions.

' Whatever else I am, however, I am not a hypocrite. I do not pretend to be anything more than a common swindler. If I return you your papers intact, it is only on the same principle as that of the Australian bushranger, who made a lady *a present* of her own watch because she had sung to him and reminded him of England. In other words, he did not take it from her. In like manner, when I found you had behaved, for once, like a gentleman, contrary to my expectation, I declined to go on with the trick I then meditated. Which does not mean to say I may not hereafter play you some other. *That* will depend upon your future good behaviour.

' Why, then, did I get White Heather to purloin your dispatch-box, with intent to return it ? Out of pure lightness of heart ? Not so ; but in order to let you see I really meant it. If I had gone off with no swag, and then written you this letter, you would not have believed me. You would have thought it was merely another of my failures. But when I have actually got all your papers into my hands, and give them up again of my own free will, you must see that I mean it.

'I will end, as I began, seriously. My trade has not quite crushed out of me all germs or relics of better feeling; and when I see a millionaire behave like a man, I feel ashamed to take advantage of that gleam of manliness.

STILL A ROGUE.

'Yours, with a tinge of penitence, but still a rogue,   CUTHBERT CLAY.'

The first thing Charles did on receiving this strange communication was to bolt downstairs and inquire for the dispatch-box. It had just arrived by Eagle Express Company. Charles rushed up to our rooms again, opened it feverishly, and counted his documents. When he found them all safe, he turned to me with a hard smile. ' This letter,' he said, with quivering lips, ' I consider still more insulting than all his previous ones.'

But, for myself, I really thought there was a ring of truth about it. Colonel Clay was a rogue, no doubt—a most unblushing rogue ; but even a rogue, I believe, has his better moments.

And the phrase about the ' position of trust and responsibility' touched Charles to the quick, I suppose, *in re* the Slump in Cloetedorp Golcondas. Though, to be sure, it was a hit at me as well, over the ten per cent commission.

X

THE EPISODE OF THE GAME OF POKER

'SEYMOUR,' my brother-in-law said, with a deep-drawn sigh, as we left Lake George next day by the Rennselaer and Saratoga Railroad, 'no more Peter Porter for me, *if* you please! I'm sick of disguises. Now that we know Colonel Clay is here in America, they serve no good purpose ; so I may as well receive the social consideration and proper respect to which my rank and position naturally entitle me.'

'And which they secure for the most part (except from hotel clerks), even in this republican land,' I answered briskly.

For in my humble opinion, for sound copper-bottomed snobbery, registered A1 at Lloyd's, give *me* the free-born American citizen.

We travelled through the States, accordingly, for the next four months, from Maine to California, and from Oregon to Florida, under our own true names, 'Confirming the churches,' as Charles facetiously put it—or in other words, looking into the management and control of railways, syndicates, mines, and cattle-ranches. We inquired about everything. And the result of our investigations appeared to be, as Charles further remarked, that the Sabeans who so troubled the sons of Job seemed to have migrated in a body to Kansas and Nebraska, and that several thousand head of cattle seemed mysteriously to vanish, *à la* Colonel Clay, into the pure air of the prairies just before each branding.

However, we were fortunate in avoiding the incursions of the Colonel himself, who must have migrated meanwhile on some enchanted carpet to other happy hunting-grounds.

It was chill October before we found ourselves safe back in New York, *en route* for England.   So long a term of freedom from the Colonel's depredations (as Charles fondly imagined—but I will not anticipate) had done my brother-in-law's health and spirits a world of good ; he was so lively and cheerful that he began to fancy his tormentor must have succumbed to yellow fever, then raging in New Orleans, or eaten himself ill, as we nearly did ourselves, on a generous mixture of clam-chowder, terrapin, soft-shelled crabs, Jersey peaches, canvas-backed ducks, Catawba wine, winter cherries, brandy cocktails, strawberry-shortcake, ice-creams, corn-dodger, and a judicious brew commonly known as a Colorado corpse-reviver.   However that may be, Charles returned to New York in excellent trim ; and, dreading in that great city the wiles of his antagonist, he cheerfully accepted the invitation of his brother millionaire, Senator Wrengold of Nevada, to spend a few days before sailing in the Senator's magnificent and newly-finished palace at the upper end of Fifth Avenue.

'There, at least, I shall be safe, Sey,' he said to me plaintively, with a weary smile. 'Wrengold, at any rate, won't try to take me in—except, of course, in the regular way of business.'

Boss-Nugget Hall (as it is popularly christened) is perhaps the handsomest brown stone mansion in the Richardsonian style on all Fifth Avenue. We spent a delightful week there. The lines had fallen to us in pleasant places. On the night we arrived Wrengold gave a small bachelor party in our honour. He knew Sir Charles was travelling without Lady Vandrift, and rightly judged he would prefer on his first night an informal party, with cards and cigars, instead of being bothered with the charming, but still somewhat hampering addition of female society.

The guests that evening were no more than seven, all told, ourselves included—making up, Wrengold said, that perfect number, an octave. He was a *nouveau riche* himself—the newest of the new —commonly known in exclusive old-fashioned New York society as the Gilded Squatter; for he 'struck his reef' no more than ten years ago; and he was therefore doubly anxious, after the American style, to be 'just dizzy with culture.' In his capacity of Mæcenas, he had invited amongst others the latest of English literary arrivals in New York—Mr.

Algernon Coleyard, the famous poet, and leader of the Briar-rose school of West-country fiction.

'You know him in London, of course?' he observed to Charles, with a smile, as we waited dinner for our guests.

'No,' Charles answered stolidly. 'I have not had that honour. We move, you see, in different circles.'

I observed by a curious shade which passed over Senator Wrengold's face that he quite misapprehended my brother-in-law's meaning. Charles wished to convey, of course, that Mr. Coleyard belonged to a mere literary and Bohemian set in London, while he himself moved on a more exalted plane of peers and politicians. But the Senator, better accustomed to the new-rich point of view, understood Charles to mean that *he* had not the entrée of that distinguished coterie in which Mr. Coleyard posed as a shining luminary. Which naturally made him rate even higher than before his literary acquisition.

At two minutes past the hour the poet entered. Even if we had not been already familiar with his portrait at all ages in *The Strand Magazine*, we should have recognised him at once for a genuine bard by his impassioned eyes, his delicate mouth, the artistic twirl of one gray lock upon his expansive brow, the grizzled moustache that gave point and force to the genial smile, and the two white rows of perfect teeth behind it. Most of our fellow-guests had met Coleyard before at a reception given by the

Lotus Club that afternoon, for the bard had reached
New York but the previous evening ; so Charles and
I were the only visitors who remained to be intro-

THE LION OF THE HOUR.

duced to him.   The lion of the hour was attired in
ordinary evening dress, with no foppery of any kind,
but he wore in his buttonhole a dainty blue flower
whose name I do not know ; and as he bowed

distantly to Charles, whom he surveyed through his
eyeglass, the gleam of a big diamond in the middle
of his shirt-front betrayed the fact that the Briar-rose
school, as it was called (from his famous epic), had
at least succeeded in making money out of poetry.
He explained to us a little later, in fact, that he was
over in New York to look after his royalties. ' The
beggars,' he said, ' only gave me eight hundred
pounds on my last volume. I couldn't stand *that*,
you know ; for a modern bard, moving with the age,
can only sing when duly wound up ; so I've run
across to investigate. Put a penny in the slot,
don't you see, and the poet will pipe for you.'

' Exactly like myself,' Charles said, finding a
point in common. ' *I'm* interested in mines ; and I,
too, have come over to look after my royalties.'

The poet placed his eyeglass in his eye once
more, and surveyed Charles deliberately from head
to foot. ' Oh,' he murmured slowly. He said not
a word more ; but somehow, everybody felt that
Charles was demolished. I saw that Wrengold,
when we went in to dinner, hastily altered the
cards that marked their places. He had evidently
put Charles at first to sit next the poet ; he varied
that arrangement now, setting Algernon Coleyard
between a railway king and a magazine editor. I
have seldom seen my respected brother-in-law so
completely silenced.

The poet's conduct during dinner was most peculiar.
He kept quoting poetry at inopportune moments.

'Roast lamb or boiled turkey, sir?' said the footman.

'Mary had a little lamb,' said the poet. 'I shall imitate Mary.'

Charles and the Senator thought the remark undignified.

I SHALL IMITATE MARY.

After dinner, however, under the mellowing influence of some excellent Roederer, Charles began to expand again, and grew lively and anecdotal. The poet had made us all laugh not a little with various capital stories of London literary society—at least two of them, I think, new ones; and Charles was moved by generous emulation to contribute his

own share to the amusement of the company. He
was in excellent cue. He is not often brilliant ; but
when he chooses, he has a certain dry vein of caustic
humour which is decidedly funny, though not perhaps
strictly without being vulgar. On this particular
night, then, warmed with the admirable Wrengold
champagne—the best made in America—he launched
out into a full and embroidered description of the
various ways in which Colonel Clay had deceived
him. I will not say that he narrated them in full
with the same frankness and accuracy that I have
shown in these pages ; he suppressed not a few of
the most amusing details—on no other ground,
apparently, than because they happened to tell
against himself ; and he enlarged a good deal on the
surprising cleverness with which several times he had
nearly secured his man ; but still, making all
allowances for native vanity in concealment and
addition, he was distinctly funny—he represented
the matter for once in its ludicrous rather than in its
disastrous aspect. He observed also, looking around
the table, that after all he had lost less by Colonel
Clay in four years of persecution than he often lost
by one injudicious move in a single day on the
London Stock Exchange ; while he seemed to imply
to the solid men of New York, that he would cheerfully sacrifice such a fleabite as that, in return for
the amusement and excitement of the chase which
the Colonel had afforded him.

The poet was pleased. ' You are a man of spirit,

Sir Charles,' he said. ' I love to see this fine old
English admiration of pluck and adventure ! The
fellow must really have some good in him, after all.
I should like to take notes of a few of those stories ;
they would supply nice material for basing a romance
upon.'

' I hardly know whether I'm exactly the man to
make the hero of a novel,' Charles murmured, with
complacence. And he certainly didn't look it.

' *I* was thinking rather of Colonel Clay as the
hero,' the poet responded coldly.

' Ah, that's the way with you men of letters,'
Charles answered, growing warm. ' You always have
a sneaking sympathy with the rascals.'

' That may be better,' Coleyard retorted, in an icy
voice, ' than sympathy with the worst forms of Stock
Exchange speculation.'

The company smiled uneasily. The railway king
wriggled. Wrengold tried to change the subject
hastily. But Charles would not be put down.

' You must hear the end, though,' he said.
' That's not quite the worst. The meanest thing
about the man is that he's also a hypocrite. He
wrote me *such* a letter at the end of his last trick
—here, positively here, in America.' And he proceeded to give his own version of the Quackenboss
incident, enlivened with sundry imaginative bursts of
pure Vandrift fancy.

When Charles spoke of Mrs. Quackenboss the
poet smiled. ' The worst of married women,' he

said, 'is—that you can't marry them; the worst of
unmarried women is—that they want to marry you.'
But when it came to the letter, the poet's eye was
upon my brother-in-law. Charles, I must fain
admit, garbled the document sadly. Still, even
so, some gleam of good feeling remained in its
sentences. But Charles ended all by saying, 'So,
to crown his misdemeanours, the rascal shows himself a whining cur and a disgusting Pharisee.'

'Don't you think,' the poet interposed, in his
cultivated drawl, 'he may have really meant it?
Why should not some grain of compunction have
stirred his soul still?—some remnant of conscience
made him shrink from betraying a man who confided
in him? I have an idea, myself, that even the worst
of rogues have always some good in them. I notice
they often succeed to the end in retaining the
affection and fidelity of women.'

'Oh, I said so!' Charles sneered. 'I told you
you literary men have always an underhand regard
for a scoundrel.'

'Perhaps so,' the poet answered. 'For we are all
of us human. Let him that is without sin among
us cast the first stone.' And then he relapsed into
moody silence.

We rose from table. Cigars went round. We
adjourned to the smoking-room. It was a Moorish
marvel, with Oriental hangings. There, Senator
Wrengold and Charles exchanged reminiscences of
bonanzas and ranches and other exciting post-

prandial topics; while the magazine editor cut in
now and again with a pertinent inquiry or a quaint
and sarcastic parallel instance.   It was clear he had
an eye to future copy.   Only Algernon Coleyard

MOODY.

sat brooding and silent, with his chin on one hand,
and his brow intent, musing and gazing at the
embers in the fireplace.   The hand, by the way,
was remarkable for a curious, antique-looking ring,
apparently of Egyptian or Etruscan workmanship,

with a projecting gem of several large facets. Once only, in the midst of a game of whist, he broke out with a single comment.

'Hawkins was made an earl,' said Charles, speaking of some London acquaintance.

'What for?' asked the Senator.

'Successful adulteration,' said the poet tartly.

'Honours are easy,' the magazine editor put in.

'And two by tricks to Sir Charles,' the poet added.

Towards the close of the evening, however—the poet still remaining moody, not to say positively grumpy—Senator Wrengold proposed a friendly game of Swedish poker. It was the latest fashionable variant in Western society on the old gambling round, and few of us knew it, save the omniscient poet and the magazine editor. It turned out afterwards that Wrengold proposed that particular game because he had heard Coleyard observe at the Lotus Club the same afternoon that it was a favourite amusement of his. Now, however, for a while he objected to playing. He was a poor man, he said, and the rest were all rich ; why should he throw away the value of a dozen golden sonnets just to add one more pinnacle to the gilded roofs of a millionaire's palace? Besides, he was half-way through with an ode he was inditing to Republican simplicity. The pristine austerity of a democratic senatorial cottage had naturally inspired him with memories of Dentatus, the Fabii, Camillus. But

Wrengold, dimly aware he was being made fun of somehow, insisted that the poet must take a hand with the financiers. 'You can pass, you know,' he said, 'as often as you like; and you can stake low, or go it blind, according as you're inclined to. It's a democratic game; every man decides for himself how high he will play, except the banker; and you needn't take bank unless you want it.'

'Oh, if you insist upon it,' Coleyard drawled out, with languid reluctance, 'I'll play, of course. I won't spoil your evening. But remember, I'm a poet; I have strange inspirations.'

The cards were 'squeezers'—that is to say, had the suit and the number of pips in each printed small in the corner, as well as over the face, for ease of reference. We played low at first. The poet seldom staked; and when he did — a few pounds — he lost, with singular persistence. He wanted to play for doubloons or sequins, and could with difficulty be induced to condescend to dollars. Charles looked across at him at last; the stakes by that time were fast rising higher, and we played for ready money. Notes lay thick on the green cloth. 'Well,' he murmured provokingly, 'how about your inspiration? Has Apollo deserted you?'

It was an unwonted flight of classical allusion for Charles, and I confess it astonished me. (I discovered afterwards he had cribbed it from a review in that evening's *Critic*.) But the poet smiled.

' No,' he answered calmly, ' I am waiting for one now. When it comes, you may be sure you shall have the benefit of it.'

Next round, Charles dealing and banking, the poet staked on his card, unseen as usual. He staked like a gentleman. To our immense astonishment he pulled out a roll of notes, and remarked, in a quiet tone, ' I have an inspiration now. *Half-hearted* will do. I go five thousand.' That was dollars, of course ; but it amounted to a thousand pounds in English money—high play for an author.

Charles smiled and turned his card. The poet turned his—and won a thousand.

' Good shot ! ' Charles murmured, pretending not to mind, though he detests losing.

' Inspiration ! ' the poet mused, and looked once more abstracted.

Charles dealt again. The poet watched the deal with boiled-fishy eyes. His thoughts were far away. His lips moved audibly. ' *Myrtle*, and *kirtle*, and *hurtle*,' he muttered. ' They'll do for three. Then there's *turtle*, meaning dove ; and that finishes the possible. *Laurel* and *coral* make a very bad rhyme. Try *myrtle ;* don't you think so ? '

' Do you stake ? ' Charles asked, severely, interrupting his reverie.

The poet started. ' No, pass,' he replied, looking down at his card, and subsided into muttering. We caught a tremor of his lips again, and heard something like this : ' Not less but more republican than thou, Half-hearted watcher by the Western sea, After long years I come to visit thee, And test thy fealty to that maiden vow, That bound thee in thy budding prime For Freedom's bride——'

'Stake?' Charles interrupted, inquiringly, again.

'Yes, five thousand,' the poet answered dreamily, pushing forward his pile of notes, and never ceasing from his murmur: 'For Freedom's bride to all succeeding time. *Succeeding; succeeding;* weak word, *succeeding.* Couldn't go five dollars on it.'

Charles turned his card once more. The poet had won again. Charles passed over his notes. The poet raked them in with a far-away air, as one who looks at infinity, and asked if he could borrow a pencil and paper. He had a few priceless lines to set down which might otherwise escape him.

'This is play,' Charles said pointedly. '*Will* you kindly attend to one thing or the other?'

The poet glanced at him with a compassionate smile. 'I told you I had inspirations,' he said. 'They always come together. I can't win your money as fast as I would like, unless at the same time I am making verses. Whenever I hit upon a good epithet, I back my luck, don't you see? I won a thousand on *Half-hearted*, and a thousand on *budding*; if I were to back *succeeding*, I should lose, to a certainty. You understand my system?'

'I call it pure rubbish,' Charles answered. 'However, continue. Systems were made for fools—and to suit wise men. Sooner or later you *must* lose at such a stupid fancy.'

The poet continued. ' For Freedom's bride to all *ensuing* time.'

' Stake!' Charles cried sharply. We each of us staked.

' *Ensuing,*' the poet murmured. ' To all *ensuing* time. First-rate epithet that. I go ten thousand, Sir Charles, on *ensuing.*'

We all turned up. Some of us lost, some won ; but the poet had secured his two thousand sterling.

' I haven't that amount about me,' Charles said, in that austerely nettled voice which he always assumes when he loses at cards ; ' but—I'll settle it with you to-morrow.'

' Another round ? ' the host asked, beaming.

' No, thank you,' Charles answered ; ' Mr. Coleyard's inspirations come too pat for my taste. His luck beats mine. I retire from the game, Senator.'

Just at that moment a servant entered, bearing a salver, with a small note in an envelope. ' For Mr. Coleyard,' he observed ; ' and the messenger said, *urgent.*'

Coleyard tore it open hurriedly. I could see he was agitated. His face grew white at once.

' I—I beg your pardon,' he said. ' I—I must go back instantly. My wife is dangerously ill—quite a sudden attack. Forgive me, Senator. Sir Charles, you shall have your revenge to-morrow.'

It was clear that his voice faltered. We felt at least he was a man of feeling. He was obviously frightened. His coolness forsook him. He shook hands as in a dream, and rushed downstairs for his dust-coat. Almost as he closed the front door, a new guest entered, just missing him in the vestibule.

WE BURST DOWN THE STAIRS IN A BODY.

'Halloa, you men,' he said, 'we've been taken in, do you know? It's all over the Lotus. The man we made an honorary member of the club to-day is *not* Algernon Coleyard. He's a blatant impostor. There's a telegram come in on the tape to-night saying Algernon Coleyard is dangerously ill at his home in England.'

Charles gasped a violent gasp. 'Colonel Clay!' he shouted, aloud. 'And once more he's done me. There's not a moment to lose. After him, gentlemen! after him!'

Never before in our lives had we had such a close shave of catching and fixing the redoubtable swindler. We burst down the stairs in a body, and rushed out into Fifth Avenue. The pretended poet had only a hundred yards' start of us, and he saw he was discovered. But he was an excellent runner. So was I, weight for age; and I dashed wildly after him. He turned round a corner; it proved to lead nowhere, and lost him time. He darted back again, madly. Delighted with the idea that I was capturing so famous a criminal, I redoubled my efforts—and came up with him, panting. He was wearing a light dust-coat. I seized it in my hands. 'I've got you at last!' I cried; 'Colonel Clay, I've got you!'

He turned and looked at me. 'Ha, old Ten Per Cent!' he called out, struggling. 'It's you, then, is it? Never, never to *you*, sir!' And as he spoke, he somehow flung his arms straight out behind him, and let the dust-coat slip off, which it easily did, the sleeves being new and smoothly silk-lined. The suddenness of the movement threw me completely off my guard, and off my legs as well. I was clinging to the coat and holding him. As the support gave way I rolled over backward, in the mud of the street, and hurt my back seriously. As

for Colonel Clay, with a nervous laugh, he bolted off
at full speed in his evening coat, and vanished round
a corner.

It was some seconds before I had sufficiently

I ROLLED BACKWARD.

recovered my breath to pick
myself up again, and ex-
amine my bruises. By this
time Charles and the other
pursuers had come up, and
I explained my condition to them. Instead of
commending me for my zeal in his cause—which
had cost me a barked arm and a good evening suit
—my brother-in-law remarked, with an unfeeling

sneer, that when I had so nearly caught my man I might as well have held him.

'I have his coat, at least,' I said. 'That may afford us a clue.' And I limped back with it in my hands, feeling horribly bruised and a good deal shaken.

When we came to examine the coat, however, it bore no maker's name; the strap at the back, where the tailor proclaims with pride his handicraft, had been carefully ripped off, and its place was taken by a tag of plain black tape without inscription of any sort. We searched the breast-pocket. A handkerchief, similarly nameless, but of finest cambric. The side-pockets—ha, what was this? I drew a piece of paper out in triumph. It was a note—a real find—the one which the servant had handed to our friend just before at the Senator's.

We read it through breathlessly :—

'DARLING PAUL,—I *told* you it was too danger- ous. You should have listened to me. You ought *never* to have imitated any real person. I happened to glance at the hotel tape just now, to see the quotations for Cloetedorps to-day, and what do you think I read as part of the latest telegram from England? "Mr. Algernon Coleyard, the famous poet, is lying on his death-bed at his home in Devonshire." By this time all New York knows. Don't stop one minute. Say I'm dangerously ill, and come away at once. Don't return to the hotel.

I am removing our things. Meet me at Mary's.
Your devoted,   MARGOT.'

'This is *very* important,' Charles said. 'This
does give us a clue. We know two things now :
his real name is Paul—whatever else it may be, and
Madame Picardet's is Margot.'

I searched the pocket again, and pulled out a
ring. Evidently he had thrust these two things
there when he saw me pursuing him, and had
forgotten or neglected them in the heat of the *mêlée*.

I looked at it close. It was the very ring I had
noticed on his finger while he was playing Swedish
poker. It had a large compound gem in the centre,
set with many facets, and rising like a pyramid to a
point in the middle. There were eight faces in all,
some of them composed of emerald, amethyst, or
turquoise. But *one* face—the one that turned at a
direct angle towards the wearer's eye—was *not* a
gem at all, but an extremely tiny convex mirror.
In a moment I spotted the trick. He held this
hand carelessly on the table while my brother-in-law
dealt ; and when he saw that the suit and number
of his own card mirrored in it by means of the
squeezers were better than Charles's, he had 'an
inspiration,' and backed his luck—or rather his
knowledge—with perfect confidence. I did not
doubt, either, that his odd-looking eyeglass was a
powerful magnifier which helped him in the trick.
Still, we tried another deal, by way of experiment—

I wearing the ring ; and even with the naked eye I
was able to distinguish in every case the suit and
pips of the card that was dealt me.

'Why, that was almost dishonest,' the Senator
said, drawing back. He wished to show us that
even far-Western speculators drew a line somewhere.

'Yes,' the magazine editor echoed. 'To back
your skill is legal ; to back your luck is foolish ; to
back your knowledge is——'

'Immoral,' I suggested.

'Very good business,' said the magazine editor.

'It's a simple trick,' Charles interposed. 'I
should have spotted it if it had been done by any
other fellow. But his patter about inspiration put
me clean off the track. That's the rascal's dodge.
He plays the regular conjurer's game of distracting
your attention from the real point at issue—so well
that you never find out what he's really about till
he's sold you irretrievably.'

We set the New York police upon the trail of
the Colonel ; but of course he had vanished at once,
as usual, into the thin smoke of Manhattan. Not a
sign could we find of him. 'Mary's,' we found an
insufficient address.

We waited on in New York for a whole fortnight. Nothing came of it. We never found
'Mary's.' The only token of Colonel Clay's presence
vouchsafed us in the city was one of his customary
insulting notes. It was conceived as follows :—

'O ETERNAL GULLIBLE!—Since I saw you on
Lake George, I have run back to London, and
promptly come out again. I had business to
transact there, indeed, which I have now completed ;
the excessive attentions of the English police sent
me once more, like great Orion, 'sloping slowly to
the west.' I returned to America in order to see
whether or not you were still impenitent. On the
day of my arrival I happened to meet Senator
Wrengold, and accepted his kind invitation solely
that I might see how far my last communication
had had a proper effect upon you. As I found
you quite obdurate, and as you furthermore persisted
in misunderstanding my motives, I determined to
read you one more small lesson. It nearly failed ;
and I confess the accident has affected my nerves a
little. I am now about to retire from business
altogether, and settle down for life at my place in
Surrey. I mean to try just one more small *coup ;*
and, when that is finished, Colonel Clay will hang
up his sword, like Cincinnatus, and take to farming.
You need no longer fear me. I have realised
enough to secure me for life a modest competence ;
and as I am not possessed like yourself with an
immoderate greed of gain, I recognise that good
citizenship demands of me now an early retirement
in favour of some younger and more deserving
rascal. I shall always look back with pleasure upon
our agreeable adventures together ; and as you hold
my dust-coat, together with a ring and letter to

which I attach importance, I consider we are quits, and I shall withdraw with dignity. Your sincere well-wisher, CUTHBERT CLAY, *Poet.*'

'Just like him!' Charles said, 'to hold this one last *coup* over my head *in terrorem.* Though even when he has played it, why should I trust his word? A scamp like that may say it, of course, on purpose to disarm me.'

For my own part, I quite agreed with 'Margot.' When the Colonel was reduced to dressing the part of a known personage I felt he had reached almost his last card, and would be well advised to retire into Surrey.

But the magazine editor summed up all in a word. 'Don't believe that nonsense about fortunes being made by industry and ability,' he said. 'In life, as at cards, two things go to produce success—the first is chance; the second is cheating.'

XI

THE EPISODE OF THE BERTILLON METHOD

WE had a terrible passage home from New York. The Captain told us he 'knew every drop of water in the Atlantic personally'; and he had never seen them so uniformly obstreperous. The ship rolled in the trough; Charles rolled in his cabin, and would not be comforted. As we approached the Irish coast, I scrambled up on deck in a violent gale, and retired again somewhat precipitately to announce to my brother-in-law that we had just come in sight of the Fastnet Rock Lighthouse. Charles merely turned over in his berth and groaned. 'I don't believe it,' he answered. 'I expect it is probably Colonel Clay in another of his manifold disguises!'

At Liverpool, however, the Adelphi consoled him. We dined luxuriously in the Louis Quinze restaurant, as only millionaires can dine, and proceeded next day by Pullman car to London.

We found Amelia dissolved in tears at a domestic cataclysm. It seemed that Césarine had given notice.

Charles was scarcely home again when he began

to bethink him of the least among his investments. Like many other wealthy men, my respected connection is troubled more or less, in the background of his consciousness, by a pervading dread that he will die a beggar. To guard against this misfortune —which I am bound to admit nobody else fears for him—he invested, several years ago, a sum of two hundred thousand pounds in Consols, to serve as a nest-egg in case of the collapse of Golcondas and South Africa generally. It is part of the same amiable mania, too, that he will not allow the dividend-warrants on this sum to be sent to him by post, but insists, after the fashion of old ladies and country parsons, upon calling personally at the Bank of England four times a year to claim his interest. He is well known by sight to not a few of the clerks ; and his appearance in Threadneedle Street is looked forward to with great regularity within a few weeks of each lawful quarter-day.

So, on the morning after our arrival in town, Charles observed to me, cheerfully, ' Sey, I must run into the City to-day to claim my dividends. There are two quarters owing.'

I accompanied him in to the Bank. Even that mighty official, the beadle at the door, unfastened the handle of the millionaire's carriage. The clerk who received us smiled and nodded. ' How much ? ' he asked, after the stereotyped fashion.

' Two hundred thousand,' Charles answered, looking affable.

The clerk turned up the books. 'Paid!' he said, with decision. 'What's your game, sir, if I may ask you?'

SHOW ME THE SIGNATURE.

'Paid!' Charles echoed, drawing back.

The clerk gazed across at him. 'Yes, Sir Charles,' he answered, in a somewhat severe tone. 'You must remember you drew a quarter's dividend from myself—last week —at this very counter.'

Charles stared at him fixedly. 'Show me the signature,' he said at last, in a slow, dazed fashion. I suspected mischief.

The clerk pushed the book across to him. Charles examined the name close.

'Colonel Clay again!' he cried, turning to me
with a despondent air. 'He must have dressed the
part. I shall die in the workhouse, Sey! That
man has stolen away even my nest-egg from me.'

I saw it at a glance. 'Mrs. Quackenboss!' I
put in. 'Those portraits on the *Etruria*! It was
to help him in his make-up! You recollect, she
sketched your face and figure at all possible angles.'

'And last quarter's?' Charles inquired, staggering.

The clerk turned up the entry. 'Drawn on the
10th of July,' he answered, carelessly, as if it
mattered nothing.

Then I knew why the Colonel had run across to
England.

Charles positively reeled. 'Take me home, Sey,'
he cried. 'I am ruined, ruined! He will leave me
with not half a million in the world. My poor, poor
boys will beg their bread, unheeded, through the
streets of London!'

(As Amelia has landed estate settled upon her
worth a hundred and fifty thousand pounds, this
last contingency affected me less to tears than Charles
seemed to think necessary.)

We made all needful inquiries, and put the police
upon the quest at once, as always. But no redress
was forthcoming. The money, once paid, could not
be recovered. It is a playful little privilege of
Consols that the Government declines under any
circumstances to pay twice over. Charles drove
back to Mayfair a crushed and broken man. I think

if Colonel Clay himself could have seen him just then, he would have pitied that vast intellect in its grief and bewilderment.

After lunch, however, my brother-in-law's natural buoyancy reasserted itself by degrees. He rallied a little. 'Seymour,' he said to me, 'you've heard, of course, of the Bertillon system of measuring and registering criminals.'

'I have,' I answered. 'And it's excellent as far as it goes. But, like Mrs. Glasse's jugged hare, it all depends upon the initial step. "First catch your criminal." Now, we have never caught Colonel Clay——'

'Or, rather,' Charles interposed unkindly, 'when you *did* catch him, you didn't hold him.'

I ignored the unkindly suggestion, and continued in the same voice, 'We have never secured Colonel Clay ; and until we secure him, we cannot register him by the Bertillon method. Besides, even if we had once caught him and duly noted the shape of his nose, his chin, his ears, his forehead, of what use would that be against a man who turns up with a fresh face each time, and can mould his features into what form he likes, to deceive and foil us ?'

'Never mind, Sey,' my brother-in-law said. 'I was told in New York that Dr. Frank Beddersley, of London, was the best exponent of the Bertillon system now living in England ; and to Beddersley I shall go. Or, rather, I'll invite him here to lunch to-morrow.'

'Who told you of him?' I inquired. '*Not*
Dr. Quackenboss, I hope; nor yet Mr. Algernon
Coleyard?'

Charles paused and reflected. 'No, neither of
them,' he answered, after a short internal delibera-
tion. 'It was that magazine editor chap we met at
Wrengold's.'

'*He's* all right,' I said; 'or, at least, I think so.'

So we wrote a polite invitation to Dr. Beddersley,
who pursued the method professionally, asking him
to come and lunch with us at Mayfair at two next
day.

Dr. Beddersley came—a dapper little man, with
pent-house eyebrows, and keen, small eyes, whom I
suspected at sight of being Colonel Clay himself in
another of his clever polymorphic embodiments. He
was clear and concise. His manner was scientific.
He told us at once that though the Bertillon method
was of little use till the expert had seen the criminal
once, yet if we had consulted him earlier he might
probably have saved us some serious disasters. 'A
man so ingenious as this,' he said, 'would no doubt
have studied Bertillon's principles himself, and would
take every possible means to prevent recognition by
them. Therefore, you might almost disregard the
nose, the chin, the moustache, the hair, all of which
are capable of such easy alteration. But there
remain some features which are more likely to persist
—height, shape of head, neck, build, and fingers;
the *timbre* of the voice, the colour of the iris. Even

these, again, may be partially disguised or concealed ;
the way the hair is dressed, the amount of padding,
a high collar round the throat, a dark line about the
eyelashes, may do more to alter the appearance of a
face than you could readily credit.'

'So we know,' I answered.

'The voice, again,' Dr. Beddersley continued.
'The voice itself may be most fallacious.   The man
is no doubt a clever mimic.   He could, perhaps, com-
press or enlarge his larynx.   And I judge from what
you tell me that he took characters each time which
compelled him largely to alter and modify his tone
and accent.'

'Yes,' I said.   'As the Mexican Seer, he had of
course a Spanish intonation.   As the little curate,
he was a cultivated North-countryman.   As David
Granton, he spoke gentlemanly Scotch.   As Von
Lebenstein, naturally, he was a South-German, trying to express himself in French.   As Professor
Schleiermacher, he was a North-German speaking
broken English.   As Elihu Quackenboss, he had a
fine and pronounced Kentucky flavour.   And as
the poet, he drawled after the fashion of the clubs,
with lingering remnants of a Devonshire ancestry.'

'Quite so,' Dr. Beddersley answered.   'That is
just what I should expect.   Now, the question is,
do you know him to be one man, or is he really a
gang ?   Is he a name for a syndicate ?   Have you
any photographs of Colonel Clay himself in any of
his disguises ? '

'Not one,' Charles answered. 'He produced some himself, when he was Medhurst the detective.

DR. BEDDERSLEY.

But he pocketed them at once; and we never recovered them.'

'Could you get any?' the doctor asked. 'Did you note the name and address of the photographer?'

'Unfortunately, no,' Charles replied. 'But the police at Nice showed us two. Perhaps we might borrow them.'

'Until we get them,' Dr. Beddersley said, 'I don't know that we can do anything. But if you can once give me two distinct photographs of the real man, no matter how much disguised, I could tell you whether they were taken from one person; and, if so, I think I could point out certain details in common which might aid us to go upon.'

All this was at lunch. Amelia's niece, Dolly Lingfield, was there, as it happened; and I chanced to note a most guilty look stealing over her face all the while we were talking. Suspicious as I had learned to become by this time, however, I did not suspect Dolly of being in league with Colonel Clay; but, I confess, I wondered what her blush could indicate. After lunch, to my surprise, Dolly called me away from the rest into the library. 'Uncle Seymour,' she said to me—the dear child calls me Uncle Seymour, though of course I am not in any way related to her—'*I* have some photographs of Colonel Clay, if you want them.'

'*You?*' I cried, astonished. 'Why, Dolly, how did you get them?'

For a minute or two she showed some little hesitation in telling me. At last she whispered, 'You won't be angry if I confess?' (Dolly is just nineteen, and remarkably pretty.)

'My child,' I said, 'why *should* I be angry?
You may confide in me implicitly.' (With a blush
like that, who on earth could be angry with
her?)

'And you won't tell Aunt Amelia or Aunt
Isabel?' she inquired somewhat anxiously.

'Not for worlds,' I answered. (As a matter of
fact, Amelia and Isabel are the last people in the
world to whom I should dream of confiding anything
that Dolly might tell me.)

'Well, I was stopping at Seldon, you know, when
Mr. David Granton was there,' Dolly went on;
'—or, rather, when that scamp pretended he was
David Granton; and—and—you won't be angry
with me, will you?—one day I took a snap-shot
with my kodak at him and Aunt Amelia!'

'Why, what harm was there in that?' I asked,
bewildered. The wildest stretch of fancy could
hardly conceive that the Honourable David had
been *flirting* with Amelia.

Dolly coloured still more deeply. 'Oh, you
know Bertie Winslow?' she said. 'Well, he's
interested in photography—and—and also in *me*.
And he's invented a process, which isn't of the
slightest practical use, he says; but its peculiarity is,
that it reveals textures. At least, that's what Bertie
calls it. It makes things come out so. And he
gave me some plates of his own for my kodak—
half-a-dozen or more, and—I took Aunt Amelia
with them.'

' I still fail to see,' I murmured, looking at her comically.

' Oh, Uncle Seymour,' Dolly cried.   ' How blind

HOW BLIND YOU MEN ARE !

you men are !   If Aunt Amelia knew she would never forgive me.   Why, you *must* understand. The—the rouge, you know, and the pearl powder ! '

' Oh, it comes out, then, in the photograph ? '   I inquired.

'Comes out! I should *think* so! It's like little black spots all over auntie's face. *Such* a guy as she looks in it!'

'And Colonel Clay is in them too?'

'Yes; I took them when he and auntie were talking together, without either of them noticing. And Bertie developed them. I've three of David Granton. Three beauties; *most* successful.'

'Any other character?' I asked, seeing business ahead.

Dolly hung back, still redder. 'Well, the rest are with Aunt Isabel,' she answered, after a struggle.

'My dear child,' I replied, hiding my feelings as a husband, 'I will be brave. I will bear up even against that last misfortune!'

Dolly looked up at me pleadingly. 'It was here in London,' she went on; '—when I was last with auntie. Medhurst was stopping in the house at the time; and I took him twice, *tête-à-tête* with Aunt Isabel!'

'Isabel does not paint,' I murmured, stoutly.

Dolly hung back again. 'No, but—her hair!' she suggested, in a faint voice.

'Its colour,' I admitted, 'is in places assisted by a—well, you know, a restorer.'

Dolly broke into a mischievous sly smile. 'Yes, it is,' she continued. 'And, oh, Uncle Sey, where the restorer has—er—restored it, you know, it comes out in the photograph with a sort of brilliant iridescent metallic sheen on it!'

'Bring them down, my dear,' I said, gently patting her head with my hand. In the interests of justice, I thought it best not to frighten her.

Dolly brought them down. They seemed to me poor things, yet well worth trying. We found it possible, on further confabulation, by the simple aid of a pair of scissors, so to cut each in two that all trace of Amelia and Isabel was obliterated. Even so, however, I judged it best to call Charles and Dr. Beddersley to a private consultation in the library with Dolly, and not to submit the mutilated photographs to public inspection by their joint subjects. Here, in fact, we had five patchy portraits of the redoubtable Colonel, taken at various angles, and in characteristic unstudied attitudes. A child had outwitted the cleverest sharper in Europe !

The moment Beddersley's eye fell upon them, a curious look came over his face. ' Why, these,' he said, 'are taken on Herbert Winslow's method, Miss Lingfield.'

' Yes,' Dolly admitted timidly. ' They are. He's —a friend of mine, don't you know ; and—he gave me some plates that just fitted my camera.'

Beddersley gazed at them steadily. Then he turned to Charles. ' And this young lady,' he said, ' has quite unintentionally and unconsciously succeeded in tracking Colonel Clay to earth at last. They are genuine photographs of the man—as he is —*without* the disguises !'

' They look to me most blotchy,' Charles murmured. 'Great black lines down the nose, and such spots on the cheek, too!'

'Exactly,' Beddersley put in. 'Those are *differences in texture*. They show just how much of the man's face is human flesh——'

'And how much wax,' I ventured.

'Not wax,' the expert answered, gazing close. 'This is some harder mixture. I should guess, a composition of gutta-percha and india-rubber, which takes colour well, and hardens when applied, so as to lie quite evenly, and resist heat or melting. Look here; that's an artificial scar, filling up a real hollow; and *this* is an added bit to the tip of the nose; and *those* are shadows, due to inserted cheek-pieces, within the mouth, to make the man look fatter!'

'Why, of course,' Charles cried. 'India-rubber it must be. That's why in France they call him *le Colonel Caoutchouc!*'

'Can you reconstruct the real face from them?' I inquired anxiously.

Dr. Beddersley gazed hard at them. 'Give me an hour or two,' he said—'and a box of water-colours. I *think* by that time—putting two and two together—I can eliminate the false and build up for you a tolerably correct idea of what the actual man himself looks like.'

We turned him into the library for a couple of hours, with the materials he needed; and by tea-time he had completed his first rough sketch of the elements common to the two faces. He brought it

out to us in the drawing-room. I glanced at it
first. It was a curious countenance, slightly wanting
in definiteness, and not unlike those 'composite
photographs' which Mr. Galton produces by exposing two negatives on the same sensitised paper
for ten seconds or so consecutively. Yet it struck
me at once as containing something of Colonel Clay
in every one of his many representations. The little
curate, in real life, did not recall the Seer ; nor did
Elihu Quackenboss suggest Count von Lebenstein
or Professor Schleiermacher. Yet in this compound
face, produced only from photographs of David
Granton and Medhurst, I could distinctly trace a certain
underlying likeness to every one of the forms which
the impostor had assumed for us. In other words,
though he could make up so as to mask the likeness
to his other characters, he could not make up so as
to mask the likeness to his own personality. He
could not wholly get rid of his native build and his
genuine features.

Besides these striking suggestions of the Seer and
the curate, however, I felt vaguely conscious of having
seen and observed *the man himself* whom the water-
colour represented, at some time, somewhere. It
was not at Nice ; it was not at Seldon ; it was not at
Meran ; it was not in America. I believed I had
been in a room with him somewhere in London.

Charles was looking over my shoulder. He gave
a sudden little start. 'Why, I know that fellow!'
he cried. 'You recollect him, Sey ; he's Fingle-

more's brother—the chap that didn't go out to China!'

Then I remembered at once where it was that I had seen him—at the broker's in the city, before we sailed for America.

'What Christian name?' I asked.

Charles reflected a moment. 'The same as the one in the note we got with the dust-coat,' he answered, at last. 'The man is Paul Finglemore!'

'You will arrest him?' I asked.

'Can I, on this evidence?'

'We might bring it home to him.'

Charles mused for a moment. 'We shall have nothing against him,' he said slowly, 'except in so far as we can swear to his identity. And that may be difficult.'

Just at that moment the footman brought in tea. Charles wondered apparently whether the man, who had been with us at Seldon when Colonel Clay was David Granton, would recollect the face or recognise having seen it. 'Look here, Dudley,' he said, holding up the water-colour, 'do you know that person?'

Dudley gazed at it a moment. 'Certainly, sir,' he answered briskly.

'Who is it?' Amelia asked. We expected him to answer, 'Count von Lebenstein,' or 'Mr. Granton,' or 'Medhurst.'

Instead of that, he replied, to our utter surprise, 'That's Césarine's young man, my lady.'

'Césarine's young man?' Amelia repeated, taken

aback. 'Oh, Dudley, surely, you *must* be mistaken !'

'No, my lady,' Dudley replied, in a tone of conviction. 'He comes to see her quite reg'lar ; he have come to see her, off and on, from time to time, ever since I've been in Sir Charles's service.'

'When will he be coming again ?' Charles asked, breathless.

'He's downstairs now, sir,' Dudley answered, unaware of the bombshell he was flinging into the midst of a respectable family.

Charles rose excitedly, and put his back against the door. 'Secure that man,' he said to me sharply, pointing with his finger.

'*What* man ?' I asked, amazed. 'Colonel Clay? The young man who's downstairs now with Césarine ? '

'No,' Charles answered, with decision ; 'Dudley !'

I laid my hand on the footman's shoulder, not understanding what Charles meant. Dudley, terrified, drew back, and would have rushed from the room ; but Charles, with his back against the door, prevented him.

'I—I've done nothing to be arrested, Sir Charles,' Dudley cried, in abject terror, looking appealingly at Amelia. 'It—it wasn't me as cheated you.' And he certainly didn't look it.

'I daresay not,' Charles answered. 'But you don't leave this room till Colonel Clay is in custody. No, Amelia, no ; it's no use your speaking to me. What he says is true. I see it all now. This

villain and Césarine have long been accomplices!
The man's downstairs with her now. If we let
Dudley quit the room he'll go down and tell them;
and before we know where we are, that slippery eel
will have wriggled through our fingers, as he always
wriggles. He *is* Paul Finglemore; he *is* Césarine's
young man; and unless we arrest him now, without
one minute's delay, he'll be off to Madrid or St.
Petersburg by this evening!'

'You are right,' I answered. 'It is now or
never!'

'Dudley,' Charles said, in his most authoritative
voice, 'stop here till we tell you you may leave the
room. Amelia and Dolly, don't let that man stir
from where he's standing. If he does, restrain him.
Seymour and Dr. Beddersley, come down with me
to the servants' hall. I suppose that's where I
shall find this person, Dudley?'

'N—no, sir,' Dudley stammered out, half beside
himself with fright. 'He's in the housekeeper's
room, sir!'

We went down to the lower regions in a solid
phalanx of three. On the way we met Simpson,
Sir Charles's valet, and also the butler, whom we
pressed into the service. At the door of the housekeeper's room we paused, strategically. Voices
came to us from within; one was Césarine's, the
other had a ring that reminded me at once of
Medhurst and the Seer, of Elihu Quackenboss and
Algernon Coleyard. They were talking together

in French ; and now and then we caught the sound of stifled laughter.

We opened the door.   '*Est-il drôle, donc, ce vieux ?*' the man's voice was saying.

'*C'est à mourir de rire,*' Césarine's voice responded.

We burst in upon them, red-handed.

Césarine's young man rose, with his hat in his hand, in a respectful attitude.   It reminded me at once of Medhurst, as he stood talking his first day at Marvillier's to Charles ; and also of the little curate, in his humblest moments as the disinterested pastor.

With a sign to me to do likewise, Charles laid his hand firmly on the young man's shoulder.   I looked in the fellow's face : there could be no denying it ; Césarine's young man was Paul Finglemore, our broker's brother.

'Paul Finglemore,' Charles said severely, ' otherwise Cuthbert Clay, I arrest you on several charges of theft and conspiracy ! '

The young man glanced around him.   He was surprised and perturbed ; but, even so, his inexhaustible coolness never once deserted him. 'What, five to one ? ' he said, counting us over. ' Has law and order come down to this ?   Five respectable rascals to arrest one poor beggar of a *chevalier d'industrie!*   Why, it's worse than New York.   *There,* it was only you and me, you know, old Ten per Cent ! '

' Hold his hands, Simpson ! ' Charles cried, trembling lest his enemy should escape him.

Paul Finglemore drew back even while we held his shoulders. ' No, not *you*, sir,' he said to the man, haughtily. ' Don't dare to lay your hands upon me! Send for a constable if you wish, Sir Charles Vandrift ; but I decline to be taken into custody by a valet ! '

' Go for a policeman,' Dr. Beddersley said to Simpson, standing forward.

The prisoner eyed him up and down. ' Oh, Dr. Beddersley ! ' he said, relieved. It was evident he knew him. ' If *you*'ve tracked me strictly in accordance with Bertillon's methods, I don't mind so much. I will not yield to fools ; I yield to science. I didn't think this diamond king had sense enough to apply to you. He's the most gullible old ass I ever met in my life. But if it's *you* who have tracked me down, I can only submit to it.'

Charles held to him with a fierce grip. ' Mind he doesn't break away, Sey,' he cried. ' He's playing his old game ! Distrust the man's patter ! '

' Take care,' the prisoner put in. ' Remember Dr. Polperro ! On what charge do you arrest me ? '

Charles was bubbling with indignation. ' You cheated me at Nice,' he said ; ' at Meran ; at New York ; at Paris ! '

Paul Finglemore shook his head. ' Won't do,' he answered, calmly. ' Be sure of your ground. Outside the jurisdiction ! You can only do that on an extradition warrant.'

' Well, then, at Seldon, in London, in this house,

and elsewhere,' Charles cried out excitedly. 'Hold
hard to him, Sey; by law or without it, blessed if
he isn't going even now to wriggle away from us!'

At that moment Simpson returned with a

A CONVENIENT POLICEMAN.

convenient policeman, whom he had happened to
find loitering about near the area steps, and whom I
half suspected from his furtive smile of being a
particular acquaintance of the household.

Charles gave the man in charge formally. Paul
Finglemore insisted that he should specify the nature
of the particular accusation. To my great chagrin,
Charles selected from his rogueries, as best within
the jurisdiction of the English courts, the matter of
the payment for the Castle of Lebenstein—made in
London, and through a London banker. 'I have a
warrant on that ground,' he said. I trembled as he
spoke. I felt at once that the episode of the
commission, the exposure of which I dreaded so
much, must now become public.

The policeman took the man in charge. Charles
still held to him, grimly. As they were leaving the
room the prisoner turned to Césarine, and muttered
something rapidly under his breath, in German.
'Of which tongue,' he said, turning to us blandly,
'in spite of my kind present of a dictionary and
grammar, you still doubtless remain in your pristine
ignorance!'

Césarine flung herself upon him with wild
devotion. 'Oh, Paul, darling,' she cried, in English,
'I will not, I will not! I will never save myself at
your expense. If they send you to prison—Paul,
Paul, I will go with you!'

I remembered as she spoke what Mr. Algernon
Coleyard had said to us at the Senator's. 'Even
the worst of rogues have always some good in them.
I notice they often succeed to the end in retaining
the affection and fidelity of women.'

But the man, his hands still free, unwound her

clasping arms with gentle fingers. 'My child,' he answered, in a soft tone, 'I am sorry to say the law of England will not permit you to go with me. If it did' (his voice was as the voice of the poet we had met), '"stone walls would not a prison make, nor iron bars a cage."' And bending forward, he kissed her forehead tenderly.

WHERE'S THAT HANSOM GONE?

We led him out to the door. The policeman, in obedience to Charles's orders, held him tight with his hand, but steadily refused, as the prisoner was not violent, to handcuff him. We hailed a passing hansom. 'To Bow Street!' Charles cried, unceremoniously pushing in policeman and prisoner. The driver nodded. We called a four-wheeler ourselves, in which my brother-in-law, Dr. Beddersley and myself took our seats. 'Follow the hansom!'

Charles cried out.   'Don't let him out of your sight.
After him, close, to Bow Street!'

I looked back, and saw Césarine, half fainting,
on the front door steps, while Dolly, bathed in tears,
stood supporting the lady's-maid, and trying to
comfort her.   It was clear she had not anticipated
this end to the adventure.

'Goodness gracious!' Charles screamed out, in a
fresh fever of alarm, as we turned the first corner;
'where's that hansom gone to?   How do I know
the fellow was a policeman at all?   We should have
taken the man in here.   We ought never to have let
him get out of our sight.   For all we can tell to the
contrary, the constable himself—may only be one of
Colonel Clay's confederates!'

And we drove in trepidation all the way to Bow
Street.

XII

THE EPISODE OF THE OLD BAILEY

WHEN we reached Bow Street, we were relieved to find that our prisoner, after all, had *not* evaded us. It was a false alarm. He was there with the policeman, and he kindly allowed us to make the first formal charge against him.

Of course, on Charles's sworn declaration and my own, the man was at once remanded, bail being refused, owing both to the serious nature of the charge and the slippery character of the prisoner's antecedents. We went back to Mayfair—Charles, well satisfied that the man he dreaded was under lock and key ; myself, not too well pleased to think that the man I dreaded was no longer at large, and that the trifling little episode of the ten per cent commission stood so near discovery.

Next day the police came round in force, and had a long consultation with Charles and myself. They strongly urged that two other persons at least should be included in the charge—Césarine and the little woman whom we had variously known as Madame Picardet, White Heather, Mrs. David

Granton, and Mrs. Elihu Quackenboss. If these
accomplices were arrested, they said, we could include conspiracy as one count in the indictment,
which gave us an extra chance of conviction. Now
they had got Colonel Clay, in fact, they naturally
desired to keep him, and also to indict with him as
many as possible of his pals and confederates.

Here, however, a difficulty arose. Charles called
me aside with a grave face into the library. 'Seymour,' he said, fixing me, 'this is a serious business.
I will not lightly swear away any woman's character.
Colonel Clay himself—or, rather, Paul Finglemore—
is an abandoned rogue, whom I do not desire to
screen in any degree. But poor little Madame
Picardet—she may be his lawful wife, and she may
have acted implicitly under his orders. Besides, I
don't know whether I could swear to her identity.
Here's the photograph the police bring of the woman
they believe to be Colonel Clay's chief female accomplice. Now, I ask you, does it in the least degree
resemble that clever and amusing and charming
little creature, who has so often deceived us?'

In spite of Charles's gibes, I flatter myself I do
really understand the whole duty of a secretary. It
was clear from his voice he did not *wish* me to
recognise her; which, as it happened, I did not.
'Certainly, it doesn't resemble her, Charles,' I
answered, with conviction in my voice. 'I should
never have known her.' But I did not add that I
should no more have known Colonel Clay himself in

his character of Paul Finglemore, or of Césarine's young man, as *that* remark lay clearly outside my secretarial functions.

Still, it flitted across my mind at the time that the Seer had made some casual remarks at Nice about a letter in Charles's pocket, presumably from Madame Picardet ; and I reflected further that Madame Picardet in turn might possibly hold certain answers of Charles's, couched in such terms as he might reasonably desire to conceal from Amelia. Indeed, I must allow that under whatever disguise White Heather appeared to us, Charles was always that disguise's devoted slave from the first moment he met it. It occurred to me, therefore, that the clever little woman—call her what you will—might be the holder of more than one indiscreet communication.

'Under these circumstances,' Charles went on, in his austerest voice, 'I cannot consent to be a party to the arrest of White Heather. I—I decline to identify her. In point of fact'—he grew more emphatic as he went on—'I don't think there is an atom of evidence of any sort against her. Not,' he continued, after a pause, 'that I wish in any degree to screen the guilty. Césarine, now—Césarine we have liked and trusted. She has betrayed our trust. She has sold us to this fellow. I have no doubt at all that she gave him the diamonds from Amelia's *rivière ;* that she took us by arrangement to meet him at Schloss Lebenstein ; that she opened and

sent to him my letter to Lord Craig-Ellachie.
Therefore, I say, we *ought* to arrest Césarine. But
not White Heather—not Jessie ; not that pretty
Mrs. Quackenboss. Let the guilty suffer ; why
strike at the innocent—or, at worst, the misguided ? '

'Charles,' I exclaimed, with warmth, 'your senti-
ments do you honour. You are a man of feeling.
And White Heather, I allow, is pretty enough and
clever enough to be forgiven anything. You may
rely upon my discretion. I will swear through thick
and thin that I do not recognise this woman as
Madame Picardet.'

Charles clasped my hand in silence. 'Seymour,'
he said, after a pause, with marked emotion, 'I felt
sure I could rely upon your—er—honour and integrity. I have been rough upon you sometimes.
But I ask your forgiveness. I see you understand
the whole duties of your position.'

We went out again, better friends than we had
been for months. I hoped, indeed, this pleasant
little incident might help to neutralise the possible
ill-effects of the ten per cent disclosure, should
Finglemore take it into his head to betray me to
my employer. As we emerged into the drawing-
room, Amelia beckoned me aside towards her
boudoir for a moment.

'Seymour,' she said to me, in a distinctly
frightened tone, 'I have treated you harshly at
times, I know, and I am very sorry for it. But I
want you to help me in a most painful difficulty.

The police are quite right as to the charge of conspiracy ; that designing little minx, White Heather,
or Mrs. David Granton, or whatever else we're to

I WANT YOU TO HELP ME IN A MOST PAINFUL DIFFICULTY.

call her, ought certainly to be prosecuted—and sent
to prison, too—and have her absurd head of hair
cut short and combed straight for her.   But—and
you will help me here, I'm sure, dear Seymour—I

cannot allow them to arrest my Césarine. I don't pretend to say Césarine isn't guilty ; the girl has behaved most ungratefully to me. She has robbed me right and left, and deceived me without compunction. Still—I put it to you as a married man —*can* any woman afford to go into the witness-box, to be cross-examined and teased by her own maid, or by a brute of a barrister on her maid's information ? I assure you, Seymour, the thing's not to be dreamt of. There are details of a lady's life— known only to her maid—which *cannot* be made public. Explain as much of this as you think well to Charles, and *make* him understand that *if* he insists upon arresting Césarine, I shall go into the box—and swear my head off to prevent any one of the gang from being convicted. I have told Césarine as much ; I have promised to help her : I have explained that I am her friend, and that if *she'll* stand by *me*, *I'll* stand by *her*, and by this hateful young man of hers.'

I saw in a moment how things went. Neither Charles nor Amelia could face cross-examination on the subject of one of Colonel Clay's accomplices. No doubt, in Amelia's case, it was merely a question of rouge and hair-dye ; but what woman would not sooner confess to a forgery or a murder than to those toilet secrets ?

I returned to Charles, therefore, and spent half an hour in composing, as well as I might, these little domestic difficulties. In the end, it was arranged

that if Charles did his best to protect Césarine from
arrest, Amelia would consent to do her best in return
on behalf of Madame Picardet.

We had next the police to tackle—a more
difficult business.   Still, even *they* were reasonable.
They had caught Colonel Clay, they believed, but
their chance of convicting him depended entirely
upon Charles's identification, with mine to back it.
The more they urged the necessity of arresting the
female confederates, however, the more stoutly did
Charles declare that for his part he could by no
means make sure of Colonel Clay himself, while he
utterly declined to give evidence of any sort against
either of the women.   It was a difficult case, he said,
and he felt far from confident even about the man.
If *his* decision faltered, and he failed to identify, the
case was closed ; no jury could convict with nothing
to convict upon.

At last the police gave way.   No other course
was open to them.   They had made an important
capture ; but they saw that everything depended
upon securing their witnesses, and the witnesses, if
interfered with, were likely to swear to absolutely
nothing.

Indeed, as it turned out, before the preliminary
investigation at Bow Street was completed (with the
usual remands), Charles had been thrown into such
a state of agitation that he wished he had never
caught the Colonel at all.

'I wonder, Sey,' he said to me, 'why I didn't

offer the rascal two thousand a year to go right off
to Australia, and be rid of him for ever! It would
have been cheaper for my reputation than keeping
him about in courts of law in England. The worst
of it is, when once the best of men gets into a
witness-box, there's no saying with what shreds
and tatters of a character he may at last come
out of it!'

'In *your* case, Charles,' I answered, dutifully,
'there can be no such doubt; except, perhaps, as
regards the Craig-Ellachie Consolidated.'

Then came the endless bother of 'getting up the
case' with the police and the lawyers. Charles
would have retired from it altogether by that time,
but, most unfortunately, he was bound over to
prosecute. 'You couldn't take a lump sum to let
me off?' he said, jokingly, to the inspector. But I
knew in my heart it was one of the 'true words
spoken in jest' that the proverb tells of.

Of course we could see now the whole building-
up of the great intrigue. It had been worked out
as carefully as the Tichborne swindle. Young
Finglemore, as the brother of Charles's broker, knew
from the outset all about his affairs; and, after a
gentle course of preliminary roguery, he laid his
plans deep for a campaign against my brother-in-law.
Everything had been deliberately designed beforehand. A place had been found for Césarine as
Amelia's maid—needless to say, by means of forged
testimonials. Through her aid the swindler had

succeeded in learning still more of the family ways and habits, and had acquired a knowledge of certain facts which he proceeded forthwith to use against us. His first attack, as the Seer, had been cleverly designed so as to give us the idea that we were a mere casual prey ; and it did not escape Charles's notice now that the detail of getting Madame Picardet to inquire at the Crédit Marseillais about his bank had been solemnly gone through on purpose to blind us to the obvious truth that Colonel Clay was already in full possession of all such facts about us.   It was by Césarine's aid, again, that he became possessed of Amelia's diamonds, that he received the letter addressed to Lord Craig-Ellachie, and that he managed to dupe us over the Schloss Lebenstein business.   Nevertheless, all these things Charles determined to conceal in court ; he did not give the police a single fact that would turn against either Césarine or Madame Picardet.

As for Césarine, of course, she left the house immediately after the arrest of the Colonel, and we heard of her no more till the day of the trial.

When that great day came, I never saw a more striking sight than the Old Bailey presented.   It was crammed to overflowing.   Charles arrived early, accompanied by his solicitor.   He was so white and troubled that he looked much more like prisoner than prosecutor.   Outside the court a pretty little woman stood, pale and anxious.   A respectful crowd stared at her silently.   'Who is that?' Charles asked.

Though we could both of us guess, rather than see, it was White Heather.

'That's the prisoner's wife,' the inspector on duty

A PRETTY LITTLE WOMAN STOOD, PALE AND ANXIOUS.

replied. 'She's waiting to see him enter. I'm sorry for her, poor thing. She's a perfect lady.'

'So she seems,' Charles answered, scarcely daring to face her.

At that moment she turned.   Her eyes fell upon his.   Charles paused for a second and looked faltering.   There was in those eyes just the faintest gleam of pleading recognition, but not a trace of the old saucy, defiant vivacity.   Charles framed his lips to words, but without uttering a sound.   Unless I greatly mistake, the words he framed on his lips were these : ' I will do my best for him.'

We pushed our way in, assisted by the police. Inside the court we saw a lady seated, in a quiet black dress, with a becoming bonnet.   A moment passed before I knew—it was Césarine.   'Who is —that person ? ' Charles asked once more of the nearest inspector, desiring to see in what way he would describe her.

And once more the answer came, ' That's the prisoner's wife, sir.'

Charles started back, surprised.   ' But—I was told—a lady outside was Mrs. Paul Finglemore,' he broke in, much puzzled.

' Very likely,' the inspector replied, unmoved. ' We have plenty that way.   *When* a gentleman has as many aliases as Colonel Clay, you can hardly expect him to be over particular about having only *one* wife between them, can you ? '

' Ah, I see,' Charles muttered, in a shocked voice. ' Bigamy ! '

The inspector looked stony.   ' Well, not exactly that,' he replied, ' occasional marriage.'

Mr. Justice Rhadamanth tried the case.   ' I'm sorry

it's him, Sey,' my brother-in-law whispered in my ear.
(He said *him*, not *he*, because, whatever else Charles
is, he is *not* a pedant ; the English language as it is
spoken by most edu-
cated men is quite
good enough for his
purpose.) 'I only wish
it had been Sir Edward
Easy. Easy's a man
of the world, and a
man of society ; he
would feel for a person
in *my* position. He
wouldn't allow these
beasts of lawyers to
badger and pester me.
He would back his
order. But Rhada-

THE PRISONER.

manth is one of your modern sort of
judges, who make a merit of being what
they call "conscientious," and won't hush
up anything. I admit I'm afraid of
him. I shall be glad when it's over.'

'Oh, *you'll* pull through all right,' I
said in my capacity of secretary. But
I didn't think it.

The judge took his seat. The prisoner was brought
in. Every eye seemed bent upon him. He was
neatly and plainly dressed, and, rogue though he was,
I must honestly confess he looked at least a gentle-

man. His manner was defiant, not abject like Charles's. He knew he was at bay, and he turned like a man to face his accusers.

We had two or three counts on the charge, and, after some formal business, Sir Charles Vandrift was put into the box to bear witness against Finglemore.

Prisoner was unrepresented. Counsel had been offered him, but he refused their aid. The judge even advised him to accept their help ; but Colonel Clay, as we all called him mentally still, declined to avail himself of the judge's suggestion.

' I am a barrister myself, my lord,' he said—' called some nine years ago. I can conduct my own defence, I venture to think, better than any of these my learned brethren.'

Charles went through his examination-in-chief quite swimmingly. He answered with promptitude. He identified the prisoner without the slightest hesitation as the man who had swindled him under the various disguises of the Reverend Richard Peploe Brabazon, the Honourable David Granton, Count von Lebenstein, Professor Schleiermacher, Dr. Quackenboss, and others. He had not the slightest doubt of the man's identity. He could swear to him anywhere. I thought, for my own part, he was a trifle too cocksure. A certain amount of hesitation would have been better policy. As to the various swindles, he detailed them in full, his evidence to be supplemented by that of bank officials and other subordinates. In short, he left Finglemore not a leg to stand upon.

When it came to the cross-examination, however, matters began to assume quite a different complexion. The prisoner set out by questioning Sir Charles's identifications. Was he sure of his man ?   He handed Charles a photograph. ' Is that the person who represented himself as the Reverend Richard Peploe Brabazon ? ' he asked persuasively.

Charles admitted it without a moment's delay.

Just at that moment, a little parson, whom I had not noticed till then, rose up, unobtrusively, near the middle of the court, where he was seated beside Césarine.

' Look at that gentleman ! ' the prisoner said, waving one hand, and pouncing upon the prosecutor.

Charles turned and looked at the person indicated. His face grew still whiter. It was—to all outer appearance—the Reverend Richard Brabazon *in propriâ personâ*.

Of course I saw the trick. This was the real parson upon whose outer man Colonel Clay had modelled his little curate. But the jury was shaken. And so was Charles for a moment.

' Let the jurors see the photograph,' the judge said, authoritatively. It was passed round the jury-box, and the judge also examined it. We could see at once, by their faces and attitudes, they all re-cognised it as the portrait of the clergyman before them—not of the prisoner in the dock, who stood there smiling blandly at Charles's discomfiture.

The clergyman sat down. At the same moment the prisoner produced a second photograph.

'Now, can you tell me who *that* is?' he asked Charles, in the regular brow-beating Old Bailey voice.

With somewhat more hesitation, Charles answered, after a pause: 'That is yourself as you appeared in London when you came in the disguise of the Graf von Lebenstein.'

This was a crucial point, for the Lebenstein fraud was the one count on which our lawyers relied to prove their case most fully, within the jurisdiction.

Even while Charles spoke, a gentleman whom I had noticed before, sitting beside White Heather, with a handkerchief to his face, rose as abruptly as the parson.   Colonel Clay indicated him with a graceful movement of his hand.   'And *this* gentleman?' he asked calmly.

Charles was fairly staggered.   It was the obvious original of the false Von Lebenstein.

The photograph went round the box once more. The jury smiled incredulously.   Charles had given himself away.   His overweening confidence and certainty had ruined him.

Then Colonel Clay, leaning forward, and looking quite engaging, began a new line of cross-examination. 'We have seen, Sir Charles,' he said, 'that we cannot implicitly trust your identifications.   Now let us see how far we can trust your other evidence.   First, then, about those diamonds.   You tried to buy them, did you not, from a person who represented himself as the Reverend Richard Brabazon, because you believed he thought they were paste ; and if you could, you

would have given him £10 or so for them. *Do* you
think that was honest?'

'I object to this line of cross-examination,' our
leading counsel interposed. 'It does not bear on the
prosecutor's evidence. It is purely recriminatory.'

Colonel Clay was all bland deference. 'I wish,
my lord,' he said, turning round, 'to show that the
prosecutor is a person unworthy of credence in any
way. I desire to proceed upon the well-known legal
maxim of *falsus in uno, falsus in omnibus.* I believe
I am permitted to shake the witness's credit?'

'The prisoner is entirely within his rights,' Rhadamanth answered, looking severely at Charles. 'And
I was wrong in suggesting that he needed the advice
or assistance of counsel.'

Charles wriggled visibly. Colonel Clay perked
up. Bit by bit, with dexterous questions, Charles
was made to acknowledge that he wanted to buy
diamonds at the price of paste, knowing them to be
real; and, a millionaire himself, would gladly have
diddled a poor curate out of a couple of thousand.

'I was entitled to take advantage of my special
knowledge,' Charles murmured feebly.

'Oh, certainly,' the prisoner answered. 'But,
while professing friendship and affection for a clergyman and his wife, in straitened circumstances, you were
prepared, it seems, to take three thousand pounds'
worth of goods off their hands for ten pounds, if you
could have got them at that price. Is not that so?'

Charles was compelled to admit it.

The prisoner went on to the David Granton incident. 'When you offered to amalgamate with Lord Craig-Ellachie,' he asked, 'had you or had you not heard that a gold-bearing reef ran straight from your concession into Lord Craig-Ellachie's, and that his portion

UNWILLINGLY, SHAMEFACEDLY, CHARLES WAS
COMPELLED TO CONFESS.

of the reef was by far the larger and more important?'

Charles wriggled again, and our counsel interposed; but Rhadamanth was adamant. Charles had to allow it.

And so, too, with the incident of the Slump in Golcondas. Unwillingly, shamefacedly, by torturing steps, Charles was compelled to confess that he had

sold out Golcondas — he, the Chairman of the
company, after repeated declarations to shareholders
and others that he would do no such thing—because
he thought Professor Schleiermacher had made
diamonds worthless.   He had endeavoured to save
himself by ruining his company.   Charles tried to
brazen it out with remarks to the effect that business
was business.   'And fraud is fraud,' Rhadamanth
added, in his pungent way.

'A man must protect himself,' Charles burst out.

'At the expense of those who have put their trust in
his honour and integrity,' the judge commented coldly.

After four mortal hours of it, all to the same
effect, my respected brother-in-law left the witness-
box at last, wiping his brow and biting his lip, with
the very air of a culprit.   His character had received
a most serious blow.   While he stood in the witness-
box all the world had felt it was *he* who was the accused
and Colonel Clay who was the prosecutor.   He was
convicted on his own evidence of having tried to
induce the supposed David Granton to sell his
father's interests into an enemy's hands, and of
every other shady trick into which his well-known
business acuteness had unfortunately hurried him
during the course of his adventures.   I had but one
consolation in my brother-in-law's misfortunes—and
that was the thought that a due sense of his own short-
comings might possibly make him more lenient in
the end to the trivial misdemeanours of a poor beggar
of a secretary !

I was the next in the box. I do not desire to enlarge upon my own achievements. I will draw a decent veil, indeed, over the painful scene that ensued when I finished my evidence. I can only say I was more cautious than Charles in my recognition of the photographs; but I found myself particularly worried and harried over other parts of my cross-examination. Especially was I shaken about that misguided step I took in the matter of the cheque for the Lebenstein commission—a cheque which Colonel Clay handed to me with the utmost politeness, requesting to know whether or not it bore my signature. I caught Charles's eye at the end of the episode, and I venture to say the expression it wore was one of relief that I too had tripped over a trifling question of ten per cent on the purchase money of the castle.

Altogether, I must admit, if it had not been for the police evidence, we would have failed to make a case against our man at all. But the police, I confess, had got up their part of the prosecution admirably. Now that they knew Colonel Clay to be really Paul Finglemore, they showed with great cleverness how Paul Finglemore's disappearances and reappearances in London exactly tallied with Colonel Clay's appearances and disappearances elsewhere, under the guise of the little curate, the Seer, David Granton, and the rest of them. Furthermore, they showed experimentally how the prisoner at the bar might have got himself up in the various characters ; and, by means of a wax bust, modelled by Dr. Beddersley from observations at Bow Street, and aided by additions in the gutta-percha composition after Dolly Lingfield's photographs, they succeeded in proving that the face as it stood could be readily transformed

MODELLED BY DR. BEDDERSLEY.

into the faces of Medhurst and David Granton. Altogether, their cleverness and trained acumen made up on the whole for Charles's over-certainty, and they succeeded in putting before the jury a strong case of their own against Paul Finglemore.

The trial occupied three days. After the first of the three, my respected brother-in-law preferred, as

he said, not to prejudice the case against the prisoner
by appearing in court again. He did not even
allude to the little matter of the ten per cent commission further than to say at dinner that evening
that all men were bound to protect their own interests
—as secretaries or as principals. This I took for
forgiveness ; and I continued diligently to attend
the trial, and watch the case in my employer's
interest.

The defence was ingenious, even if somewhat
halting. It consisted simply of an attempt to prove
throughout that Charles and I had made our prisoner
the victim of a mistaken identity. Finglemore put
into the box the ingenuous original of the little
curate—the Reverend Septimus Porkington, as it
turned out, a friend of his family ; and he showed
that it was the Reverend Septimus himself who had
sat to a photographer in Baker Street for the portrait
which Charles too hastily identified as that of
Colonel Clay in his personification of Mr. Richard
Brabazon. He further elicited the fact that the
portrait of the Count von Lebenstein was really taken
from Dr. Julius Keppel, a Tyrolese music-master,
residing at Balham, whom he put into the box, and
who was well known, as it chanced, to the foreman
of the jury. Gradually he made it clear to us that
no portraits existed of Colonel Clay at all, except
Dolly Lingfield's—so it dawned upon me by degrees
that even Dr. Beddersley could only have been misled
if we had succeeded in finding for him the alleged

photographs of Colonel Clay as the count and the
curate, which had been shown us by Medhurst.
Altogether, the prisoner based his defence upon the
fact that no more than two witnesses directly
identified him ; while one of those two had positively
sworn that he recognised as the prisoner's two
portraits which turned out, by independent evidence,
to be taken from other people !

The judge summed up in a caustic way which
was pleasant to neither party. He asked the jury to
dismiss from their minds entirely the impression
created by what he frankly described as ' Sir Charles
Vandrift's obvious dishonesty.'   They must not allow
the fact that he was a millionaire—and a particularly
shady one—to prejudice their feelings in favour of
the prisoner. Even the richest—and vilest—of men
must be protected. Besides, this was a public
question. If a rogue cheated a rogue, he must still
be punished. If a murderer stabbed or shot a
murderer, he must still be hung for it. Society must
see that the worst of thieves were not preyed upon
by others. Therefore, the proved facts that Sir
Charles Vandrift, with all his millions, had meanly
tried to cheat the prisoner, or some other poor
person, out of valuable diamonds—had basely tried
to juggle Lord Craig-Ellachie's mines into his own
hands—had vilely tried to bribe a son to betray his
father—had directly tried, by underhand means, to
save his own money, at the risk of destroying the
wealth of others who trusted to his probity—these

proved facts must not blind them to the truth that the prisoner at the bar (if he were really Colonel Clay) was an abandoned swindler. To that point alone they must confine their attention ; and *if* they were convinced that the prisoner was shown to be the self-same man who appeared on various occasions as David Granton, as Von Lebenstein, as Medhurst, as Schleiermacher, they must find him guilty.

As to that point, also, the judge commented on the obvious strength of the police case, and the fact that the prisoner had not attempted in any one out of so many instances to prove an *alibi*. Surely, if he were *not* Colonel Clay, the jury should ask themselves, must it not have been simple and easy for him to do so? Finally, the judge summed up all the elements of doubt in the identification—and all the elements of probability ; and left it to the jury to draw their own conclusions.

They retired at the end to consider their verdict. While they were absent every eye in court was fixed on the prisoner. But Paul Finglemore himself looked steadily towards the further end of the hall, where two pale-faced women sat together, with handkerchiefs in their hands, and eyes red with weeping.

Only then, as he stood there, awaiting the verdict, with a fixed white face, prepared for everything, did I begin to realise with what courage and pluck that one lone man had sustained so long an unequal contest against wealth, authority, and all the Governments of Europe, aided but by his own skill and two feeble women! Only then did I feel he had played his reckless game through all those years with *this* ever before him! I found it hard to picture.

The jury filed slowly back. There was dead silence in court as the clerk put the question, 'Do you find the prisoner at the bar guilty or not guilty?'

'We find him guilty.'

THE JURY FILED SLOWLY BACK.

'On all the counts?'

'On all the counts of the indictment.'

The women at the back burst into tears, unanimously.

Mr. Justice Rhadamanth addressed the prisoner. 'Have you anything to urge,' he asked in a very stern tone, 'in mitigation of whatever sentence the Court may see fit to pass upon you?'

'Nothing,' the prisoner answered, just faltering slightly. 'I have brought it upon myself—but—I

have protected the lives of those nearest and dearest
to me. I have fought hard for my own hand. I
admit· my crime, and will face my punishment. I
only regret that, since we were both of us rogues—
myself and the prosecutor—the lesser rogue should
have stood here in the dock, and the greater in the
witness-box. Our country takes care to decorate
each according to his deserts—to him, the Grand
Cross of St. Michael and St. George ; to me, the
Broad Arrow ! '

The judge gazed at him severely. ' Paul Finglemore,' he said, passing sentence in his sardonic way,
' you have chosen to dedicate to the service of fraud
abilities and attainments which, if turned from the
outset into a legitimate channel, would no doubt
have sufficed to secure you without excessive effort
a subsistence one degree above starvation—possibly
even, with good luck, a sordid and squalid competence. You have preferred to embark them on a
lawless life of vice and crime—and I will not deny
that you seem to have had a good run for your
money. Society, however, whose mouthpiece I am,
cannot allow you any longer to mock it with im-
punity. You have broken its laws openly, and you
have been found out.' He assumed the tone of
bland condescension which always heralds his
severest moments. ' I sentence you to Fourteen
Years' Imprisonment, with Hard Labour.'

The prisoner bowed, without losing his apparent
composure. But his eyes strayed away again to the

far end of the hall, where the two weeping women, with a sudden sharp cry, fell at once in a faint on one another's shoulders, and were with difficulty removed from court by the ushers.

As we left the room, I heard but one comment all round, thus voiced by a school-boy: 'I'd a jolly sight rather it had been old Vandrift. This Clay chap's too clever by half to waste on a prison!'

But he went there, none the less—in that 'cool sequestered vale of life' to recover equilibrium; though I myself half regretted it.

I will add but one more little parting episode.

When all was over, Charles rushed off to Cannes, to get away from the impertinent stare of London. Amelia and Isabel and I went with him. We were driving one afternoon on the hills beyond the town, among the myrtle and lentisk scrub, when we noticed in front of us a nice victoria, containing two ladies in very deep mourning. We followed it, unintentionally, as far as Le Grand Pin—that big pine tree that looks across the bay towards Antibes. There, the ladies descended and sat down on a knoll, gazing out disconsolately towards the sea and the islands. It was evident they were suffering very deep grief. Their faces were pale and their eyes bloodshot. 'Poor things!' Amelia said. Then her tone altered suddenly.

'Why, good gracious,' she cried, 'if it isn't Césarine!'

So it was—with White Heather!

Charles got down and drew near them. ' I beg your pardon,' he said, raising his hat, and addressing Madame Picardet : ' I believe I have had the pleasure of meeting you. And since I have doubtless paid in the end for your victoria, *may* I venture to inquire for whom you are in mourning ? '

White Heather drew back, sobbing ; but Césarine turned to him, fiery red, with the mien of a lady. ' For *him !* ' she answered ; ' for Paul ! for our king, whom *you* have imprisoned ! As long as *he* remains there, we have both of us decided to wear mourning for ever ! '

Charles raised his hat again, and drew back without one word. He waved his hand to Amelia and walked home with me to Cannes. He seemed deeply dejected.

' A penny for your thoughts ! ' I exclaimed, at last, in a jocular tone, trying feebly to rouse him.

He turned to me, and sighed. ' I was wondering,' he answered, ' if *I* had gone to prison, would Amelia and Isabel have done as much for me ? '

For myself, I did *not* wonder. I knew pretty well. For Charles, you will admit, though the bigger rogue of the two, is scarcely the kind of rogue to inspire a woman with profound affection.

A CATALOGUE OF
SELECTED DOVER BOOKS
IN ALL FIELDS OF INTEREST

A CATALOGUE OF SELECTED DOVER
BOOKS IN ALL FIELDS OF INTEREST

RACKHAM'S COLOR ILLUSTRATIONS FOR WAGNER'S RING. Rackham's finest mature work—all 64 full-color watercolors in a faithful and lush interpretation of the *Ring*. Full-sized plates on coated stock of the paintings used by opera companies for authentic staging of Wagner. Captions aid in following complete Ring cycle. Introduction. 64 illustrations plus vignettes. 72pp. 8⅝ x 11¼.   23779-6 Pa. $6.00

CONTEMPORARY POLISH POSTERS IN FULL COLOR, edited by Joseph Czestochowski. 46 full-color examples of brilliant school of Polish graphic design, selected from world's first museum (near Warsaw) dedicated to poster art. Posters on circuses, films, plays, concerts all show cosmopolitan influences, free imagination. Introduction. 48pp. 9⅜ x 12¼.
                                                        23780-X Pa. $6.00

GRAPHIC WORKS OF EDVARD MUNCH, Edvard Munch. 90 haunting, evocative prints by first major Expressionist artist and one of the greatest graphic artists of his time: *The Scream, Anxiety, Death Chamber, The Kiss, Madonna,* etc. Introduction by Alfred Werner. 90pp. 9 x 12.
                                                        23765-6 Pa. $5.00

THE GOLDEN AGE OF THE POSTER, Hayward and Blanche Cirker. 70 extraordinary posters in full colors, from Maitres de l'Affiche, Mucha, Lautrec, Bradley, Cheret, Beardsley, many others. Total of 78pp. 9⅜ x 12¼.   22753-7 Pa. $5.95

THE NOTEBOOKS OF LEONARDO DA VINCI, edited by J. P. Richter. Extracts from manuscripts reveal great genius; on painting, sculpture, anatomy, sciences, geography, etc. Both Italian and English. 186 ms. pages reproduced, plus 500 additional drawings, including studies for *Last Supper,* Sforza monument, etc. 860pp. 7⅞ x 10¾. (Available in U.S. only)
                                    22572-0, 22573-9 Pa., Two-vol. set $15.90

THE CODEX NUTTALL, as first edited by Zelia Nuttall. Only inexpensive edition, in full color, of a pre-Columbian Mexican (Mixtec) book. 88 color plates show kings, gods, heroes, temples, sacrifices. New explanatory, historical introduction by Arthur G. Miller. 96pp. 11⅜ x 8½. (Available in U.S. only)   23168-2 Pa. $7.95

UNE SEMAINE DE BONTÉ, A SURREALISTIC NOVEL IN COLLAGE, Max Ernst. Masterpiece created out of 19th-century periodical illustrations, explores worlds of terror and surprise. Some consider this Ernst's greatest work. 208pp. 8⅛ x 11.   23252-2 Pa. $5.00

THE AMERICAN SENATOR, Anthony Trollope. Little known, long un-available Trollope novel on a grand scale. Here are humorous comment on American vs. English culture, and stunning portrayal of a heroine/villainess. Superb evocation of Victorian village life. 561pp. 5⅜ x 8½.
23801-6 Pa. $6.00

WAS IT MURDER? James Hilton. The author of *Lost Horizon* and *Good-bye, Mr. Chips* wrote one detective novel (under a pen-name) which was quickly forgotten and virtually lost, even at the height of Hilton's fame. This edition brings it back—a finely crafted public school puzzle resplendent with Hilton's stylish atmosphere. A thoroughly English thriller by the creator of Shangri-la. 252pp. 5⅜ x 8. (Available in U.S. only)
23774-5 Pa. $3.00

CENTRAL PARK: A PHOTOGRAPHIC GUIDE, Victor Laredo and Henry Hope Reed. 121 superb photographs show dramatic views of Central Park: Bethesda Fountain, Cleopatra's Needle, Sheep Meadow, the Blockhouse, plus people engaged in many park activities: ice skating, bike riding, etc. Captions by former Curator of Central Park, Henry Hope Reed, provide historical view, changes, etc. Also photos of N.Y. landmarks on park's periphery. 96pp. 8½ x 11. 23750-8 Pa. $4.50

NANTUCKET IN THE NINETEENTH CENTURY, Clay Lancaster. 180 rare photographs, stereographs, maps, drawings and floor plans recreate unique American island society. Authentic scenes of shipwreck, light-houses, streets, homes are arranged in geographic sequence to provide walking-tour guide to old Nantucket existing today. Introduction, captions. 160pp. 8⅞ x 11¾. 23747-8 Pa. $6.95

STONE AND MAN: A PHOTOGRAPHIC EXPLORATION, Andreas Feininger. 106 photographs by *Life* photographer Feininger portray man's deep passion for stone through the ages. Stonehenge-like megaliths, fortified towns, sculpted marble and crumbling tenements show textures, beauties, fascination. 128pp. 9¼ x 10¾. 23756-7 Pa. $5.95

CIRCLES, A MATHEMATICAL VIEW, D. Pedoe. Fundamental aspects of college geometry, non-Euclidean geometry, and other branches of mathematics: representing circle by point. Poincare model, isoperimetric property, etc. Stimulating recreational reading. 66 figures. 96pp. 5⅜ x 8¼.
63698-4 Pa. $2.75

THE DISCOVERY OF NEPTUNE, Morton Grosser. Dramatic scientific history of the investigations leading up to the actual discovery of the eighth planet of our solar system. Lucid, well-researched book by well-known historian of science. 172pp. 5⅜ x 8½. 23726-5 Pa. $3.00

THE DEVIL'S DICTIONARY. Ambrose Bierce. Barbed, bitter, brilliant witticisms in the form of a dictionary. Best, most ferocious satire America has produced. 145pp. 5⅜ x 8½. 20487-1 Pa. $2.00

HOUSEHOLD STORIES BY THE BROTHERS GRIMM. All the great Grimm stories: "Rumpelstiltskin," "Snow White," "Hansel and Gretel," etc., with 114 illustrations by Walter Crane. 269pp. 5⅜ x 8½.
21080-4 Pa. $3.00

SLEEPING BEAUTY, illustrated by Arthur Rackham. Perhaps the fullest, most delightful version ever, told by C. S. Evans. Rackham's best work. 49 illustrations. 110pp. 7⅞ x 10¾.
22756-1 Pa. $2.50

AMERICAN FAIRY TALES, L. Frank Baum. Young cowboy lassoes Father Time; dummy in Mr. Floman's department store window comes to life; and 10 other fairy tales. 41 illustrations by N. P. Hall, Harry Kennedy, Ike Morgan, and Ralph Gardner. 209pp. 5⅜ x 8½.
23643-9 Pa. $3.00

THE WONDERFUL WIZARD OF OZ, L. Frank Baum. Facsimile in full color of America's finest children's classic. Introduction by Martin Gardner. 143 illustrations by W. W. Denslow. 267pp. 5⅜ x 8½.
20691-2 Pa. $3.50

THE TALE OF PETER RABBIT, Beatrix Potter. The inimitable Peter's terrifying adventure in Mr. McGregor's garden, with all 27 wonderful, full-color Potter illustrations. 55pp. 4¼ x 5½. (Available in U.S. only)
22827-4 Pa. $1.25

THE STORY OF KING ARTHUR AND HIS KNIGHTS, Howard Pyle. Finest children's version of life of King Arthur. 48 illustrations by Pyle. 131pp. 6⅛ x 9¼.
21445-1 Pa. $4.95

CARUSO'S CARICATURES, Enrico Caruso. Great tenor's remarkable caricatures of self, fellow musicians, composers, others. Toscanini, Puccini, Farrar, etc. Impish, cutting, insightful. 473 illustrations. Preface by M. Sisca. 217pp. 8⅜ x 11¼.
23528-9 Pa. $6.95

PERSONAL NARRATIVE OF A PILGRIMAGE TO ALMADINAH AND MECCAH, Richard Burton. Great travel classic by remarkably colorful personality. Burton, disguised as a Moroccan, visited sacred shrines of Islam, narrowly escaping death. Wonderful observations of Islamic life, customs, personalities. 47 illustrations. Total of 959pp. 5⅜ x 8½.
21217-3, 21218-1 Pa., Two-vol. set $12.00

INCIDENTS OF TRAVEL IN YUCATAN, John L. Stephens. Classic (1843) exploration of jungles of Yucatan, looking for evidences of Maya civilization. Travel adventures, Mexican and Indian culture, etc. Total of 669pp. 5⅜ x 8½.
20926-1, 20927-X Pa., Two-vol. set $7.90

AMERICAN LITERARY AUTOGRAPHS FROM WASHINGTON IRVING TO HENRY JAMES, Herbert Cahoon, et al. Letters, poems, manuscripts of Hawthorne, Thoreau, Twain, Alcott, Whitman, 67 other prominent American authors. Reproductions, full transcripts and commentary. Plus checklist of all American Literary Autographs in The Pierpont Morgan Library. Printed on exceptionally high-quality paper. 136 illustrations. 212pp. 9⅛ x 12¼.
23548-3 Pa. $7.95

UNCLE SILAS, J. Sheridan LeFanu. Victorian Gothic mystery novel, considered by many best of period, even better than Collins or Dickens. Wonderful psychological terror. Introduction by Frederick Shroyer. 436pp. 5⅜ x 8½.   21715-9 Pa. $6.00

JURGEN, James Branch Cabell. The great erotic fantasy of the 1920's that delighted thousands, shocked thousands more. Full final text, Lane edition with 13 plates by Frank Pape. 346pp. 5⅜ x 8½.
                                                                     23507-6 Pa. $4.50

THE CLAVERINGS, Anthony Trollope. Major novel, chronicling aspects of British Victorian society, personalities. Reprint of Cornhill serialization, 16 plates by M. Edwards; first reprint of full text. Introduction by Norman Donaldson. 412pp. 5⅜ x 8½.   23464-9 Pa. $5.00

KEPT IN THE DARK, Anthony Trollope. Unusual short novel about Victorian morality and abnormal psychology by the great English author. Probably the first American publication. Frontispiece by Sir John Millais. 92pp. 6½ x 9¼.   23609-9 Pa. $2.50

RALPH THE HEIR, Anthony Trollope. Forgotten tale of illegitimacy, inheritance. Master novel of Trollope's later years. Victorian country estates, clubs, Parliament, fox hunting, world of fully realized characters. Reprint of 1871 edition. 12 illustrations by F. A. Faser. 434pp. of text. 5⅜ x 8½.   23642-0 Pa. $5.00

YEKL and THE IMPORTED BRIDEGROOM AND OTHER STORIES OF THE NEW YORK GHETTO, Abraham Cahan. Film *Hester Street* based on *Yekl* (1896). Novel, other stories among first about Jewish immigrants of N.Y.'s East Side. Highly praised by W. D. Howells—Cahan "a new star of realism." New introduction by Bernard G. Richards. 240pp. 5⅜ x 8½.   22427-9 Pa. $3.50

THE HIGH PLACE, James Branch Cabell. Great fantasy writer's enchanting comedy of disenchantment set in 18th-century France. Considered by some critics to be even better than his famous *Jurgen*. 10 illustrations and numerous vignettes by noted fantasy artist Frank C. Pape. 320pp. 5⅜ x 8½.   23670-6 Pa. $4.00

ALICE'S ADVENTURES UNDER GROUND, Lewis Carroll. Facsimile of ms. Carroll gave Alice Liddell in 1864. Different in many ways from final Alice. Handlettered, illustrated by Carroll. Introduction by Martin Gardner. 128pp. 5⅜ x 8½.   21482-6 Pa. $2.00

FAVORITE ANDREW LANG FAIRY TALE BOOKS IN MANY COLORS, Andrew Lang. The four Lang favorites in a boxed set—the complete *Red, Green, Yellow* and *Blue* Fairy Books. 164 stories; 439 illustrations by Lancelot Speed, Henry Ford and G. P. Jacomb Hood. Total of about 1500pp. 5⅜ x 8½.   23407-X Boxed set, Pa. $14.95

THE EARLY WORK OF AUBREY BEARDSLEY, Aubrey Beardsley. 157 plates, 2 in color: *Manon Lescaut, Madame Bovary, Morte Darthur, Salome,* other. Introduction by H. Marillier. 182pp. 8⅛ x 11. 21816-3 Pa. $4.50

THE LATER WORK OF AUBREY BEARDSLEY, Aubrey Beardsley. Exotic masterpieces of full maturity: *Venus and Tannhauser, Lysistrata, Rape of the Lock, Volpone,* Savoy material, etc. 174 plates, 2 in color. 186pp. 8⅛ x 11. 21817-1 Pa. $4.50

THOMAS NAST'S CHRISTMAS DRAWINGS, Thomas Nast. Almost all Christmas drawings by creator of image of Santa Claus as we know it, and one of America's foremost illustrators and political cartoonists. 66 illustrations. 3 illustrations in color on covers. 96pp. 8⅜ x 11¼.
23660-9 Pa. $3.50

THE DORÉ ILLUSTRATIONS FOR DANTE'S DIVINE COMEDY, Gustave Doré. All 135 plates from Inferno, Purgatory, Paradise; fantastic tortures, infernal landscapes, celestial wonders. Each plate with appropriate (translated) verses. 141pp. 9 x 12. 23231-X Pa. $4.50

DORÉ'S ILLUSTRATIONS FOR RABELAIS, Gustave Doré. 252 striking illustrations of *Gargantua and Pantagruel* books by foremost 19th-century illustrator. Including 60 plates, 192 delightful smaller illustrations. 153pp. 9 x 12. 23656-0 Pa. $5.00

LONDON: A PILGRIMAGE, Gustave Doré, Blanchard Jerrold. Squalor, riches, misery, beauty of mid-Victorian metropolis; 55 wonderful plates, 125 other illustrations, full social, cultural text by Jerrold. 191pp. of text. 9⅜ x 12¼. 22306-X Pa. $6.00

THE RIME OF THE ANCIENT MARINER, Gustave Doré, S. T. Coleridge. Dore's finest work, 34 plates capture moods, subtleties of poem. Full text. Introduction by Millicent Rose. 77pp. 9¼ x 12. 22305-1 Pa. $3.50

THE DORE BIBLE ILLUSTRATIONS, Gustave Doré. All wonderful, detailed plates: Adam and Eve, Flood, Babylon, Life of Jesus, etc. Brief King James text with each plate. Introduction by Millicent Rose. 241 plates. 241pp. 9 x 12. 23004-X Pa. $6.00

THE COMPLETE ENGRAVINGS, ETCHINGS AND DRYPOINTS OF ALBRECHT DURER. "Knight, Death and Devil"; "Melencolia," and more—all Dürer's known works in all three media, including 6 works formerly attributed to him. 120 plates. 235pp. 8⅜ x 11¼.
22851-7 Pa. $6.50

MAXIMILIAN'S TRIUMPHAL ARCH, Albrecht Dürer and others. Incredible monument of woodcut art: 8 foot high elaborate arch—heraldic figures, humans, battle scenes, fantastic elements—that you can assemble yourself. Printed on one side, layout for assembly. 143pp. 11 x 16.
21451-6 Pa. $5.00

AN AUTOBIOGRAPHY, Margaret Sanger. Exciting personal account of hard-fought battle for woman's right to birth control, against prejudice, church, law. Foremost feminist document. 504pp. 5⅜ x 8½.

20470-7 Pa. $5.50

MY BONDAGE AND MY FREEDOM, Frederick Douglass. Born as a slave, Douglass became outspoken force in antislavery movement. The best of Douglass's autobiographies. Graphic description of slave life. Introduction by P. Foner. 464pp. 5⅜ x 8½. 22457-0 Pa. $5.50

LIVING MY LIFE, Emma Goldman. Candid, no holds barred account by foremost American anarchist: her own life, anarchist movement, famous contemporaries, ideas and their impact. Struggles and confrontations in America, plus deportation to U.S.S.R. Shocking inside account of persecution of anarchists under Lenin. 13 plates. Total of 944pp. 5⅜ x 8½.

22543-7, 22544-5 Pa., Two-vol. set $11.00

LETTERS AND NOTES ON THE MANNERS, CUSTOMS AND CONDITIONS OF THE NORTH AMERICAN INDIANS, George Catlin. Classic account of life among Plains Indians: ceremonies, hunt, warfare, etc. Dover edition reproduces for first time all original paintings. 312 plates. 572pp. of text. 6⅛ x 9¼. 22118-0, 22119-9 Pa.. Two-vol. set $11.50

THE MAYA AND THEIR NEIGHBORS, edited by Clarence L. Hay, others. Synoptic view of Maya civilization in broadest sense, together with Northern, Southern neighbors. Integrates much background, valuable detail not elsewhere. Prepared by greatest scholars: Kroeber, Morley, Thompson, Spinden, Vaillant, many others. Sometimes called Tozzer Memorial Volume. 60 illustrations, linguistic map. 634pp. 5⅜ x 8½.

23510-6 Pa. $7.50

HANDBOOK OF THE INDIANS OF CALIFORNIA, A. L. Kroeber. Foremost American anthropologist offers complete ethnographic study of each group. Monumental classic. 459 illustrations, maps. 995pp. 5⅜ x 8½.

23368-5 Pa. $10.00

SHAKTI AND SHAKTA, Arthur Avalon. First book to give clear, cohesive analysis of Shakta doctrine, Shakta ritual and Kundalini Shakti (yoga). Important work by one of world's foremost students of Shaktic and Tantric thought. 732pp. 5⅜ x 8½. (Available in U.S. only)

23645-5 Pa. $7.95

AN INTRODUCTION TO THE STUDY OF THE MAYA HIEROGLYPHS, Syvanus Griswold Morley. Classic study by one of the truly great figures in hieroglyph research. Still the best introduction for the student for reading Maya hieroglyphs. New introduction by J. Eric S. Thompson. 117 illustrations. 284pp. 5⅜ x 8½. 23108-9 Pa. $4.00

A STUDY OF MAYA ART, Herbert J. Spinden. Landmark classic interprets Maya symbolism, estimates styles, covers ceramics, architecture, murals, stone carvings as artforms. Still a basic book in area. New introduction by J. Eric Thompson. Over 750 illustrations. 341pp. 8⅜ x 11¼.

21235-1 Pa. $6.95

THE DEPRESSION YEARS AS PHOTOGRAPHED BY ARTHUR ROTH-STEIN, Arthur Rothstein. First collection devoted entirely to the work of outstanding 1930s photographer: famous dust storm photo, ragged children, unemployed, etc. 120 photographs. Captions. 119pp. 9¼ x 10¾.
23590-4 Pa. $5.00

CAMERA WORK: A PICTORIAL GUIDE, Alfred Stieglitz. All 559 illustrations and plates from the most important periodical in the history of art photography, *Camera Work* (1903-17). Presented four to a page, reduced in size but still clear, in strict chronological order, with complete captions. Three indexes. Glossary. Bibliography. 176pp. 8⅜ x 11¼.
23591-2 Pa. $6.95

ALVIN LANGDON COBURN, PHOTOGRAPHER, Alvin L. Coburn. Revealing autobiography by one of greatest photographers of 20th century gives insider's version of Photo-Secession, plus comments on his own work. 77 photographs by Coburn. Edited by Helmut and Alison Gernsheim. 160pp. 8⅛ x 11.
23685-4 Pa. $6.00

NEW YORK IN THE FORTIES, Andreas Feininger. 162 brilliant photographs by the well-known photographer, formerly with *Life* magazine, show commuters, shoppers, Times Square at night, Harlem nightclub, Lower East Side, etc. Introduction and full captions by John von Hartz. 181pp. 9¼ x 10¾.
23585-8 Pa. $6.00

GREAT NEWS PHOTOS AND THE STORIES BEHIND THEM, John Faber. Dramatic volume of 140 great news photos, 1855 through 1976, and revealing stories behind them, with both historical and technical information. Hindenburg disaster, shooting of Oswald, nomination of Jimmy Carter, etc. 160pp. 8¼ x 11.
23667-6 Pa. $5.00

THE ART OF THE CINEMATOGRAPHER, Leonard Maltin. Survey of American cinematography history and anecdotal interviews with 5 masters—Arthur Miller, Hal Mohr, Hal Rosson, Lucien Ballard, and Conrad Hall. Very large selection of behind-the-scenes production photos. 105 photographs. Filmographies. Index. Originally *Behind the Camera.* 144pp. 8¼ x 11.
23686-2 Pa. $5.00

DESIGNS FOR THE THREE-CORNERED HAT (LE TRICORNE), Pablo Picasso. 32 fabulously rare drawings—including 31 color illustrations of costumes and accessories—for 1919 production of famous ballet. Edited by Parmenia Migel, who has written new introduction. 48pp. 9⅜ x 12¼. (Available in U.S. only)
23709-5 Pa. $5.00

NOTES OF A FILM DIRECTOR, Sergei Eisenstein. Greatest Russian filmmaker explains montage, making of *Alexander Nevsky*, aesthetics; comments on self, associates, great rivals (Chaplin), similar material. 78 illustrations. 240pp. 5⅜ x 8½.
22392-2 Pa. $4.50

SECOND PIATIGORSKY CUP, edited by Isaac Kashdan. One of the greatest tournament books ever produced in the English language. All 90 games of the 1966 tournament, annotated by players, most annotated by both players. Features Petrosian, Spassky, Fischer, Larsen, six others. 228pp. 5⅜ x 8½. 23572-6 Pa. $3.50

ENCYCLOPEDIA OF CARD TRICKS, revised and edited by Jean Hugard. How to perform over 600 card tricks, devised by the world's greatest magicians: impromptus, spelling tricks, key cards, using special packs, much, much more. Additional chapter on card technique. 66 illustrations. 402pp. 5⅜ x 8½. (Available in U.S. only) 21252-1 Pa. $3.95

MAGIC: STAGE ILLUSIONS, SPECIAL EFFECTS AND TRICK PHOTOGRAPHY, Albert A. Hopkins, Henry R. Evans. One of the great classics; fullest, most authorative explanation of vanishing lady, levitations, scores of other great stage effects. Also small magic, automata, stunts. 446 illustrations. 556pp. 5⅜ x 8½. 23344-8 Pa. $6.95

THE SECRETS OF HOUDINI, J. C. Cannell. Classic study of Houdini's incredible magic, exposing closely-kept professional secrets and revealing, in general terms, the whole art of stage magic. 67 illustrations. 279pp. 5⅜ x 8½. 22913-0 Pa. $3.00

HOFFMANN'S MODERN MAGIC, Professor Hoffmann. One of the best, and best-known, magicians' manuals of the past century. Hundreds of tricks from card tricks and simple sleight of hand to elaborate illusions involving construction of complicated machinery. 332 illustrations. 563pp. 5⅜ x 8½. 23623-4 Pa. $6.00

MADAME PRUNIER'S FISH COOKERY BOOK, Mme. S. B. Prunier. More than 1000 recipes from world famous Prunier's of Paris and London, specially adapted here for American kitchen. Grilled tournedos with anchovy butter, Lobster a la Bordelaise, Prunier's prized desserts, more. Glossary. 340pp. 5⅜ x 8½. (Available in U.S. only) 22679-4 Pa. $3.00

FRENCH COUNTRY COOKING FOR AMERICANS, Louis Diat. 500 easy-to-make, authentic provincial recipes compiled by former head chef at New York's Fitz-Carlton Hotel: onion soup, lamb stew, potato pie, more. 309pp. 5⅜ x 8½. 23665-X Pa. $3.95

SAUCES, FRENCH AND FAMOUS, Louis Diat. Complete book gives over 200 specific recipes: bechamel, Bordelaise, hollandaise, Cumberland, apricot, etc. Author was one of this century's finest chefs, originator of vichyssoise and many other dishes. Index. 156pp. 5⅜ x 8.
23663-3 Pa. $2.50

TOLL HOUSE TRIED AND TRUE RECIPES, Ruth Graves Wakefield. Authentic recipes from the famous Mass. restaurant: popovers, veal and ham loaf, Toll House baked beans, chocolate cake crumb pudding, much more. Many helpful hints. Nearly 700 recipes. Index. 376pp. 5⅜ x 8½.
23560-2 Pa. $4.50

THE COMPLETE BOOK OF DOLL MAKING AND COLLECTING, Catherine Christopher. Instructions, patterns for dozens of dolls, from rag doll on up to elaborate, historically accurate figures. Mould faces, sew clothing, make doll houses, etc. Also collecting information. Many illustrations. 288pp. 6 x 9. 22066-4 Pa. $4.50

THE DAGUERREOTYPE IN AMERICA, Beaumont Newhall. Wonderful portraits, 1850's townscapes, landscapes; full text plus 104 photographs. The basic book. Enlarged 1976 edition. 272pp. 8¼ x 11¼. 23322-7 Pa. $7.95

CRAFTSMAN HOMES, Gustav Stickley. 296 architectural drawings, floor plans, and photographs illustrate 40 different kinds of "Mission-style" homes from The Craftsman (1901-16), voice of American style of simplicity and organic harmony. Thorough coverage of Craftsman idea in text and picture, now collector's item. 224pp. 8⅛ x 11. 23791-5 Pa. $6.00

PEWTER-WORKING: INSTRUCTIONS AND PROJECTS, Burl N. Osborn. & Gordon O. Wilber. Introduction to pewter-working for amateur craftsman. History and characteristics of pewter; tools, materials, step-by-step instructions. Photos, line drawings, diagrams. Total of 160pp. 7⅞ x 10¾. 23786-9 Pa. $3.50

THE GREAT CHICAGO FIRE, edited by David Lowe. 10 dramatic, eyewitness accounts of the 1871 disaster, including one of the aftermath and rebuilding, plus 70 contemporary photographs and illustrations of the ruins—courthouse, Palmer House, Great Central Depot, etc. Introduction by David Lowe. 87pp. 8¼ x 11. 23771-0 Pa. $4.00

SILHOUETTES: A PICTORIAL ARCHIVE OF VARIED ILLUSTRATIONS, edited by Carol Belanger Grafton. Over 600 silhouettes from the 18th to 20th centuries include profiles and full figures of men and women, children, birds and animals, groups and scenes, nature, ships, an alphabet. Dozens of uses for commercial artists and craftspeople. 144pp. 8⅜ x 11¼. 23781-8 Pa. $4.00

ANIMALS: 1,419 COPYRIGHT-FREE ILLUSTRATIONS OF MAMMALS, BIRDS, FISH, INSECTS, ETC., edited by Jim Harter. Clear wood engravings present, in extremely lifelike poses, over 1,000 species of animals. One of the most extensive copyright-free pictorial sourcebooks of its kind. Captions. Index. 284pp. 9 x 12. 23766-4 Pa. $7.95

INDIAN DESIGNS FROM ANCIENT ECUADOR, Frederick W. Shaffer. 282 original designs by pre-Columbian Indians of Ecuador (500-1500 A.D.). Designs include people, mammals, birds, reptiles, fish, plants, heads, geometric designs. Use as is or alter for advertising, textiles, leathercraft, etc. Introduction. 95pp. 8¾ x 11¼. 23764-8 Pa. $3.50

SZIGETI ON THE VIOLIN, Joseph Szigeti. Genial, loosely structured tour by premier violinist, featuring a pleasant mixture of reminiscenes, insights into great music and musicians, innumerable tips for practicing violinists. 385 musical passages. 256pp. 5⅝ x 8¼. 23763-X Pa. $3.50

THE STANDARD BOOK OF QUILT MAKING AND COLLECTING, Marguerite Ickis. Full information, full-sized patterns for making 46 traditional quilts, also 150 other patterns. Quilted cloths, lame, satin quilts, etc. 483 illustrations. 273pp. 6⅞ x 9⅝. 20582-7 Pa. $4.95

ENCYCLOPEDIA OF VICTORIAN NEEDLEWORK, S. Caulfield, Blanche Saward. Simply inexhaustible gigantic alphabetical coverage of every traditional needlecraft—stitches, materials, methods, tools, types of work; definitions, many projects to be made. 1200 illustrations; double-columned text. 697pp. 8⅛ x 11. 22800-2, 22801-0 Pa., Two-vol. set $12.00

MECHANICK EXERCISES ON THE WHOLE ART OF PRINTING, Joseph Moxon. First complete book (1683-4) ever written about typography, a compendium of everything known about printing at the latter part of 17th century. Reprint of 2nd (1962) Oxford Univ. Press edition. 74 illustrations. Total of 550pp. 6⅛ x 9¼. 23617-X Pa. $7.95

PAPERMAKING, Dard Hunter. Definitive book on the subject by the foremost authority in the field. Chapters dealing with every aspect of history of craft in every part of the world. Over 320 illustrations. 2nd, revised and enlarged (1947) edition. 672pp. 5⅜ x 8½. 23619-6 Pa. $7.95

THE ART DECO STYLE, edited by Theodore Menten. Furniture, jewelry, metalwork, ceramics, fabrics, lighting fixtures, interior decors, exteriors, graphics from pure French sources. Best sampling around. Over 400 photographs. 183pp. 8⅜ x 11¼. 22824-X Pa. $6.00

Prices subject to change without notice.

Available at your book dealer or write for free catalogue to Dept. GI, Dover Publications, Inc., 180 Varick St., N.Y., N.Y. 10014. Dover publishes more than 175 books each year on science, elementary and advanced mathematics, biology, music, art, literary history, social sciences and other areas.